PRAISE FOR

Powers of Detection: Stories of Mystery & Fantasy

"Everyone's heart is in the right place, and, in the best stories, their tongues are firmly in their cheeks."

—*Mystery Scene*

"A fantastic, rewarding experience. Each tale is top rate . . . The contributors are top players in their own genres but had no problem placing a foot in an area they normally do not frequent. Each author ensured that the magical elements seemed real—drawing the reader in to become a believer for the moment—yet did not scrimp on the mystery components . . . The crossing of two genres works on all levels so that the audience of either will appreciate mayhem in a whimsical setting." —*Midwest Book Review*

"Any book featuring contributions from the likes of Bishop and Green is worthy of attention." —Rambles.net

"An anthology of mystery stories with an interesting twist . . . For readers of mystery who like the paranormal or are looking to get a taste of what's out there in fantasy without diving into a multivolume set of doorstop novels, this is the perfect pick . . . the perfect blend of mystery and magic." —*The Romance Readers Connection*

"Stabenow assembled a stellar group of writers from several genres for this unique anthology . . . every story is worthwhile." —*Romantic Times*

Ace anthologies edited by Dana Stabenow

POWERS OF DETECTION
UNUSUAL SUSPECTS

Unusual Suspects

STORIES OF MYSTERY & FANTASY

edited by Dana Stabenow

ACE BOOKS, NEW YORK

THE BERKLEY PUBLISHING GROUP
Published by the Penguin Group
Penguin Group (USA) Inc.
375 Hudson Street, New York, New York 10014, USA
Penguin Group (Canada), 90 Eglinton Avenue East, Suite 700, Toronto, Ontario M4P 2Y3, Canada
(a division of Pearson Penguin Canada Inc.)
Penguin Books Ltd., 80 Strand, London WC2R 0RL, England
Penguin Group Ireland, 25 St. Stephen's Green, Dublin 2, Ireland (a division of Penguin Books Ltd.)
Penguin Group (Australia), 250 Camberwell Road, Camberwell, Victoria 3124, Australia
(a division of Pearson Australia Group Pty. Ltd.)
Penguin Books India Pvt. Ltd., 11 Community Centre, Panchsheel Park, New Delhi—110 017, India
Penguin Group (NZ), 67 Apollo Drive, Rosedale, North Shore 0632, New Zealand
(a division of Pearson New Zealand Ltd.)
Penguin Books (South Africa) (Pty.) Ltd., 24 Sturdee Avenue, Rosebank, Johannesburg 2196,
South Africa

Penguin Books Ltd., Registered Offices: 80 Strand, London WC2R 0RL, England

This is an original publication of The Berkley Publishing Group.

This is a work of fiction. Names, characters, places, and incidents either are the product of the author's imagination or are used fictitiously, and any resemblance to actual persons, living or dead, business establishments, events, or locales is entirely coincidental. The publisher does not have any control over and does not assume any responsibility for author or third-party websites or their content.

First edition: December 2008

Library of Congress Cataloging-in-Publication Data

Unusual suspects : stories of mystery & fantasy / edited by Dana Stabenow. — 1st ed.
    p.   cm.
  ISBN 978-0-441-01637-2
  1. Fantasy fiction, American.   2. Detective and mystery stories, American.   I. Stabenow, Dana.
PS648.F3U58   2008
813'.0876608—dc22   2008037153

PRINTED IN THE UNITED STATES OF AMERICA

10 9 8 7 6 5 4 3 2

CONTENTS

Contents

Introduction

by Dana Stabenow

Evidently, enough of you enjoyed *Powers of Detection* so much that Ginjer Buchanan at Ace Books thought a second collection was a good idea. On behalf of all the authors included herein, thank you!

Most of the usual suspects are back, with the addition of Michael A. Stackpole, Laurie R. King, and Carole Nelson Douglas. Who would want to kill Sam Spade? Carole's got an answer for that, and Michael's got a new take on scapegoats that, okay, I know somebody gets killed and that's a bad thing, but I'm still laughing as I write these words.

Laurie R. King and Sharon Shinn offer up ghost stories, each with a very high goose-bump index. Interesting how the spookiest stories often have the least amount of gore.

Donna Andrews returns to the Westmarch College of Magical Studies and the adventures of Gwynn the apprentice, who this time saves master mage Justinian from a fate worse than death. Charlaine Harris returns to Bon Temps, Louisiana, where the vampires are out by night and the insurance agents by day. What's the difference, really? Sookie Stackhouse knows.

Laura Anne Gilman introduces us to a cave dragon who's a loan shark, and Simon R. Green takes us back into the Nightside for a grim little tale of justice delayed but not denied. Mike Doogan, tongue firmly in cheek, magicks up a traveling salesman story; Michael Armstrong indulges in a little global wishful thinking; and John Straley tells us where Santa Claus really goes during the off-season.

Me, I went back to Mnemosynea for another tale of Seer and Sword. Turns out I like that world so much that the Magi Guild commissioned me to write a Mnemosynean world almanac. I've even got a map now. And I admit, the ending of "A Woman's Work" involves a little wishful thinking of my own.

The great thing about fantastical fiction is its ability to put any ending on a question beginning "What if . . . ?" What if Santa goes Down Under on vacation? What if a cave dragon loan shark wants to make good on an investment? What if video games achieve the level of reality, then what rights belong to the characters created therein?

In her introduction to *The Norton Book of Science Fiction*, Ursula K. Le Guin wrote, "In a story where only what ordinarily occurs is going to occur, one can safely use such a sentence as, 'He was absorbed in the landscape.' In a story where *only the story* tells you what is likely to happen, you had best be careful about using sentences like that."

And of course the great thing about crime fiction, aside from the universal human love of a mystery, is that by the end there is always a resolution and, sometimes, justice.

Put murder in a fantasy setting, and "If you die, I'll kill you!" becomes a credible threat.

At least in here. Be careful how you go.

Lucky

by Charlaine Harris

Amelia Broadway and I were painting each other's toenails when my insurance agent knocked at the front door. I'd picked Roses on Ice. Amelia had opted for Mad Burgundy Cherry Glacé. She'd finished my feet, and I had about three toes to go on her left foot when Greg Aubert interrupted us.

Amelia had been living with me for a month, and it had been kind of nice to have someone else sharing my old house. Amelia is a witch from New Orleans, and she was hanging out with me because she had a magical misfortune she didn't want any of her witch buddies in the Big Easy to know about. Also, since Katrina, she really doesn't have anything to go home to, at least for a while. My little hometown of Bon Temps was swollen with refugees.

Greg Aubert had been to my house after I'd had a fire that caused a lot of damage. As far as I knew, I didn't have any insurance needs at the moment. I was pretty curious about his purpose, I confess.

Amelia had glanced up at Greg, found his sandy hair and

rimless glasses uninteresting, and completed painting her little toe while I ushered him to the wingback chair.

"Greg, this is my friend Amelia Broadway," I said. "Amelia, this is Greg Aubert."

Amelia looked at Greg with more interest. I'd told her Greg was a colleague of hers, in some respects. Greg's mom had been a witch, and he'd found using the craft very helpful in protecting his clients. Not a car got insured with Greg's agency without having a spell cast on it. I was the only one in Bon Temps who knew about Greg's little talent. Witchcraft wouldn't be popular in our devout little town. Greg always handed his clients a lucky rabbit's foot to keep in their new vehicles or homes.

After he turned down the obligatory offer of iced tea or water or Coke, Greg sat on the edge of the chair while I resumed my seat on one end of the couch. Amelia had the other end.

"I felt the wards when I drove up," Greg told Amelia. "Very impressive." He was trying real hard to keep his eyes off my tank top. I would have put on a bra if I'd known we were going to have company.

Amelia tried to look indifferent, and she might have shrugged if she hadn't been holding a bottle of nail polish. Amelia, tan and athletic, with short glossy brown hair, is not only pleased with her looks but really proud of her witchcraft abilities. "Nothing special," she said, with unconvincing modesty. She smiled at Greg, though.

"What can I do for you today, Greg?" I asked. I was due to go to work in an hour, and I had to change and pull my long hair up in a ponytail.

"I need your help," he said, yanking his gaze up to my face.

No beating around the bush with Greg.

"Okay, how?" If he could be direct, so could I.

"Someone's sabotaging my agency," he said. His voice was suddenly passionate, and I realized Greg was really close to a major breakdown. He wasn't quite the broadcaster Amelia was—I could read most thoughts Amelia had as clearly as if she'd spoken them—but I could certainly read his inner workings.

"Tell us about it," I said, because Amelia could not read Greg's mind.

"Oh, thanks," he said, as if I'd agreed to do something. I opened my mouth to correct this idea, but he plowed ahead.

"Last week I came into the office to find that someone had been through the files."

"You still have Marge Barker working for you?"

He nodded. A stray beam of sunlight winked off his glasses. It was September, and still very warm in northern Louisiana. Greg got out a snowy handkerchief and patted his forehead. "I've got my wife, Christy, she comes in three days a week for half a day, and I've got Marge full-time." Christy, Greg's wife, was as sweet as Marge was sour.

"How'd you know someone had been through the files?" Amelia asked. She screwed the top on the polish bottle and put it on the coffee table.

Greg took a deep breath. "I'd been thinking for a couple of weeks that someone had been in the office at night. But nothing was missing. Nothing was changed. My wards were okay. But two days ago, I got into the office to find that one of the drawers on our main filing cabinet was open. Of course, we lock them at night," he said. "We've got one of those filing systems that locks up when you turn a key in the top drawer. Almost all of the client files were at risk. But every day, last thing in the afternoon, Marge goes around and locks all that cabinet. What if someone suspects . . . what I do?"

I could see how that would shiver Greg down to his liver. "Did you ask Marge if she remembered locking the cabinet?"

"Sure I asked her. She got mad—you know Marge—and said she definitely did. My wife had worked that afternoon, but she couldn't remember if she watched Marge lock the cabinets or not. And Terry Bellefleur had dropped by at the last minute, wanting to check again on the insurance for his damn dog. He might have seen Marge lock up."

Greg sounded so irritated that I found myself defending Terry. "Greg, Terry doesn't like being the way he is, you know," I said, trying to gentle my voice. "He got messed up fighting for our country, and we got to cut him some slack."

Greg looked grumpy for a minute. Then he relaxed. "I know, Sookie," he said. "He's just been so hyped up about this dog."

"What's the story?" Amelia asked. If I have moments of curiosity, Amelia has an imperative urge. She wants to know everything about everybody. The telepathy should have gone to her, not me. She might actually have enjoyed it, instead of considering it a disability.

"Terry Bellefleur is Andy's cousin," I said. I knew Amelia had met Andy, a police detective, at Merlotte's. "He comes in after closing and cleans the bar. Sometimes he substitutes for Sam. Maybe not the few evenings you were working." Amelia filled in at the bar from time to time.

"Terry fought in Vietnam, got captured, and had a pretty bad time of it. He's got scars inside and out. The story about the dogs is this: Terry loves hunting dogs, and he keeps buying himself these expensive Catahoulas, and things keep happening to them. His current bitch has had puppies. He's just on pins and needles lest something happen to her and the babies."

"You're saying Terry is a little unstable?"

"He has bad times," I said. "Sometimes he's just fine."

"Oh," Amelia said, and a lightbulb might as well have popped on above her head. "He's the guy with the long graying auburn hair, going bald at the front? Scars on his cheek? Big truck?"

"That's him," I said.

Amelia turned to Greg. "You said for at least a couple of weeks you'd felt someone had been in the building after it closed. That couldn't be your wife, or this Marge?"

"My wife is with me all evening unless we have to take the kids to different events. And I don't know why Marge would feel she had to come back at night. She's there during the day, every day, and often by herself. Well, the spells that protect the building seem okay to me. But I keep recasting them."

"Tell me about your spells," Amelia said, getting down to her favorite part.

She and Greg talked spells for a few minutes, while I listened but didn't comprehend. I couldn't even understand their thoughts.

Then Amelia said, "What do you want, Greg? I mean, why did you come to us?"

He'd actually come to me, but it was kind of nice to be an "us."

Greg looked from Amelia to me, and said, "I want Sookie to find out who opened my files, and why. I worked hard to become the best-selling Pelican State agent in northern Louisiana, and I don't want my business fouled up now. My son's about to go to Rhodes in Memphis, and it ain't cheap."

"Why are you coming to me instead of the police?"

"I don't want anyone else finding out what I am," he said, embarrassed but determined. "And it might come up if the police start looking into things at my office. Plus, you know, Sookie, I got you a real good payout on your kitchen."

My kitchen had been burned down by an arsonist months before. I'd just finished getting it all rebuilt. "Greg, that's your job," I said. "I don't see where the gratitude comes in."

"Well, I have a certain amount of discretion in arson cases," he said. "I could have told the home office that I thought you did it yourself."

"You wouldn't have done that," I said calmly, though I was seeing a side of Greg I didn't like. Amelia practically had flames coming out of her nose, she was so incensed. But I could tell that Greg was already ashamed of bringing up the possibility.

"No," he said, looking down at his hands. "I guess I wouldn't. I'm sorry I said that, Sookie. I'm scared someone'll tell the whole town what I do, why people I insure are so . . . lucky. Can you see what you can find out?"

"Bring your family into the bar for supper tonight, give me a chance to look them over," I said. "That's the real reason you want me to find out, right? You suspect your family might be involved. Or your staff."

He nodded, and he looked wretched.

"I'll try to get in there tomorrow to talk to Marge. I'll say you wanted me to drop by."

"Yeah, I make calls from my cell phone sometimes, ask people to come in," he said. "Marge would believe it."

Amelia said, "What can I do?"

"Well, can you be with her?" Greg said. "Sookie can do things you can't, and vice versa. Maybe between the two of you . . ."

"Okay," Amelia said, giving Greg the benefit of her broad and dazzling smile. Her dad must have paid dearly for the perfect white smile of Amelia Broadway, witch and waitress.

Bob the cat padded in just at that moment, as if belatedly realizing we had a guest. Bob jumped up on the chair right beside Greg and examined him with care.

Greg looked down at Bob just as intently. "Have you been doing something you shouldn't, Amelia?"

"There's nothing strange about Bob," Amelia said, which was not true. She scooped up the black-and-white cat in her arms and nuzzled his soft fur. "He's just a big ole cat. Aren't you, Bob?" She was relieved when Greg dropped the subject. He got up to leave.

"I'll be grateful for anything you can do to help me," he said. With an abrupt switch to his professional persona, he said, "Here, have an extra lucky rabbit's foot," and reached in his pocket to hand me a lump of fake fur.

"Thanks," I said, and decided to put it in my bedroom. I could use some luck in that direction.

After Greg left, I scrambled into my work clothes (black pants and white boatneck T-shirt with MERLOTTE'S embroidered over the left breast), brushed my long blond hair and secured it in a ponytail, and left for the bar, wearing Teva sandals to show off my beautiful toenails. Amelia, who wasn't scheduled to work that night, said she might go have a good look around the insurance agency.

"Be careful," I said. "If someone really is prowling around there, you don't want to run into a bad situation."

"I'll zap 'em with my wonderful witch powers," she said,

only half-joking. Amelia had a fine opinion of her own abilities, which led to mistakes like Bob. He had actually been a thin young witch, handsome in a nerdy way. While spending the night with Amelia, Bob had been the victim of one of her less successful attempts at major magic. "Besides, who'd want to break into an insurance agency?" she said quickly, having read the doubt on my face. "This whole thing is ridiculous. I do want to check out Greg's magic, though, and see if it's been tampered with."

"You can do that?"

"Hey, standard stuff."

To my relief, the bar was quiet that night. It was Wednesday, which is never a very big day at supper time, since lots of Bon Temps citizens go to church on Wednesday night. Sam Merlotte, my boss, was busy counting cases of beer in the storeroom when I got there; that was how light the crowd was. The waitresses on duty were mixing their own drinks.

I stowed my purse in the drawer in Sam's desk that he keeps empty for them, then went out front to take over my tables. The woman I was relieving, a Katrina evacuee I hardly knew, gave me a wave and departed.

After an hour, Greg Aubert came in with his family as he'd promised. You seated yourself at Merlotte's, and I surreptitiously nodded to a table in my section. Dad, Mom, and two teenagers, the nuclear family. Greg's wife, Christy, had medium-light hair like Greg, and like Greg she wore glasses. She had a comfortable middle-aged body, and she'd never seemed exceptional in any way. Little Greg (and that's what they called him) was about three inches taller than his father, about thirty pounds heavier, and about ten IQ points smarter. That is, book smart. Like most nineteen-year-olds, he was pretty dumb about the world. Lindsay, the daughter, had lightened her hair five shades and squeezed herself into an outfit at least a size too small, and could hardly wait to get away from her folks so she could meet the Forbidden Boyfriend.

While I took their drink and food orders, I discovered that (a) Lindsay had the mistaken idea that she looked like Christina Aguilera, (b) Little Greg thought he would never go into insurance because it was so boring, and (c) Christy thought Greg might be interested in another woman because he'd been so distracted lately. As you can imagine, it takes a lot of mental doing to separate what I'm getting from people's minds from what I'm hearing directly from their mouths, which accounts for the strained smile I often wear—the smile that's led some people to think I'm just crazy.

After I'd brought them their drinks and turned in their food order, I puttered around studying the Aubert family. They seemed so typical it just hurt. Little Greg thought about his girlfriend mostly, and I learned more than I wanted to know.

Greg was just worried.

Christy was thinking about the dryer in their laundry room, wondering if it was time to get a new one.

See? Most people's thoughts are like that. Christy was also weighing Marge Barker's virtues (efficiency, loyalty) against the fact that she seriously disliked the woman.

Lindsay was thinking about her secret boyfriend. Like teenage girls everywhere, she was convinced her parents were the most boring people in the universe and had pokers up their asses besides. They didn't understand *anything*. Lindsay herself didn't understand why Dustin wouldn't take her to meet his folks, why he wouldn't let her see where he lived. No one but Dustin knew how poetic her soul was, how fascinating she truly could be, how misunderstood she was.

If I had a dime for every time I'd heard that from a teenager's brain, I'd be as rich as John Edward, the psychic.

I heard the bell ding in the service window, and I trotted over to get the Auberts' order from our current cook. I loaded my arms with the plates and hustled them over to the table. I had to endure a full-body scan from Little Greg, but that was par for the course, too. Guys can't help it. Lindsay didn't register me at all. She was wondering why Dustin was so secretive about his daytime activities. Shouldn't he be in school?

Okay, now. We were getting somewhere.

But then Lindsay began thinking about her D in algebra and how she was going to get grounded when her parents found out and then she wouldn't get to see Dustin for a while unless she climbed out of her bedroom window at two in the morning. She was seriously considering going all the way.

Lindsay made me feel sad and old. And very smart.

By the time the Aubert family paid their bill and left, I was tired of all of them, and my head was exhausted (a weird feeling, and one I simply can't describe).

I plodded through work the rest of the night, glad to the very ends of my Roses on Ice toenails when I headed out the back door.

"Psst," said a voice from behind me while I was unlocking my car door.

With a stifled shriek, I swung around with my keys in my hand, ready to attack.

"It's me," Amelia said gleefully.

"Dammit, Amelia, don't sneak up on me like that!" I sagged against the car.

"Sorry," she said, but she didn't sound very sorry. "Hey," she continued, "I've been over by the insurance agency. Guess what!"

"What?" My lack of enthusiasm seemed to register with Amelia.

"You tired or something?" she asked.

"I just had an evening of listening in to the world's most typical family," I said. "Greg's worried, Christy's worried, Little Greg is horny, and Lindsay has a secret love."

"I know," Amelia said. "And guess what?"

"He might be a vamp."

"Oh." She sagged. "You already knew?"

"Not for sure. I know other fascinating stuff, though. I know he understands Lindsay as she's never been understood before in her whole underappreciated life, that he just might be The One, and that she's thinking of having sex with this goober."

"Well, I know where he lives. Let's go by there. You drive; I need to get some stuff ready." We got into Amelia's car. I took the driver's seat. Amelia began fumbling in her purse through the many little Ziplocs that filled it. They were all full of magic ready to go: herbs and other ingredients. Bat wings, for all I knew.

"He lives by himself in a big house with a FOR SALE sign in the front yard. No furniture. Yet he looks like he's eighteen." Amelia pointed at the house, which was dark and isolated.

"Hmmm." Our eyes met.

"What do you think?" Amelia asked.

"Vampire, almost surely."

"Could be. But why would a strange vampire be in Bon Temps? Why don't any of the other vamps know about him?" It was all right to be a vampire in today's America, but the vamps were still trying to keep a low profile. They regulated themselves rigorously.

"How do you know they don't? Know about him, that is."

Good question. Would the area vampires be obliged to tell me? It wasn't like I was an official vampire greeter or anything.

"Amelia, you went looking around after a vampire? Not smart."

"It wasn't like I knew he might be fangy when I started. I just followed him after I saw him cruising around the Auberts' house."

"I think he's in the middle of seducing Lindsay," I said. "I better make a call."

"But does this have anything to do with Greg's business?"

"I don't know. Where is this boy now?"

"He's at Lindsay's house. He finally just parked outside. I guess he's waiting for her to come out."

"Crap." I pulled in a little way down the street from the Auberts' ranch style. I flipped open my cell phone to call Fangtasia. Maybe it's not a good sign when the area vampire bar is on your speed dial.

"Fangtasia, the bar with a bite," said an unfamiliar voice. Just as Bon Temps and our whole area was saturated with human evacuees, the vampire community in Shreveport was, too.

"This is Sookie Stackhouse. I need to speak with Eric, please," I said.

"Oh, the telepath. Sorry, Miss Stackhouse. Eric and Pam are out tonight."

"Maybe you can tell me if any of the new vampires are staying in my town, Bon Temps?"

"Let me inquire."

The voice was back after a few minutes. "Clancy says no." Clancy was like Eric's third in command, and I was not his favorite person. You'll notice Clancy didn't even ask the phone guy to find out why I needed to know. I thanked the unknown vampire for his trouble and hung up.

I was stumped. Pam, Eric's second in command, was sort of a buddy of mine, and Eric was, occasionally, something more than that. Since they weren't there, I'd have to call our local vampire, Bill Compton.

I sighed. "I'm going to have to call Bill," I said, and Amelia knew enough of my history to understand why the idea was so traumatic. And then I braced myself and dialed.

"Yes?" said a cool voice.

Thank goodness. I'd been scared the new girlfriend, Selah, would answer.

"Bill, this is Sookie. Eric and Pam are out of touch, and I have a problem."

"What?"

Bill has always been a man of few words.

"There's a young man in town we think is a vampire. Have you met him?"

"Here in Bon Temps?" Bill was clearly surprised and displeased.

That answered my question. "Yes, and Clancy told me they hadn't farmed out any new vamps to Bon Temps. So I thought maybe you'd encountered this individual?"

"No, which means he's probably taking care not to cross my path. Where are you?"

"We're parked outside the Auberts' house. He's interested in the daughter, a teenager. We've pulled into a house for sale across the street, middle of the block on Hargrove."

"I'll be there very soon. Don't approach him."

As if I would. "He thinks I'm stupid enough—" I began, and Amelia already had her "Indignant for You" face on when the driver's door was yanked open and a white hand latched on to my shoulder. I squawked until the other hand clamped over my mouth.

"Shut up, breather," said a voice that was even colder than Bill's. "Are you the one that's been following me around all night?"

Then I realized that he didn't know Amelia was in the passenger's seat. That was good.

Since I couldn't speak, I nodded slightly.

"Why?" he growled. "What do you want with me?" He shook me like I was a dustcloth, and I thought all my bones would come disjointed.

Then Amelia leaped from the other side of the car and darted over to us, tossing the contents of a Ziploc on his head. Of course, I had no idea what she was saying, but the effect was dramatic. After a jolt of astonishment, the vampire froze. The problem was, he froze with me clasped with my back to his chest in an unbreakable hold. I was mashed against him, and his left hand was still hard over my mouth, his right hand around my waist. So far, the investigative team of Sookie Stackhouse, telepath, and Amelia Broadway, witch, was not doing a top-flight job.

"Pretty good, huh?" Amelia said.

I managed to move my head a fraction. "Yes, if I could breathe," I said. I wished I hadn't wasted breath speaking.

Then Bill was there, surveying the situation.

"You stupid woman, Sookie's trapped," Bill said. "Undo the spell."

Under the streetlight, Amelia looked sullen. Undoing was not her best thing, I realized with some anxiety. I couldn't do anything else, so I waited while she worked on the counter-spell.

"If this doesn't work, it'll only take me a second to break his arm," Bill told me. I nodded . . . well, I moved my head a fraction of an inch . . . because that was all I could do. I was getting pretty breathless.

Suddenly there was a little *pop!* in the air, and the younger vampire let go of me to launch himself at Bill—who wasn't there. Bill was behind him, and he grabbed one of the boy's arms and twisted it up and back. The boy screamed, and down they went to the ground. I wondered if anyone was going to call the police. This was a lot of noise and activity for a residential neighborhood after one o'clock. But no lights came on.

"Now, talk." Bill was absolutely determined, and I guess the boy knew it.

"What's your problem?" the boy demanded. He had spiked brown hair and a lean build, and a couple of diamond studs in his nose. "This woman's been following me around. I need to know who she is."

Bill looked up at me questioningly. I jerked my head toward Amelia.

"You didn't even grab the right woman," Bill said. He sounded kind of disappointed in the youngster. "Why are you here in Bon Temps?"

"Getting away from Katrina," the boy said. "My sire was staked by a human when we ran out of bottled blood substitute after the flood. I stole a car outside of New Orleans, changed the license plates, and got out of town. I reached here at daylight. I found an empty house with a FOR SALE sign and a windowless bathroom, so I moved in. I've been going out with a local girl. I take a sip every night. She's none the wiser," he sneered.

"What's your interest?" Bill asked me.

"Have you two been going into her dad's office at night?" I asked.

"Yeah, once or twice." He smirked. "Her dad's office has a couch in it." I wanted to slap the shit out of him, maybe smacking the jewelry in his nose just by accident.

"How long have you been a vampire?" Bill asked.

"Ah . . . maybe two months."

Okay, that explained a lot. "So that's why he didn't know to check in with Eric. That's why he doesn't realize what he's doing is foolish and liable to get him staked."

"There's only so much excuse for stupidity," Bill said.

"Have you gone through the files in there?" I asked the boy, who was looking a little dazed.

"What?"

"Did you go through the files in the insurance office?"

"Uh, no. Why would I do that? I was just loving up the girl, to get a little sip, you know? I was real careful not to take too much. I don't have any money to buy artificial stuff."

"Oh, you are *so dumb*." Amelia was fed up with this kid. "For goodness' sake, learn something about your condition. Stranded vampires can get help just like stranded people. You just ask the Red Cross for some synthetic blood, and they dole it out free."

"Or you could have found out who the sheriff of the area

is," Bill said. "Eric would never turn away a vampire in need. What if someone had found you biting this girl? She's under the age of consent, I gather?" For blood "donation" to a vampire.

"Yeah," I said, when Dustin looked blank. "It's Lindsay, daughter of Greg Aubert, my insurance agent. He wanted us to find out who'd been going into his building at night. Called in a favor to get me and Amelia to investigate."

"He should do his own dirty work," Bill said quite calmly. But his hands were clenched. "Listen, boy, what's your name?"

"Dustin." He'd even given Lindsay his real name.

"Well, Dustin, tonight we go to Fangtasia, the bar in Shreveport that Eric Northman uses as his headquarters. He will talk to you there, decide what to do with you."

"I'm a free vampire. I go where I want."

"Not within Area Five, you don't. You go to Eric, the area sheriff."

Bill marched the young vampire off into the night, probably to load him into his car and get him to Shreveport.

Amelia said, "I'm sorry, Sookie."

"At least you stopped him from breaking my neck," I said, trying to sound philosophical about it. "We still have our original problem. It wasn't Dustin who went through the files, though I'm guessing it was Dustin and Lindsay going into the office at night that disturbed the magic. How could they get past it?"

"After Greg told me his spell, I realized he wasn't much of a witch. Lindsay's a member of the family. With Greg's spell to ward against outsiders, that made a difference," Amelia said. "And sometimes vampires register as a void on spells created for humans. After all, they're not alive. I made my 'freeze' spell vampire specific."

"Who else can get through magic spells and work mischief?"

"Magical nulls," she said.

"Huh?"

"There are people who can't be affected by magic," Amelia said. "They're rare, but they exist. I've only met one before."

"How can you detect nulls? Do they give off a special vibration or something?"

"Only very experienced witches can detect nulls without casting a spell on them that fails," Amelia admitted. "Greg probably has never encountered one."

"Let's go see Terry," I suggested. "He stays up all night."

The baying of a dog announced our arrival at Terry's cabin. Terry lived in the middle of three acres of woods. Terry liked being by himself most of the time, and any social needs he might feel were satisfied by an occasional stint of working as a bartender.

"That'll be Annie," I said, as the barking rose in intensity. "She's his fourth."

"Wife? Or dog?"

"Dog. Specifically, a Catahoula. The first one got hit by a truck, I think, and one got poisoned, and one got bit by a snake."

"Gosh, that is bad luck."

"Yeah, unless it's not chance at all. Maybe someone's making it happen."

"What are Catahoulas for?"

"Hunting. Herding. Don't get Terry started on the history of the breed, I'm begging you."

Terry's trailer door opened, and Annie launched herself off

the steps to find out if we were friends or foes. She gave us a good bark, and when we stayed still, she eventually remembered she knew me. Annie weighed about fifty pounds, I guess, a good-sized dog. Catahoulas are not beautiful unless you love the breed. Annie was several shades of brown and red, and one shoulder was a solid color while her legs were another, though her rear half was covered with spots.

"Sookie, did you come to pick out a puppy?" Terry called. "Annie, let them by." Annie obediently backed up, keeping her eyes on us as we began approaching the trailer.

"I came to look," I said. "I brought my friend Amelia. She loves dogs."

Amelia was thinking she'd like to slap me upside the head because she was definitely a cat person.

Annie's puppies and Annie had made the small trailer quite doggy, though the odor wasn't really unpleasant. Annie herself maintained a vigilant stance while we looked at the three pups Terry still had. Terry's scarred hands were gentle as he handled the dogs. Annie had encountered several gentleman dogs on her unplanned excursion, and the puppies were diverse. They were adorable. Puppies just are. But they were sure distinctive. I picked up a bundle of short reddish fur with a white muzzle, and felt the puppy wiggle against me and snuffle my fingers. Gee, it was cute.

"Terry," I said, "have you been worried about Annie?"

"Yeah," he said. Since he was off base himself, Terry was very tolerant of other people's quirks. "I got to thinking about the things that have happened to my dogs, and I began to wonder if someone was causing them all."

"Do you insure all your dogs with Greg Aubert?"

"Naw, Diane at Liberty South insured the others. And see what happened to them? I decided to switch agents, and everyone says Greg is the luckiest son of a bitch in Renard Parish."

The puppy began chewing on my fingers. Ouch. Amelia was looking around her at the dingy trailer. It was clean enough, but the furniture arrangement was strictly utilitarian, like the furniture itself.

"So, did you go through the files at Greg Aubert's office?"

"No, why would I do that?"

Truthfully, I couldn't think of a reason. Fortunately, Terry didn't seem interested in why I wanted to know. "Sookie," he said, "if anyone in the bar thinks about my dogs, knows anything about 'em, will you tell me?"

Terry knew about me. It was one of those community secrets that everyone knows but no one ever discusses. Until they need me.

"Yes, Terry, I will." It was a promise, and I shook his hand. Reluctantly, I set the puppy back in its improvised pen, and Annie checked it over anxiously to make sure it was in good order.

We left soon after, none the wiser.

"So, who've we got left?" Amelia said. "You don't think the family did it, the vampire boyfriend is cleared, and Terry, the only other person on the scene, didn't do it. Where do we look next?"

"Don't you have some magic that would give us a clue?" I asked. I pictured us throwing magic dust on the files to reveal fingerprints.

"Uh. No."

"Then let's just reason our way through it. Like they do in crime novels. They just talk about it."

"I'm game. Saves gas."

We got back to the house and sat across from each other at the kitchen table. Amelia brewed a cup of tea for herself, while I got a caffeine-free Coke.

I said, "Greg is scared that someone is going through his files at work. We solved the part about someone being in his office. That was the daughter and her boyfriend. So we're left with the files. Now, who would be interested in Greg's clients?"

"There's always the chance that some client doesn't think Greg paid out enough on a claim, or maybe thinks Greg is cheating his clients." Amelia took a sip of her tea.

"But why go through the files? Why not just bring a complaint to the national insurance agents' board, or whatever?"

"Okay. Then there's . . . the only other answer is another insurance agent. Someone who wonders why Greg has such phenomenal luck in what he insures. Someone who doesn't believe it's chance or those cheesy synthetic rabbits' feet."

It was so simple when you thought about it, when you cleared away the mental debris. I was sure the culprit had to be someone in the same business.

I was pretty sure I knew the other three insurance agents in Bon Temps, but I checked the phone book to be sure.

"I suggest we go from agent to agent, starting with the local ones," Amelia said. "I'm relatively new in town, so I can tell them I want to take out some more insurance."

"I'll come with you, and I'll scan them."

"During the conversation, I'll bring up the Aubert Agency, so they'll be thinking about the right thing." Amelia had asked enough questions to understand how my telepathy worked.

I nodded. "First thing tomorrow morning."

We went to sleep that night with a pleasant tingle of anticipation. A plan was a beautiful thing. Stackhouse and Broadway swing into action.

The next day didn't start exactly like we'd planned. For one thing, the weather had decided to be fall. It was cool. It was pouring rain. I put my shorts and tank tops away sadly, knowing I probably wouldn't wear them again for several months.

The first agent, Diane Porchia, was guarded by a meek clerk. Alma Dean crumpled like a fender when we insisted on seeing the actual agent. Amelia, with her bright smile and gorgeous teeth, simply beamed at Ms. Dean until she called Diane out of her office. The middle-aged agent, a stocky woman in a green pantsuit, came out to shake our hands. I said, "I've been taking my friend Amelia around to all the agents in town, starting with Greg Aubert." I was listening as hard as I could to the result, and all I got was professional pride . . . and a hint of desperation. Diane Porchia was scared by the number of claims she had processed lately. It was abnormally high. All she was thinking of was selling. Amelia gave me a little hand wave. Diane Porchia was not a magical null.

"Greg Aubert thought he'd had someone break into his office at night," Amelia said.

"Us, too," Diane said, seeming genuinely astonished. "But nothing was taken." She rallied and got back to her purpose. "Our rates are very competitive with anything Greg can offer you. Take a look at the coverage we provide, and I think you'll agree."

Shortly after that, our heads filled with figures, we were on our way to Bailey Smith. Bailey was a high school class-mate of my brother Jason's, and we had to spend a little longer there playing "What's he/she doing now?" But the result was the same. Bailey's only concern was getting Amelia's business, and maybe getting her to go out for a drink with him if he could think of a place to take her that his wife wouldn't hear about.

He had had a break-in at his office, too. In his case, the window had been shattered. But nothing had been taken. And I heard directly from his brain that business was down. Way down.

At John Robert Briscoe's we had a different problem. He didn't want to see us. His clerk, Sally Lundy, was like an angel with a flaming sword guarding the entrance to his private office. We got our chance when a client came in, a little withered woman who'd had a collision the month before. She said, "I don't know how this could be, but the minute I signed with John Robert, I had an accident. Then a month goes by, and I have another one."

"Come on back, Mrs. Hanson." Sally gave us a mistrustful look as she took the little woman to the inner sanctum. The minute they were gone, Amelia went through the stack of paperwork in the in-box, to my surprise and dismay.

Sally came back to her desk, and Amelia and I took our departure. I said, "We'll come back later. We've got another appointment right now."

"They were all claims," Amelia said, when we were out of the door. "Every one of them." She pushed back the hood on her slicker since the rain had finally stopped.

"There's something wrong with that. John Robert has been hit even harder than Diane or Bailey."

We stared at each other. Finally, I said what we were both thinking. "Did Greg upset some balance by claiming more than his fair share of good luck?"

"I never heard of such a thing," Amelia said. But we both believed that Greg had unwittingly tipped over a cosmic applecart.

"There weren't any nulls at any of the other agencies," Amelia said. "It's got to be John Robert or his clerk. I didn't get to check either of them."

"He'll be going to lunch any minute," I said, glancing down at my watch. "Probably Sally will be, too. I'll go to the back where they park and stall them. Do you just have to be close?"

"If I have one of my spells, it'll be better," she said. She darted over to the car and unlocked it, pulling out her purse. I hurried around to the back of the building, just a block off the main street but surrounded by crepe myrtles.

I managed to catch John Robert as he left his office to go to lunch. His car was dirty. His clothes were disheveled. He slumped. I knew him by sight, but we'd never had a conversation.

"Mr. Briscoe," I said, and his head swung up. He seemed confused. Then his face cleared, and he tried to smile.

"Sookie Stackhouse, right? Girl, it's been an age since I saw you."

"I guess you don't come in Merlotte's much."

"No, I pretty much go home to the wife and kids in the evening," he agreed. "They've got a lot of activities."

"Do you ever go over to Greg Aubert's office?" I asked, trying to sound gentle.

He stared at me for a long moment. "No, why would I do that?"

And I could tell, hear from his head directly, that he absolutely didn't know what I was talking about. But there came Sally Lundy, steam practically coming out of her ears at the sight of me talking to her boss when she'd done her best to shield him.

"Sally," John Robert said, relieved to see his right-hand woman, "this young woman wants to know if I've been to Greg's office lately."

"I'll just bet she does," Sally said, and even John Robert blinked at the venom in her voice.

And I got it then, the name I'd been waiting for.

"It's you," I said. "You're the one, Ms. Lundy. What are you doing that for?" If I hadn't known I had backup, I would've been scared. Speaking of backup . . .

"What am I doing it for?" she screeched. "You have the gall, the nerve, the, the, *balls* to ask me that?"

John Robert couldn't have looked more horrified if she'd sprouted horns.

"Sally," he said, very anxiously. "Sally, maybe you need to sit down."

"You can't see it!" she shrieked. "You can't see it. That Greg Aubert, he's dealing with the devil! Diane and Bailey are in the same boat we are, and it's sinking! Do you know how many claims he had to handle last week? Three! Do you know how many new policies he wrote? Thirty!"

John Robert literally staggered when he heard the numbers. He recovered enough to say, "Sally, we can't make wild accusations against Greg. He's a fine man. He'd never . . ."

But Greg had, however blindly.

Sally decided it would be a good time to kick me in the shins, and I was really glad I was wearing jeans instead of shorts that day. *Okay, anytime now, Amelia,* I thought. John Robert was windmilling his arms and yelling at Sally— though not moving to restrain her, I noticed—and Sally was yelling back at the top of her lungs and venting her feelings about Greg Aubert and that bitch Marge who worked for him. She had a lot to say about Marge. No love lost there.

By that time I was holding Sally off at arm's length, and I was sure my legs would be black-and-blue the next day.

Finally, *finally*, Amelia appeared, breathless and disarranged. "Sorry," she panted, "you're not going to believe this, but my foot got stuck between the car seat and the doorsill, then I fell, and my keys went under the car . . . anyway, *Congelo!*"

Sally's foot stopped in midswing, so she was balancing on one skinny leg. Greg had both hands in the air in a gesture of despair. I touched his arm, and he felt as hard as the frozen vampire had the other night. At least he wasn't holding me.

"Now what?" I asked.

"I thought you knew!" she said. "We've got to get them off thinking about Greg and his luck!"

"The problem is, I think Greg's used up all the luck going around," I said. "Look at the problems you had just getting out of the car here."

She looked intensely thoughtful. "Yeah, we have to have a chat with Greg," she said. "But first, we got to get out of this situation." Holding out her right hand toward the two frozen people, she said, "Ah—*amicus cum Greg Aubert.*"

They didn't look any more amiable, but maybe the change was taking place in their hearts. "*Regelo,*" Amelia said, and Sally's foot came down to the ground hard. The older woman lurched a bit, and I caught her. "Watch out, Miss Sally," I said, hoping she wouldn't kick me again. "You were a little off balance there."

She looked at me in surprise. "What are you doing back here?"

Good question. "Amelia and I were just cutting through

the parking lot on our way to McDonald's," I said, gesturing toward the golden arches that stuck up one street over. "We didn't realize that you had so many high bushes around the back, here. We'll just return to the front parking lot and get our car and drive around."

"That would be better," John Robert said. "That way we wouldn't have to worry about something happening to your car while it was parked in our parking lot." He looked gloomy again. "Something's sure to hit it, or fall on top of it. Maybe I'll just call that nice Greg Aubert and ask him if he's got any ideas about breaking my streak of bad luck."

"You do that," I said. "Greg would be glad to talk to you. He'll give you lots of his lucky rabbits' feet, I bet."

"Yep, that Greg sure is nice," Sally Lundy agreed. She turned to back into the office, a little dazed but none the worse for wear.

Amelia and I went over to the Pelican State office. We were both feeling pretty thoughtful about the whole thing.

Greg was in, and we plopped down on the client side of his desk.

"Greg, you've got to stop using the spells so much," I said, and I explained why.

Greg looked frightened and angry. "But I'm the best agent in Louisiana. I have an incredible record."

"I can't make you change anything, but you're sucking up all the luck in Renard Parish," I said. "You gotta let loose of some of it for the other guys. Diane and Bailey are hurting so much they're thinking about changing professions. John Robert Briscoe is almost suicidal." To do Greg credit, once we explained the situation, he was horrified.

"I'll modify my spells," he said. "I'll accept some of the bad luck. I just can't believe I was using up everyone else's share." He still didn't look happy, but he was resigned. "And the people in the office at night?" Greg asked meekly.

"Don't worry about it," I said. "Taken care of." At least, I hoped so. Just because Bill had taken the young vampire to Shreveport to see Eric didn't mean that he wouldn't come back again. But maybe the couple would find somewhere else to conduct their mutual exploration.

"Thank you," Greg said, shaking our hands. In fact, Greg cut us a check, which was also nice, though we assured him it wasn't necessary. Amelia looked proud and happy. I felt pretty cheerful myself. We'd cleaned up a couple of the world's problems, and things were better because of us.

"We were fine investigators," I said, as we drove home.

"Of course," said Amelia. "We weren't just good. We were lucky."

Bogieman

by Carole Nelson Douglas

Sam Spade's splayed body was a symphony in black and white on the hellfire orange carpet of the Inferno Hotel.

It had that pale and wan look down pat. His skin was ashen, his hair and beard stubble gray, his suit pin-striped in silver and dark charcoal, the nearby fedora a soft gray. Only his eyebrows and hatband were black.

So. Who would want to kill Sam Spade?

Who would want to kill Humphrey Bogart, for that matter?

And, legally, could either one of them be murdered?

Here's the deal. This is Las Vegas, after all. I live and work here. Delilah Street, PI. PI as in Paranormal Investigator. Lucky me.

A lot in Las Vegas in 2013 is unlucky, including the pervasive presence of all the unhumans released by the Millennium Revelation. Instead of Apocalypse Now at the Turn, we got Apocalypse Now and Forever. The two-thousand-year millennium didn't bring the much-vaunted end of the world, only the end of the world as we knew it. All the legendary bogeymen and women of history and myth showed up, maybe not exactly as advertised in our nightmares, but there. Witches and werewolves and zombies, oh, my!

Sam Spade sprang from the black type on white paper Dashiell Hammett had rolled through his manual typewriter almost ninety years ago. Humphrey Bogart had been a human actor, but dead for almost sixty years, since 1957.

Add a little high-tech enterprise to exploit the new supernatural population, and you had what lay before me, either dead or merely unplugged: one of the fabulous Las Vegas CinSims. The CinSim that lay immobile on the carpet was an amalgam of character and actor that had been moving and "living" until person or persons unknown—or unpersons unknown—had driven a corkscrew from the Inferno Bar into its all-too-solid chest.

And there was yet a third persona present, last but not least. That would be whoever's resurrected dead body had been the medium upon which the silver-screen icon Humphrey Bogart, who played Sam Spade in the 1941 film classic *The Maltese Falcon*, had been re-created.

The corkscrew was spiraled into the dead man's chest, but was an ordinary mortal weapon capable of killing a CinSim? That's short for Cinema Simulacrum, and Vegas was teeming with them. They had been reanimated, certainly, but were they capable of dying? Of being murdered?

And why was I standing here contemplating all these unknowns?

Because besides being Delilah Street, Paranormal Investigator, I'm a silver medium. I have an unexplained affinity for any kind of silver . . . the sterling kind in jewelry, mirror backings, mercury glass, and the silver nitrate that was used in the black-and-white film strips from which the CinSim personas are stripped.

CinSims are the billion-dollar baby of a literal Industrial Light and Magic post-Spielberg special-effects company. They exist by the mating of a complex copyright network that leases the Silver Screen characters to entertainment venues, and of the grave robbers employed by the Immortality Mob to provide the flesh-and-bone "canvas" on which the animated effect is achieved. Smuggling zombies into the U.S. is against the law. Once they get here and disappear into their CinSim overlay, they're just hard-to-trace illegal aliens, like ordinary live border-crossers.

It's no coincidence that most of the zombies are imported from Mexico.

CinSims are one of latter-day Las Vegas's most enduringly popular attractions. Wouldn't you like to shoot the breeze with John Wayne as the Ringo Kid or Bette Davis as Jezebel? They are also one of its most morally ambiguous creations.

I knew and liked a lot of CinSims around town, and the feeling was mutual. Yeah, CinSims have feelings, which almost nobody knows. They make terrific snitches. Everyone treats them like trained dogs it's safe to talk in front of. We get along because I treat them like real people. So I mourned Sam Spade/Humphrey Bogart, even though we'd never met.

"What do you think, Miss Street?" The voice was brusque. This bizarre case, the first dead CinSim ever, had brought out the Las Vegas Metropolitan Police Department's captain of homicide, Kennedy Malloy. "Getting any useful 'vibes' off the so-called body?"

Kennedy Malloy was not a man. Yeah, I thought that too when I first heard the name.

I first heard the name in connection with my sudden personal interest and sometime professional partner, Ricardo Montoya, ex-FBI guy and a secret dowser for the dead. He was good at dowsing a lot of things, including me. Ric was the zombie expert, but he was consulting in Juarez. Malloy had been a professional friend of his until I came along and snagged the benefits. She still was his friend. And no friend of mine.

"You're supposed to have this rapport with the CinSims." She was a trim blonde with hazel eyes and the hard-edged moxie of women moving up in a man's profession.

"Usually they're alive," I said. "Or at least moving and talking, like the motion pictures that spawned them."

"I'm giving you two hours. You'll have to deal with the various entities that 'own' the remains. They came out like maggots the minute this was called in. Then we cart this . . . stuff away. We'll call the Metropolitan Waste Department. I don't see what an autopsy could do. The body's already long dead. It'll stink soon, for sure. And burial doesn't seem necessary."

Behind her, Nick Charles, another Dashiell Hammett creation known as the Thin Man for the title of his first novelistic case, clicked his teeth. "It isn't nice for a public servant to disrespect discriminated-against minorities," he said.

Malloy spun on him. "A bleeding heart like Street here can go all gooey over this character running out of film, but you CinSims have no civil rights in this town or this country. You're all copyrighted and leased entertainment entities."

"At least," Nick Charles said in his slightly soused but

shrewd way, "somebody cared enough to copyright us. I don't see a Kennedy Malloy Barbie in your future, Captain."

I swallowed a giggle. Nick Charles was from back in the day when a smart comeback was all the rage, and he still had them in . . . er, spades.

"I like a modern dame," he commented to me, as the captain stomped away, "but one with a clever lip on her as well as looks. Like my esteemed spouse, Nora. And like you, my dear Miss Street."

"Thanks, Nicky." His tux was a symphony in black-tie and black-and-white all over. I sighed as I regarded the possible corpse. "Did you know this CinSim?"

"Not personally. He was attached to the Club Noir in the hotel's Lower Depths, Circle One. We are all chained to our particular entertainment venues, you know."

I did know. All CinSim have internal chips that keep them from wandering away from their home hotel or bar or brothel.

Nicky went on after a graciously swallowed hiccup. "I can't leave this bar for the life of me. Not that I mind." He took another tipsy sip from the martini glass perpetually in hand.

"The life of me" was an ironic expression coming from his pearl gray lips. I was maybe the only mortal who knew that the CinSims craved more freedom. A fortunate few had film histories that helped them avoid detection, so they could ditch their chips and skip out on their home assignments. Like the Invisible Man, a pal of Nicky's, and therefore of mine.

I was particularly fond of Nick Charles, not only for his jazz-age detective history, but because his "cousin"—both played by the same long-dead actor William Powell—was my boss's "man Godfrey" from another film of the thirties. My boss was Hector Nightwine, producer of the Las-Vegas-and-beyond-set *CSI: Crime Scene Instincts* TV series that had been the rage since God made maggots and the profit motive.

It still freaked me out that various versions of roles played by the same actor had been resurrected as utterly individual CinSim. Even now, as we contemplated the death of the Sam Spade incarnation, I remembered that Humphrey Bogart was alive in some Hemingway novel made into film at a hotel down the Strip.

"I would have never given up Mary Astor," Nicky mused, speaking of the actress who played *The Maltese Falcon*'s femme fatale. "A good-looker and really classy dame. What's a little deception between film-noir lovers?"

That's when it occurred to me. A CinSim could have offed Sam Spade. Say, the woman who loved him . . . who he turned in to the police in *The Maltese Falcon*. Say, that greedy kingpin, Gutman, the "Fat Man" from the film. A lot of them are alive and semiwell in Las Vegas these days. Who was to say cinematic loves and hates didn't transfer with their portrayals?

But the prime problem was who had been killed: the zombie body, the film character applied over it, or the actor who'd originated the film role?

Only God can make a tree, but these days, man can make, and remake, anything. Including original sin, the first murder of a CinSim.

I didn't relish interviewing the interested parties leaning against the bar.

I recognized the lawyer for the Immortality Mob from the way he clutched his faux-crocodile briefcase. He was over-dressed for Vegas's desert climate in a gray sharkskin suit and vintage Op Art tie. The Incorporated FX and Magic Show technician who fine-tunes and places the CinSims lounged beside him, long-haired, laid-back, and wearing tattooed blue jeans.

The third figure was the Inferno's head honcho, a rock superstar I'd both tangled and tangoed with, Cocaine, an updated, albino Elvis in tight white leather pants, long white hair, and mirror shades. No one quite knew what he was—vampire? fallen angel? con man? CEO?—besides sexy.

I was an ex–TV reporter, so I sashayed right over.

"Miss Delilah Street," Cocaine said in his belly-tightening bass voice. His stage costume included a flowing white poet's shirt open to the navel. Despite the two-hour show, his albino skin was dry as a bone. No one had ever seen him sweat. No one had ever seen his eyes, either. I didn't care to.

"Who owns the body?" I asked.

"Just what we were discussing," the dead-croc hugger said. "I'm Peter Eddy, the intellectual property rights attorney for IFX-MS, Industrial Special Effects and Magic Show. Mr. Cocaine here is refusing to let our technician download what's left of the persona into his computer. And the police captain has been none too friendly either."

"Police captains don't get promoted by being friendly. Any suspects?"

"None," squeaked Eddy at the very idea. "An unfortunate accident. The CinSim must have fallen on a bar implement. Perhaps it was drinking. The technicians can't control their every move. Yet."

I eyed the tech guy. "Aren't they chained to their venues?

This guy should have never left the Club Noir level to come up here."

"Absolutely right." His hands with their bitten-to-the-quick nails smoothed the small, unmarked silver case slung over his shoulder.

"Your name is?" I always like a full cast of suspects.

"Reggie Owens. Our program prevents unauthorized wanderings. Someone must have hacked into the programming to move him here. I could upload Bogart and Spade right now, and let the police and Mr. Eddy dispose of the Z-canvas, but Mr. Christophe won't okay it."

"Christophe" was Cocaine's supposed real name, first and last, but the fans in the mosh pit screamed themselves hoarse begging for their drug of choice by the nickname they gave him. His friends called him Snow, and so did I, even though I wasn't exactly a friend. Call me a thorn in the side.

I lifted an interrogatory eyebrow in his direction.

"Nobody," he said, "is disabling an Inferno Hotel CinSim on my premises. I want to know who offed it, and how and why. And I want Miss Street to do the job."

Goodie. Put me on the hot seat between three quarreling superpowers in Las Vegas. I decided to let them fight over the retread corpse and excused myself to hunt up any possible witnesses.

Nick Charles was lighting a cigarette for a willowy woman in sleek Nora Charles evening velvet. He had quite a following at the Inferno Bar. Like Snow, the CinSims had their devoted fans. Called CinSymbs, for CinSim Symbiants—yes, if you're good at tongue twisters, this is your subculture—they dressed in vintage clothes, but in black and white, including their clown white made-up skin and vamp black dyed hair.

"Thanks, Nicky," she said, patting her pale gray hair in a grandmotherly way.

He turned to me with relief.

"Now that we're alone, what did you see?" I asked him.

"The bar was mobbed from the Seven Deadly Sins performance, a monster mash of Cocaine groupies, the usual Cin-Symbs doing both the rock concert and the bar scene, tourists milling around with their plugged-in communication cameras. Drugs, sex, and rock and roll. A little gin was all it took to get high in my day, and the sex came without that blaring musical accompaniment. Maybe just a little Noel Coward."

"And a lot of gin in your case, Nicky."

"Guilty. But not of this CinSim's current condition."

"You don't say 'dead'?"

"It's debatable, isn't it? The . . . personage was discovered when the crowd began to thin after the Sins concert. Just there." He pointed.

"Had you ever seen him before?"

"No, but I knew of him. He was the coming thing, with that tough-guy stuff. No white tie and tails and smooth patter for him. And it was ironic that Sam Spade was portrayed by an actual swell, like Bogart, who'd been expelled from a fancy Eastern prep school. Film can be fickle."

I lowered my voice. "Are you aware of other CinSims leaving their, um, moorings."

"Well, our Invisible friend gets around."

I checked the neighboring empty barstools for a betraying depression in the middle, but they were all undimpled red leather.

"Not tonight. Not that I know of. I was distracted, of course," Nick said, sipping from his martini glass. His pleasantly hazy eyes sharpened. "It's as if the body was planted here. When the crowd parted like the Red Sea, voilà! Somebody wanted it to be found, and publicly."

I accepted what Nicky offered: the Albino Vampire cocktail I'd invented from white chocolate liqueur and vanilla vodka to piss off Snow. He'd merely appropriated it for the bar and made a mint.

While I sipped and thought, I felt a sharp bite on my rear. No, the barstools didn't have teeth and claws. The Invisible Man was announcing his presence. Being Invisible, he hadn't had a date since the 1940s and pinching unsuspecting women was his kick. Since he'd once saved my life, I put up with his idea of a pickup line.

"I knew," he whispered in my ear, "Sam was going to make a run for it. Humphrey was hankering to visit another venue."

"You saw him get to the bar area?" I mumbled to my glass rim. The dame with the cigarette gave me an "are you nuts?" glance.

"Hell, I helped him get off Circle One. He mixed with the CinSymbs up here, blended right in. I lost him until Nick and everyone saw him frozen on the floor when the crowd cleared. Talk about a still life."

"Why the corkscrew?"

"I don't have the faintest, Miss Street. Umm, you smell good."

"It's not me, it's my Albino Vampire."

"How naughty of Christophe to rip you off like that. You want me to put quinine in his onstage bottled water?"

I shook my head, getting another look from the woman on my right.

"Can I have a sip?" the Invisible Man cajoled.

"I guess." I watched the smooth white liquid in my martini glass descend an inch. "Sip?"

"Umhmm, good. They never feed or water me. The corkscrew? I don't know. Someone hurled a switchblade at me once. It stuck, but it didn't hurt, and it didn't do any damage. It was like it hit corkboard. These borrowed bodies are sturdy."

"How'd they manage to make you invisible?"

"It comes with the character, not the canvas." I felt a chocolate buss on the cheek. " 'Bye, baby." Sweet.

I glanced at the triumvirate with ownership interests in the Bogart/Spade CinSim. The lawyer and the techie were sweating bullets, but Snow seemed cool as an ice cube. I ambled over to eavesdrop.

"While you let this Street woman pretend to investigate, I don't trust the police to guard our property," Eddy told Snow. "Some of these rubbernecking tourists might violate our copyright and tear away pieces of its clothing."

True, the crime scene was surrounded by tourists five feet deep, not to mention the Inferno's hovering airborne flock of mirror-ball security cameras.

Cocaine/Christophe sighed and reached up to the pink ruby-dotted black leather collar circling his dead white neck. He pressed a faceted black gemstone separating the rubies.

"I'll have my head of security watch the . . . er, canvas . . . while I escort Miss Street to the CinSim's home environment."

A six-hundred-pound white tiger with green eyes stalked past the people and the police CSI crew to stand by the body. The tourists moved back. Way back.

"Nicky," Snow said. "Get the gentlemen some drinks while I escort Miss Street below."

"Charmed," Nick Charles said. "I recommend gin. And gin. And gin. What would you like, sir? A gin rickey? Martini? Gimlet?"

"You checked your security satellites?" I asked Snow, as we moved away. He was an Invisible Man himself once off-stage. I don't know how he managed it, but he avoided being mobbed. Some things you don't want to know in post–Millennium Revelation Las Vegas. I had my secrets too.

"Checked them immediately. The crowd around the bar was too thick to isolate anyone. Whatever stopped Sam Spade cold, it happened during my . . . er, curtain call."

Except there was no curtain, just the band drawn back onstage by clapping, hooting, digital screams. I could picture every eye fixed onstage as he bent down to uplift a dozen lucky, screaming female fans for the Brimstone Kiss. It wasn't just a hasty smooch, either. Perfect timing for an unprecedented murder.

"You know you won't win custody in court," I told Snow, as we headed toward the roaring dragon's mouth that housed the elevators to the Inferno Hotel's lower depths. "You're just a lessee. And no one will claim the anonymous, illegally resurrected body."

"Sure this isn't your FBI friend Ric's work?"

"Ex-FBI. And Ric dowses for the dead, he doesn't create them. He doesn't trifle with the resurrected dead like you Vegas moguls do."

The brushed stainless-steel doors opened between flaming jaws seven feet wide and high. I admit to a tremor. I'd never been below the Inferno's main floor, which was bad enough.

In the elevator, Snow tilted his head back against the stainless-steel-mirror walls.

"This is important, Delilah. My people are my people, CinSims or not. No one messes with me and mine. Not even you. Find whoever, or whatever, did this. I'll handle the cops and the corporations."

"Haven't you got people to do that? Attorneys, muscle?"

"I run a hands-on operation."

I was sure the eyes behind those glossy black lenses were giving me a lazy and provocative half stare.

Or maybe they were eyeing the Elsa Peretti sapphire-studded sterling-silver bangle on my left wrist. I can't afford that kind of bracelet, but silver is a sort of familiar of mine.

This particular piece of it had a literal lock on me, having started out as a lock of Snow's angel white hair. When I touched it, it climbed my wrist and became the bracelet. When I confronted Snow about it later, he claimed if he gave me some of his power, I wouldn't try to take it all.

I'd only touched the damn strand because it reminded me of my white Lhasa apso, Achilles, lost to a vampire bite. He bit the vampire, mind you, but died of blood poisoning. Or maybe not. He kept turning up alive in my dreams. Anyway, my weakness for Achilles had led to having Snow's creepy lock of hair as a permanent fashion accessory–cum–martial arts attachment.

"Besides," he was saying, "I didn't want to miss the opportunity of working with you."

"Why? You know I despise you and all your works."

"That's why. You're totally objective."

"Just show me where the dead CinSim was supposed to be."

"This level is all key clubs," he said, waiting for me to exit the flaming dragon's mouth on Circle One. I knew what that meant. The first of the nine circles of Hell from Dante's *Inferno*.

"Fantasy enviros," Snow went on, proud of his hellfire clubs. "Club Noir offers all the famous names and faces from the era. Here's *The Maltese Falcon* boutique hotel and bistro. Please don't be hard on Peter Lorre; he gets kicked around enough in the film."

By then we'd entered a pair of etched-glass double doors bearing the film's name. Beyond them lay a moving wax museum of movie moments: walls playing the famous scenes in 3-D, the reel characters moving around, mumbling lines, intermixing with real-life visitors to Vegas who'd paid for the privilege.

Peter Lorre as Joel Cairo caught my eye, and scuttled away. He didn't know much in the film, and he wouldn't know much now. Snow was right. He was too pathetic to bother with, as Sam Spade had determined.

"I'm bad," Mary Astor, as Brigid O'Shaughnessy, was breathing at a fat man in a Hawaiian shirt and baggy shorts. "I'm so bad."

I'd seen at a glance that Bogie was missing from the scenery, so I stepped into Mary's bar-side seduction scene.

"Get lost, tourist," I said. The guy bristled, but obeyed. "So did you do in Sam?" I asked Brigid.

"Who are you to ask questions like that? You're not in the script."

"Neither was an offed Sam Spade. When did you last see him?"

"Sam? Dead? It can't be."

"It is. 'Fess up, sister. You know you had the hots for him, and he was ready to send you up the river on a murder rap. Why wouldn't you drive a corkscrew into his chest if you had a chance?"

"No! I loved him. I'd never kill him."

"Seems like you set him up a few times, for just that re-sult."

"That was the script! I had to do it. I hated the ending. Sam would never have sold me out. He didn't give a toot about his partner, Miles Archer. He'd been screwing Archer's wife, Iva, but then he met and loved me. He really loved me. Then the scriptwriters messed us up. Why don't you ask Iva where she was when Sam got corkscrewed?"

Good point. I racked my brain for the cast list from the film. Snow stepped into the scene, a handheld computer showing just what I'd wanted.

"Thanks, Jeeves." I was getting into the fact that maybe he really needed me to solve this. If that entitled me to hand him some lip without personal peril, it was pretty sweet.

Okay. Iva Archer. Miles Archer had been Sam Spade's partner until he was killed. Iva had been the femme fatale in the threesome until Brigid O'Shaughnessy had shown up. Was Sam Spade's "death" part of the backstory mayhem of *The Maltese Falcon* novel and film?

I found Iva having a hasty talk with Peter Lorre/Joel Cairo. She was a refined beauty for a cheap PI's wife.

"Sam Spade has left the building," I told her. The Elvis reference meant nothing, but her face turned a whiter shade of pale gray.

"I don't know what you're talking about. I live here. I'm a widow, don't you know that? Who'd walk out on a widow? Sam wouldn't leave me. Don't you say that he would!"

Women in film noir sure were hair-trigger. "Okay, okay. I just wanted to talk to him. I have a case."

She eyed me. "Yeah, all you dames have cases, all right." She looked around. Looked harder. No Sam Spade to be found. "Get outa here! You're crazy."

I backed off, but I didn't stop considering which one of these fictional characters made flesh would want to kill the leading man. And how had they lured him out of his safe, scripted environment for a date with death in the Inferno Bar?

I left *The Maltese Falcon* enviro, Snow at my side.

"This is complicated," I said.

"This is Las Vegas."

I glanced around at the double-doored entries to many cinema worlds. We were in a freaking CinSim multiplex!

"Is this an all-Bogart level?" I asked.

"No. All noir. Only two of the clubs center on Bogart."

"*Casablanca*?"

"My favorite. You want to see?"

Snow, hooked on true love and self-sacrifice? Sell me another bridge in Brooklyn.

"You must like the hot, dry climate," I hazarded.

"Hot is my sexual preference."

"It was Satan's too." We went through another pair of frosted-glass doors into Rick's Café Américain bar.

Bogie was here, in a slightly wilted white evening jacket, leaning over an upright piano on which a black guy played "As Time Goes By." Customers in Bermuda shorts and Hawaiian shirts looked a lot more at home here. Ingrid Bergman sat alone at a table, looking pensive while being chatted up by two surfer dudes. And Peter Lorre lurked around the fringes, having played the same conniving, cringing lowlife he was so good at in *The Maltese Falcon*.

I ankled over, and his beady eyes lit up. He wasn't used to women seeking him out.

"Hi, cutie, can I buy you a gin rickey?" I didn't even know what a gin rickey was, except it evoked the name of the bar's fictional owner . . . and of my own personal cutie, Ric Montoya, come to think of it.

He would have looked good at Rick's place. Much better-looking than Bogart.

"You can buy me some information," I said, melding into forties noir-speak. "Have there been any attempts on Rick's life lately?"

"This is Casablanca. If the local occupying Nazis aren't after you, the international rat pack is. Rick can take care of himself." Lorre eyed Bergman. "That dame is no good for him. That's the kind of classy dame even a hardheaded guy could lose his sense of self-preservation over."

"He did," I said. "Do you ever trespass on your 'cousin's' scenario in the next club over?"

"Never! We are forbidden to meet. It's in our contracts."

"Aren't you even tempted?"

"No. He's a weaselly little rat who will never get the girl. Here, I get to talk to you, cutie."

"Not anymore."

I looked around for Snow. He was hanging over the top of the small, white upright piano, singing along to Sam's soulful rendition of "As Time Goes By." I suppose even a rock star harbors visions of crooning classics.

On the "a kiss is just a kiss," he turned those blind-man glasses my way.

A kiss is just a kiss, my eye! His Brimstone Kiss after the show addicted the clamoring mosh-pit females to a repeat

performance that would never happen. These pathetic Cocaine junkies attended every performance, living their lives
only to support their doomed habit. I was secretly working to
rehabilitate them, for my own reasons.

"We done here?" I asked as I walked over.

He finished the phrase. Then, since the fundamentals still
apply, he escorted me to the Circle One lobby.

"Got any ideas?" he asked.

"Just a couple more questions."

He waited.

"The CinSims are strictly tied to their performance areas,
right?"

"Theoretically. It depends how diligent the hotelier is
about keeping a leash on them."

"And you?"

"I'd find it more interesting if they would depart from the
script. Call me contrary, but tourists like the unexpected."

"So you don't have them tied down as tightly as some."

"No."

"And Sam Spade might have gotten up to the Inferno Bar
on his own."

"If he'd had the will. That's the intriguing part. Does a
CinSim have free will?"

"Humans do."

"They seem to think so."

"And an unhuman like you?"

"Are you certain I'm unhuman, or what kind of unhuman
I might be?"

The rumor said master vampire. I wasn't so sure. "No.
That's your devilish charm."

I doubt many people made Snow laugh, but I did then.

"That's my devilish charm," I said.

But he didn't answer, only reached down and snapped his forefinger on my bracelet, my bond, his former lovelock, making it chime.

"What else did you want to know?" he asked.

"Which other hotels host Bogart CinSim, and what incarnations they use."

"Easy. My office computer has stats on all the competition."

On the way back up in the elevator, the pink ruby collar buzzed. His forefinger stabbed the black onyx stone.

"The police and interested CinSim parties are getting restless, boss," came a deep, growly voice.

"Keep them busy. I'll want them in my office in a bit. We may have something for them soon."

I was indignant. " 'We,' white man?" Well, he was literally white from crown to toe, as far as I know, or ever wish to know.

"You've got an idea on this CinSim murder, haven't you?"

"Yes. Maybe you can just read my mind and take it."

"Maybe I like you working for a living."

Me, too. I'd been an unemployed TV reporter until this paranormal investigator gig evolved. Actually, I enjoyed working for someone other than Hector Nightwine, my landlord and somewhat ghoulish mentor.

Snow's office sported a lot of glossy black furniture and a huge, tufted white leather executive chair.

Even the laptop computer case was glossy black.

I saw myself, darkly, in its reflective surface while his pale hands with their china white fingernails punched keys and scrolled and hunted.

"All right," he said at last. "The Gehenna has the only other Bogart film leased."

"*To Have and Have Not*, right?"

"Is that a proposal or a question?"

I made a face. I'd always known that Snow had designs on me. I just didn't know what for. Or why.

"Not one of Hemingway's best novels," he said. "Or Bogart's best roles."

"Can I see the screen?"

He spun the laptop to face me.

I started punching my own buttons, looking up the original cast and the reviewer notes.

Aha!

That film had debuted Bogart's future wife, long, lean model Lauren Bacall, and had made them into "Bogie and Bacall" for eternity. Her character in the movie was even nicknamed "Slim." That was the film where she had taunted the Bogart character that he knew how to whistle, didn't he? "Just pucker up your lips and blow."

It's amazing what passed for racy seventy-some years ago.

"I know who killed the Sam Spade CinSim. And why."

"Good."

"It's all your fault, you know."

"My fault?"

"You like your CinSims on a loose leash."

"Free will is a noble concept, especially for indentured servants."

"Sorta free will. Get Captain Malloy and the interested parties in here."

"Oh, excellent. You're going to do the pin-the-rap-on-the-perp shtick. Classic mystery finish."

I said no more, waiting.

Within ten minutes, the interested parties were herded into the room by the huge white tiger, who shifted into a skinny, six-foot-something black woman with long white hair like Snow's, green eyes, and red-painted nails long and sharp enough to eviscerate an adult male. She was wearing purple leather Escada and it looked good on her.

"We'll take the Inferno to court," croco-man Peter Eddy was sputtering as he took a seat, "if you deny our substantial financial interest in the now-useless CinSim."

"We'll take you to jail," Captain Malloy told Snow as she took her seat, "if you're ducking any wrongdoing on your part here."

Reggie, the IFX-MS technician, slouched into another leather tub chair and shrugged his disdain for the whole inquiry. "It doesn't matter what all you honchos decide. I just need to strip our programming pronto. Then you all can fight over the remains."

"Sure you really need to deprogram the fallen CinSim?" I asked. "Let me see your portable programmer."

"No! It's IFX-MS property." He clutched the slim case to his side, but Grizelle, Snow's security chief, leaned over to slash through the leather shoulder sling with one red, tigerish claw. She slung the item down on the desk in front of me.

I tapped around and found I couldn't get anywhere without an entry code.

Everyone was watching me. Malloy was irritated. The lawyer was fixated. The tech guy was looking constipated, and who knew what Snow was thinking behind those impervious shades.

Okay. Time for a little silver-medium work. These CinSim were my people, peeled from silver nitrate and given latter-day life. I let my fingers wander, like a musician's. I was looking for the one right note in Sam Spade's key . . . a code name Sam/Humphrey would know and love.

Effie. The name of Spade's loyal secretary. Every private dick in those days had one. Nothing. Iva. Nothing. Brigid. Rhymes with "frigid." Hammett named the "Fat Man" Gutman, so he was trying to tell us something. Nothing. None of the story dames registered. It had to be a woman. I tried the actress names, Mary Astor, Lee Patrick, Gladys George. Nothing.

Leather chairs creaked as representatives of three powerful forces in Las Vegas grew impatient.

Nothing from the fourth and key figure, Snow.

I entered an all-American name. Betty. Betty Bacall, before the "Lauren" became her screen moniker.

Suddenly I was in the Sam Spade file. *Yes!* What was left of it. Hopefully, all.

"You've already uploaded the Spade and Bogart personas." I looked up to accuse Reggie, the tech guy. "You erased the canvas. You stuck the dead man's chest with a redundant corkscrew to hide the fact that the canvas was already empty. Why?"

"Me? I'm only the tech zombie. I just do my job."

"The whole CinSim was right in your porta-puter all the time. You were going to pretend to upload the personas from the 'mysteriously' dead CinSim body. Why the subterfuge?"

Reggie squirmed in his chair, but Grizelle's red-taloned hands held him still. She leaned her face close to his and gave one of those Big Cat snarls

"S-s-secret orders. Get this thing away from me!" Grizelle backed off her face, but not her claws. "There's nothing illegal here. No murder. This CinSim was rogue. The chip told us he was trying to leave his venue. That's why I had to waste

him in the Inferno Lounge. One CinSim wanders off its con-
tracted premises, it's history, like it was before."

"Why not just withdraw the lease?"

"Too many questions. Money loss. Besides, Mr. Christophe is not a team player." He glared at our host.

I tapped some commands into the console. Up came a
screenful of gobbledygook.

"Why?" Captain Malloy wanted to know. "Why get a
crime-scene team out here for nonsense? You can't kill a Cin-
Sim."

"Only by computer" I said. "I'm guessing the IFX-MS
brass didn't want to antagonize Christophe. He's a good cus-
tomer, if willful. They canceled the contract without having
to pay a kill fee. Created a mystery. A philosophical conun-
drum. The CinSim is indeed their property, but it was wandering and the contract hadn't run out. An executive decision.
This tech man is only the hired hand who did the take-
down."

Captain Kennedy arched a pale eyebrow. "Not everybody
can take down Sam Spade." She eyed Christophe. "You want
to charge fraud?"

"I want my CinSim back. I'll say if it's out of bounds, not
IFX-MS."

I spun the tech's computer across Snow's desk to face him.
"Be my guest."

Captain Malloy stood. "There's no crime here. Don't call
the police the next time you corporate zombie-lovers have a
spat. There are some things we expect you dealers in immortality to work out for yourselves. We work the real-dead
beat."

She left.

The lawyer bowed out too. "It's obvious that a CinSim

can't die. My job is done. You tech geeks and ghouls and girls work it out between you."

It was just the three of us. And the gigabytes of Sam Spade and Humphrey Bogart.

"Your company doesn't like my operation," Snow said softly, "you come to me. You don't sneak onto my premises to off my CinSims. Got it?"

The guy was just a low-level techie, following orders. He swallowed, glanced at Grizelle, then fled, leaving his porta-puter.

"He's all here?" Snow asked me. "Role and actor?"

"I think so."

He nodded at Grizelle and she left with the computer and file, walking with one Jimmy Choo spike swaggering in front of the other, like a big cat stalking. Sam Spade would soon be restored to his rightful starring place in the Inferno firmament.

Snow leaned back in his infinitely programmable executive chair, running his dead white fingers through his dead white hair.

"So, Delilah. It was just unsanctioned industrial sabotage. The Immortality Mob needed a comeuppance. Thanks for the quick solve. Your fee will be waiting at your cottage on Nightwine's estate."

"That may not be enough in this case."

"No? We had a deal."

"You realize why Sam was wandering."

"He could."

"You're a generous slaveholder, but no."

"I give them leeway. Why leave my hotel?"

"Because you don't lease Betty Bacall."

"What? You're saying he needed a girlfriend?"

"I'm saying Bogie needed his wife."

Snow was silent, taking in all the implications. Then he sat up, wired.

"The CinSims want a life? Real life?"

"They're a blend of actor and role . . . and corporeal canvas. The role is written. The actor has a soul. Humphrey Bogart wanted to play a part that united him with the woman he loved in the real world."

"Lauren Bacall, not 'Slim' Browning?"

I nodded. "I wouldn't expect you to understand."

"I understand that this is a most . . . interesting development. More interesting than IFX-MS's tawdry attempt to confuse the issues with a phony homicide."

"I agree."

"I'll have to pay a bundle for the *Casablanca* cast. Ingrid Bergman was a much bigger star than Mary Astor. The Gehenna will want more for *To Have and Have Not* and Lauren Bacall. On the other hand, I always thought she was a classy dame."

"Noir does not become you, Snow. And while you're arranging for new CinSims, I have a suggestion."

"Suggestion?"

"Demand."

"And you want—?"

"Given the soul you've now discovered in the CinSims, I think, at the least, that Nick Charles deserves a Nora Charles at the Inferno bar."

"What a romantic you are, Delilah Street. And pretty pricey yourself." Snow made a note on the laptop. "I'll look into a Myrna Loy/Nora Charles lease in the morning. I suppose you want the damn dog too?"

My hand unconsciously went to the damned silver bracelet,

once a lock of Snow's hair as white and supple as my lost Lhasa apso's floor-length coat.

"And Asta, the wire-haired terrier," Snow said as he typed, long, white fingers playing the keyboard like a piano. "One dead dog, coming up."

Didn't I wish.

Looks Are Deceiving

by Michael A. Stackpole

For a murder victim, Duke Serean Darikean looked surprisingly lively. The Iron Duke sat there amid a pack of hunting dogs, lazily scratching one of the Wurmhounds behind an ear. He looked better than he had when I last saw him, but none of us retreating from The City Beyond The Sea had been at our best.

The death of an Age will sap life from even the most resilient.

The dogs dwarfed every man there save one, Kellach, whom I thought of as a friend, but who likely saw me as a curious acquaintance. By temperament Kellach was more wolf than man. Had the Duke set one of the hounds on him, the beast would have fared badly. The Iron Duke's having again employed Kellach underscored the seriousness of his situation. Darikean could have called up Legions, but this problem was one to be handled in secrecy and shadows.

The hawk-nosed Duke smiled as if wondering how quick

a meal one of the brindle Wurmhounds would make of me. I'd be a bite. Barely. I could have walked beneath one and only touched its belly if I stretched.

Touched physically, that is.

Two servants dragged a chair over, and the Duke waited until I struggled up into it before speaking.

"We had our differences in Aviantis, Primin. I would apologize, but . . ."

"An apology without remorse means nothing."

The man's dark eyes sharpened. "I regret having lost your home."

Only for the tarnish on your reputation.

"We did what we could." I shrugged. "My friend convinced me to come because he said you'd been murdered."

"And you wanted to see for yourself." The Skorpantine noble raised a hand and flicked a nail against a dark ring on his little finger. "I am being poisoned. Someone switched another ring for mine."

The Duke's new house wizard tugged on his beard sagely. "You are familiar with a Bloodlock?"

I scratched my chin. "Old magick, Sepheri magick, but common enough now. The curse had to be sworn through a god."

"I have made the temple rounds, made the right sacrifices, paid the proper bribes." Darikean frowned. "The ring remains."

I shook my head. "If a god won't release you, only the oathtakers' blood can." I opened my arms and looked around the hunting villa. "Did you fail to pay the artists for these murals?"

Darikean's hand closed into a fist. He would have struck me, but he wanted my help. More importantly he feared me. All of them did save Kellach. What my twisted body lacked in physical stature, it made up for beyond the Veils.

The Skorpantine sorcerer waved that suggestion away. "This is far more vile than some ruse to extract payments. Whoever it is truly wants our lord deceased."

"Not a short list." The sorcerer and the two courtiers grew angry, but the Duke just stroked Wurmhound fur. "Who benefits from your death?"

"Another long list." The Duke shook his head. "Of those who benefit, only four could have made the substitution. My wife, two sons, and my daughter. None of them, however, has the skill to work such magick."

"I'm to find their accomplice?"

"I am rather counting on it."

The sorcerer opened his hands. "The Duke has a week to live, perhaps less."

"You've been able to curtail some of the effects?"

"And mask others."

The Iron Duke sat forward. "Primin, I shall reward you substantially."

I admired the lack of concern in his voice, but I did not credit it to courage. The man just could not conceive of his dying in such a manner, so it would not be happening. Whoever had betrayed him would die, and the matter forgotten much as the death of my city had been.

"You most certainly will." I slid from the chair and held a hand up. The Wurmhound lowered his muzzle to it, sniffed, then licked it in a manner that was so gentle, and such a sharp contrast to their tearing young dragons apart. "I'll find your killer. I'll stop him."

I felt I had to.

After all, I didn't want someone else doing the job I'd already set for myself.

Kellach and I made an unlikely pair. He, tall and massive, with raven's-wing hair and emerald eyes, striding along fluidly. Men catching even a glimpse of him—hard men, with scars, beards, and ferocious attitudes—splashed through the open sewer to get out of his way. They stared at him slack-jawed and shuddered.

Each man shivering as if his shadow passed over his grave.

Trailing in his wake I passed unnoticed. Tiny and warped, with a gait best described as a lopsided skip, I tried to keep up with him. His long legs wolfishly devoured distance. That he didn't turn and offer to carry me was a mark of respect. Others might pity me, or see me as a curiosity, but he took me as I was.

For that I was grateful.

He paused at the entry to the market. He wore a dark leather jerkin and pair of plaid trousers. I doubted they were his clan pattern, but they were of Cengar manufacture. A dagger topped each boot, and a short sword rode at his left hip. In Aviantis he'd preferred an ax or a mace, but here in the city, things sharp and pointy would serve him best.

He read the street names on the corner post, a finger tracing each letter of the Imperial High script. "Now where?"

I made a sign and parted the first of the Veils, allowing me to see more. One name on the signpost had been underlined with a glowing purple arrow. It pointed east. "That way."

He headed off, but the set of his shoulders betrayed his displeasure. The Southerner could have thrived all alone for

months in the Empire of Trees or the Carse-el-Dael; but being trapped here in a crowd wore on him as being trapped on
the bottom of the Akkanean Sea would have me. I'd not seen
him this discomfited in Aviantis, but the city was locked in
war, to which he took even better than to the wilderness.

"Why did you remain in Dedecian? I had thought you
had other plans."

"There was work. Bandits." His grin was predatory. "The
Duke pays well."

"You've had time to study the family. What do you
think?"

The Cengar smiled. "Hastatean hates his father."

"Still?"

"Forever."

Hastatean Darikean had been the Skorpantine garrison
commander at Aviantis but had been stripped of command
and sent home. His father had overseen his disgrace and replaced him. There had been rumors of the son's wanting to
challenge his father to an honor-duel over the matter, but
entreaties by his mother and sister dissuaded him.

With a well-placed slap on the buttocks, Kellach convinced a vendor of sour wine to move his cart so we could
squeeze past. "Olivina is betrothed to some princeling in Akkanis. Pretty but not evil enough to survive at court. Cinteana loves her husband more than required by law."

"Left here." The Duke had been a widower for most of the
time he first commanded the garrison in Aviantis. Cinteana
had been his brother's wife, and they took care of his eldest
son, Nitidean, while the Duke was away. When his brother
died, he took Cinteana to wife as prescribed by Skorpantine
law. He had two more children by her, Olivina and Hastatean. That she had come to love him I found hard to believe.

The Duke's bronze statue at city center would have been more capable of returning any sentiment than his bodily incarnation. But, working with magick, I had seen far stranger things, and seldom were they as strong as the bonds of even one-sided love.

The alley closed in on both sides. The wine cart could have passed down it, but the merchant would have been fast stuck. The buildings tugged at Kellach's shoulders. I got to dance from right to left, skipping over the trickle of sewage running down the center of the cobblestone street.

"What of the other son?"

"A weakling. A poet, not even a bard. Black flux killed his mother. He survived. He's not right." The giant shook his head. "So worthless that Death ignores him."

"But he will inherit over his brother, despite the family's military tradition?"

"The stupidity of law."

"Stop, Kellach, here."

He turned at the sound of my voice and frowned. "It is a wall."

I held a hand up and he stooped to take it. "That's what you see, but it's not what's here." Because I had the First Veil parted, the door stood out easily, only partially hidden by an illusion as thick as fog. I led him through the doorway and let the sigil-decorated door swing shut behind us.

His tension, as communicated through his hand, eased only slightly. The low ceiling and smoke-dimmed lights made the place seem terribly familiar. Sorcerers and wizards sat at tables. Attendants moved among them, serving refreshment or guiding folk to the tiers of pallets lining the back wall. There dozens lay as if eaters of Lotus. While their physical forms rested, they pierced the Third Veil, or farther.

They remained physically vulnerable while off working great magicks, hence came to an establishment like this to be cared for while they were away.

"I have no liking for this place."

Judged by the expressions of those present, the place had no liking for us. Being a stranger, a dwarf, and having brought a Blind companion along, endeared me to no one. We got a lot of interest, not all of it healthy.

Still, no one cared to hold my stare for long.

Then she emerged from beyond a curtain. Tall and slender, with long hair the perfect contrast to Kellach's and dark eyes rimmed with kohl, she drifted forward to meet us. Kellach stared, for to him she did drift. I could see past much of the glamour hiding her movement, but I didn't try too hard. I thoroughly enjoyed just watching her move.

In many, such profligate use of illusion would have masked insecurity. She did not shy from my gaze and seemed to find Kellach little more threatening than a kitten.

"Do you bind yourself, friend, with the peace of sanctuary?"

"Save where another has violated it." Formalities concluded, I bowed as I was able. "I am Primin Aviantin, but am called Min."

"And I am Veneceana." She gestured. Suddenly there was a table between us, and I'd been lifted onto a stool almost tall enough to make us equals. "How may we serve?"

"I have come seeking news of Sepheri ruins lately manifested."

She laughed easily. "Another seeker of power? I should have thought you graced with quite enough."

"Can one ever have too much?"

"Better to quest for knowledge." She curled a white lock

around a finger. "Dedecian is built near what was a Sepheri provincial capital, but it is still scattered."

I nodded. The Sepheri, who still existed in the west in a much-degraded state, had once been the masters of a magickal empire encompassing the known world. The empire collapsed, but not into dust as do the dreams of men. The Sepheri people and holdings were scattered through time. When they did appear, they usually took umbrage at the spread and independence of men, since we had long been their slaves.

The Sepheri used Bloodlocks as slave restraints. Others had adapted them to more nefarious purposes. They required an oath sworn to a god, and if none of the human gods would release the Duke, I thought it possible a Sepheri god might have obliged in the Bloodlock's creation.

"Had you heard something to suggest the opposite, my friend, Min?" She cocked her head. "This would be valuable news."

"Rumor only, born of bored speculation. I have a friend, an outlander, who scarce believes the Sepheri ever existed." I spoke, of course, of Kellach, but could not refer to him by name. In places of magick, the Blind did not exist. "I thought I would show him evidence of his ignorance."

"Most of the ruins were drowned in the sea." She wrinkled her nose in a most distracting way. "Fisherfolk always bring up strange things, especially after the sea rages."

"I had heard the Duke's first wife died of the blood flux, and that often betokens Sepheri meddling."

Veneceana smiled. "But it was not the blood flux, friend Min. It was the black flux. The mother brought her child to me, desperate that he survive. I did what I could, and he grew well. It had all taken a toll on his mother, however, and she succumbed. The uncle took charge of the boy and raised him as his own."

I studied her more closely, but either her magick could not be penetrated, or the years had been very kind to her.

"I am sorry, Min, that you shall disappoint your friend. A caution, however. It is seldom wise to seek what the past has buried. The Sepheri are gone, and the sooner they are forgotten, the better."

I was ready to be well away from there, but Kellach stopped in the street and loosened his trousers. Without ceremony, and with a certain apparent satisfaction, he urinated on the sanctuary door. The stream disappeared into the illusion, then flowed steaming into the trickle at the alley's heart.

"I meant you no disrespect, Kellach. There are protocols."

He tied his trousers up again. "I know there are Sepheri. I have killed Sepheri. I told you the mother died of the black flux, not blood flux."

"You weren't there. You didn't see."

"I had it from the Duke."

My eyes narrowed. "He did not see, either. He was in Aviantis. I recall the year of mourning."

My companion's face darkened. "The boy blames the father for his mother's death?"

"Or fears a reconciliation between Hastatean and the Iron Duke. He must know he is a disappointment."

"Possible."

"Many things are possible." I scrubbed a hand over my face. "Where do I find Nitidean?"

"Scarlet Crow or Cloven Snake." He pointed back toward the market and hills beyond. "Come."

"I'll find it."

He frowned at me.

"I want to study him covertly, my friend. You will attract notice."

He laughed. "And you shall not?"

"You should remember, my friend, that I can be very good at not being seen."

It didn't require a Wurmhound to sniff out the Scarlet Crow. The largest public house at the base of the nobles' hill district, it allowed the blooded and the moneyed to mix. Intrigue ran thicker than pipe smoke and darker than candle soot. Wine came in bottles instead of pitchers. Food arrived on individual plates, not heaped on platters to be fought over like carrion. The doorpost's chalked notice advertised "an entertainment" by Nitidean for that evening, so I found myself a quiet corner and settled in to wait.

I'd met the Duke's younger son in Aviantis, though I did not know him socially. I had seen him in action and thought well of him. He'd led troops bravely and only suffered disgrace when the priests of several Orders conspired against him. Even though that conspiracy had become common knowledge, the Duke, acting at the behest of the King, had no choice but to recall his son and replace him.

Hastatean had made no effort to hide his hatred for his father, but I had a hard time believing he'd use a Bloodlock to kill him. Most soldiers despised Bloodlocks since they have been used to keep conscripts in line. He might have opted for it to humiliate his father, but Hastatean had always seemed interested in honor and fighting, not resting on his laurels as so many other leaders were. While his demotion could have unhinged him, he'd always seemed too strong for that.

Assassins and women favor poison, but Bloodlocks take too long to work. The whole point of one is to get someone to realize they're in danger and that they need to do something to rectify the situation. But there was no behavior to rectify, so the only use of the Bloodlock could have been to cause the Duke to dread his impending death.

The daughter, whose future lay coupled with that of a prince in Akkanis, would benefit little from her father's death. In fact, his death would hurt her, as he would not be able to support her at court. And his wife seemed little likely to want him dead. For most women—if they act when passions are running high—can kill but usually do so quickly.

An angry wife will feed you spoiled mussels laced with arsenic and offer hemlock to wash it all down.

Though he arrived quietly, Nitidean stood out from the crowd. The elder son lived down to Kellach's description, to which I added a pasty complexion and lifelessly straight black hair. Had one stuck his feet in the ground, watered him and weeded, in ten years he might have grown into Kellach, but a decade of sunshine could not have erased his mournful expression.

Clad head to toe in black, save for a lapis pectoral that matched his eyes, Nitidean took his place behind a podium. He unlaced a thick folio and sorted through yellowed leaves. His audience grew quiet, save for those who gossiped concerning other attendees or shared hopes that an old favorite might be repeated.

Kellach had decried him as a poet, not a bard; and the source of his disdain made itself readily apparent from the first. Nitidean's voice grated, equal parts of a trapped mouse's squeals and the yowls of a gutted cat. The sounds did resolve themselves into words, but they seemed almost randomly chosen. He paid no heed to rhyme or meter. Likewise I found no story or moral in his work.

I do recall one piece:

> Sun's shadow fades,
> Night's black glows fastly hot.
> A leaf curls to no purpose.

I have heard entertainers opine that one should leave the audience wanting more, but I doubt this is what they meant. The audience seemed willing to supply "the more," in whispered speculation, confident interpretation, and lusty applause.

It made no sense to me, which prompted the mistake of looking about for any sign of comprehension among my companions. In short, I abandoned the attempt to remain unseen. This brought a servant in my direction but also attracted other unwanted notice.

A strongly built man crossed the room and took the chair beside me. "And why would you be here, Min? I had heard you'd been dropped in Akkanis."

"You honor me by remembering me, Lord Hastatean."

"And you dodge my question."

"I am here as you, my lord, to hear the poet's work." I smiled, piercing the First Veil. Nothing out of the ordinary. The serpentine scar on his cheek had healed nicely. I rather liked that he'd not paid some wizard to fashion an illusion to hide it.

"Come to see my brother, have you? The monster?"

I arched an eyebrow.

"Look at him. Weak as you, yet has none of your skills."

With my eyes Veiled, I did see a glamour cast on his pec-toral. It made Nitidean appear more noble, which he cer-tainly needed. His shoulders slumped a bit without it and one eye drooped, but I really expected nothing more.

"It would appear, my lord, that he has those who appreci-ate his gifts with the arts."

"They will find his gibberish cold comfort the day he as-cends to my father's position."

"A day far in the future, surely."

"By all the gods, yes, a long way in the future." He stood and waved his half brother over. The poet stared blankly for a moment, then came like a dog. He clutched a single page that trembled mightily. "Nitidean, this is Min, late of Aviantis."

"Most pleased, Master Min." The man bowed, then shoved the page toward me.

"I couldn't."

"It would please me greatly."

I took it. His hands were as soft and gentle as the script in which the poem had been written. I glanced at it, reading but not comprehending, then rolled it up tightly. "You are most generous, my lord."

"I please people as I can." He smiled, then glanced at his brother. "I shall read more?"

"Yes, please." The flash of pain on Hastatean's face mocked the lighter tone of voice.

Despite his brother having withdrawn to the front of the room, I whispered. "Why are you here?"

"There are those who would do him harm. Those here see him as a genius. Others regard him as an imbecile who will

rule over them someday. They would eliminate him. I will
not have that."

"Even though he is your competition?"

"I may hate my father, but I respect the law. By birth he is
my superior. If he comes to harm, Skorpanis comes to harm.
I will not have it." He gave me a nod and withdrew.

I resumed my anonymity.

The vehemence of Hastatean's words meant one of two
things. Either he had no part in his father's murder, or the
man had practiced long and hard at acting. The Veiled glance
detected no glamours that affected his voice or made his expression more sincere, enchantments not uncommon among
actors, which is why, as a class, they are held in such low es-
teem. After all, their only chore is to add emotion and sincer-
ity to the words of others, and if they cannot do that without
sorcery, then they are nothing.

But Nitidean's career as a poet did not really position him
much higher in Skorpantine society. Though many sons and
daughters of the lesser nobility found their way into "the
arts"—not including magick—that was not usually permitted
for those in line to inherit. Nitidean's appearance there, though
pleasing to some, was the black flux to any political career.

Why the Duke indulged his first son in such a pursuit I
could not imagine. Another father might have done it out of
love since the son seemed so devoted to his art. Guilt, perhaps, that he'd not been present as the boy grew up. I couldn't
be certain. I had to ask the Duke. His answer might be what
provided a solution to the puzzle.

Other Veiled glances revealed nothing out of the
ordinary—ordinary including a few benign glamours that
thickened thinning hair, made bosoms appear larger or bellies smaller. From the glow half of them came from unguents

smeared on the appropriate body part. Once again, I made a mental note to work out a pomade that would actually grow hair and thereby make my fortune.

The crowd began to thin. Hastatean had vanished, and Nitidean sat with fawning courtiers. The hour-candle had burned down toward midnight. I thought about returning to my home for sleep, but none would come. So if I was not going to be sleeping, no reason the Duke should. His sons knew I was here, so the need for secrecy evaporated. I'd let him yell at me for being discovered, then I would have answers to my questions.

Skorpanis's second city, Dedecian, is large enough for most people, but I grew up in Aviantis, the city where worlds met. The whole of Dedecian could have fit into the slums, and in many points would have fared worse by comparison. The Aviantine Spice Market alone dwarfed the whole of Dedecian's market.

Thus it was with big-city arrogance that I traveled dark byways with little sense of danger. I hiked through alleys, and they must have anticipated me. One followed, cutting off my retreat, while two others, slightly winded, emerged from shadows in an apartment building's courtyard. One tugged a dagger from the sheath at the small of his back. No magick, just razored steel.

I slipped the coin-pouch from my belt and tossed it toward him, playing my part in the charade. "You don't want to hurt me."

"Alas, we are paid to hurt you."

I reached past the Second Veil, summoning a fistful of power. While my hands are tiny, beyond the Veils they are like shovels. I cloaked myself in shadow and slid left, avoiding the man coming at my back. He raced past harmlessly, then with his compatriots, pulled his headband down over his eyes and spoke a word of power.

I needed no magesight to reveal that enchantment. They could see me, perhaps as nothing more than a glowing blob, but I wasn't hidden. They came on, filling both hands with daggers and the courtyard with their laughter.

I reached back, pulling double handfuls of power. I clapped them together. They erupted in a gout of flame that took the leader square in the chest. He bounced back, a living torch, and slammed into a wall. His compatriots reeled away, then darkness stole back in.

"You don't want to hurt me."

The leader gasped, then sat up, which summoned a gasp from me. He slapped both hands to his chest, powdering what was left of his tunic. He came up to one knee, unconcerned that his trousers had similarly been reduced to ash. He recovered one of his daggers, then a white smile split his soot black face.

He waved a confederate forward. "Your turn."

The man made a show of twirling his daggers and drew one back to throw. He smiled.

Then the ax split his smile.

The other two, blood-spattered, stared at the twitching corpse. Daggers clattered musically on cobblestones. Somehow they knew I couldn't have thrown that ax. They'd been prepared for danger, well prepared, but they were expecting magick and that ax was anything but.

Silent as a Wurmhound bounding after prey, Kellach burst into the courtyard. He closed the gap in a heartbeat. The short sword swung in a brief arc. More musical daggers accompanied the thump of a head. A cry for mercy gurgled into silence, then he stood there, sword dripping, watching, waiting, preternaturally aware.

A cart hurriedly creaked past in the streets. Kellach started for it, pausing only to wrench his ax from the first assassin's skull.

I called for him to hold and wiped blood from my face. "Don't bother. It's just a carter. He'll have three goats in cages. One of them will be roasted."

My friend glowered silently.

I slipped from shadow and knelt beside the man I'd burned. A leather collar had slipped from his neck stump. It was unremarkable save that it had a single broken link hanging from it. A Veiled glance suggested nothing more than I expected it would.

Kellach, squatting, grunted. "Scapegoat."

"Exactly." The goats would have worn identical collars, cut from the same leather. The links would have once been paired. The magickal energy I'd unleashed had passed through the chains, roasting the goat instead of the man. While not unknown, scapegoat magick was not easy to do, which was why its use had surprised us at Aviantis.

I stood, which did not remove me nearly far enough from the carnage. "This confirms three things. First, a magician is involved here. Second, my identity has revealed to this person that I'm a threat. Unfortunately, this is not terribly illuminative."

Kellach grunted.

It always amused him when I used words bigger than myself. Much of my education had been in the Imperial High tongue, so I tended to think in it. Thinking was not doing me much good, however, since I'd not narrowed the field down to any suspects.

I smiled. "The third thing is that you're getting very good at concealing yourself in a city. I had no idea you were following me all evening."

"I wasn't." He tore the tunic from one of the other bodies and wiped his weapons off. "I was sent to fetch you."

I raised an eyebrow.

"The Duke is dead."

If not for the black veins and his skin's ashen hue, Duke Darikean might simply have been sleeping on the daybed. They'd laid him out in the villa's central sunroom, with his feet toward dawn and his arms crossed over his breast. The rectangular slit in the roof would allow the sun to wash down over him, first touching his face, then caressing his body. For one last time it would warm him, then, that night, he would be burned.

The veins, which spiderwebbed his body and contrasted with the white scars, gave the illusion he'd died of the black flux. The fluxes—the black flux being the worst of those occurring naturally—unbalanced humors, creating a vile venom. The poison affected nerves, occasionally agitating them but most often dulling them. With the black flux, the victim's lungs become paralyzed. The victim suffocates.

Whoever had created the Bloodlock had wanted the Iron Duke dead in the worst way. While I doubted the ring had actually caused the disease, I had no desire to get close to the corpse. His pet wizard could stand vigil there if he wanted to, but I would keep my distance.

I'd seen enough disease close up in Aviantis, and my magicks had never been strong in the healing arts. I dabbled, but such diseases required more powerful magicks.

Cloaked and hooded in mourning dress, Darikean's wife and daughter sat in a corner weeping, holding each other. No distasteful keening, that would come later when professional mourners arrived. For now the simple and heart-wrenching sobs of true anguish serenaded the dead man, and I almost felt sorry for him.

My hatred for him had been born in the destruction of Aviantis. Perhaps I knew, deep inside, that the siege would have succeeded eventually, but who can watch the city of his birth die without wanting another week or month or year for it? His choice to abandon Aviantis likely did have to be made, and might have been the correct one. I couldn't accept it, however, as my hatred kept my grief at bay.

Nitidean arrived, took one look at the corpse, and became even more pale. Still in black from his performance, he joined the women. He had the presence of mind to remove the pectoral before he embraced them. His sobs joined theirs, and his voice seemed somehow sweeter.

Then, deeper in the villa, someone screamed. I ran from the room, once again following Kellach. I don't know if the others heard, but none followed us immediately. We raced through a garden courtyard, chipped marble crunching like snow beneath our feet. A serving woman lay huddled on the ground crying outside a far door. Kellach ignored her and stopped in the doorway.

I slipped past easily enough. Hastatean slumped in a chair with a short sword plunged hilt deep in his belly. I pierced the First Veil but saw no magick lingering on him or the blade. I caught a glow in the corner of my eye, but when I turned to look, there was nothing odd on the desk where he sat.

"Kellach, bring me that chair. Put it next to the desk, please."

The Cengar complied, then lifted me onto the seat. I studied the desktop carefully, but again saw nothing I'd not expect to find there. Hastatean had written out a suicide note. He'd sealed it at the bottom, but left it open for anyone to read.

Consumed by hatred, I murdered my father. I have not been a man since he humiliated me. Consumed now by guilt, I must render judgment unto myself. I pray to be forgiven and beg to share the flames of the man I have so unjustly murdered.

"He should be thrown to the dogs." The Cengar growled.

"A priest will appreciate his remorse and—with promises of the proper sacrifices—will grant his last wish. It will preserve the family's dignity. Hastatean will have killed himself out of grief over his father's death, but will have saved everyone the melodrama of throwing himself on the pyre."

"Paper lies and appearances are for fools. The gods know the truth."

Paper lies. Something sparked in the back of my mind. I set the suicide note aside, then pulled a fresh piece of paper from the folio and inked a pen. I handed both to Kellach.

He stared at them as if I'd given him an old viper or a newborn babe.

"Write down what you see on the note."

"I am not a scribe."

"Don't write it. Draw. Make an exact copy—every line, every dot."

He gave me a hard look.

"Kellach, this is no lark." I moved a candle to better illu-

minate the note. "Your copy will tell us who killed both father and son. After that, we'll have to stop them from killing
again."

We emerged in minutes from Hastatean's chamber with the
evidence of Nitidean's perfidy firmly in hand. Kellach repro-
duced the text faithfully, as he saw it. It came out in Cengar
runes, while the original had been written in the Imperial
High script. The Cengar insisted Hastatean had written in
his language, and I felt equally as strong about High Imperial, and this exposed the whole matter.

The glamours had been spectacular work. The spells were
designed to avoid casual discovery, hence a simple Veiled
glance revealed nothing. Moreover, the glamours led the
viewer to see what he expected to see. It subtly confirmed
innate prejudices. The suicide note read exactly the way I
thought it should, which meant I'd have no impetus to question its validity.

Once I realized what was happening, I took the glamour
apart. The note's text, while identical to what I'd read, had
been written in a soft hand. And thanks to Nitidean's gift, I
had a sample for comparison.

Nitidean, with his arms around both grieving women's
shoulders, stopped at the garden's far edge. His dull expression evaporated. His hands slid up to their necks, then he
shook them once, hard. Their necks popped, and their limp
bodies fell away as the poet charged us.

I could have used magick to strip the glamours from him,
but Nitidean shed them in an eyeblink. The large-eyed poet
burst through the illusion, doubling in height, tripling in
mass. Crocodile flesh covered his body, all of it sand gold,

save for black specks like pepper. His face had flattened, with his nose becoming slits and ears tiny holes. Fangs protruded from a scale-lipped mouth, and huge muscles rippled beneath the bony flesh. Hands and feet ended in blunt black talons that were never meant to tear, but would still do frightful damage to a man.

And especially to one as tiny as I.

I reached back beyond the Second Veil to summon power, but I had no idea what to do. It wasn't that I didn't have lethal magick available, but this was a *tellek bicha*, a sorcerous automaton of Sepheri manufacture. In creating them each was given a flaw that would make destroying it simple, if you knew what it was. Most were created for combat, so their flaw would be a chronologically limited life span, providing an easy way to retire your invincible army once you'd done all your conquering. This automaton had impersonated Nitidean for years, making it much more complex and powerful.

It drove at me, spraying stones in its wake. A clawed hand rose. I decided on fire—always a good choice in combat—then remembered the Sepheri worshipped fire. I hesitated. I froze.

I prepared to die.

Then Kellach tackled the beast. It went down hard. Kellach rolled over its chest. His tunic caught on a fang and tore, spinning him around. He came to his feet in a heartbeat, then kicked Nitidean in the head.

The *tellek bicha* hissed and came up, then swiped a paw at the Cengar. Kellach dodged back, then slashed with his short sword. Bones cracked, but no blood flew. The monster roared outrage that echoed threateningly throughout the villa. Undaunted, the Cengar darted forward and thrust the blade into the monster's belly.

The blade snapped.

Nitidean swatted the Cengar down, then kicked him. My friend flew back, smashing into the villa's wall. Plaster cracked and hunks of mural honoring the Duke rained down over his dead wife and daughter.

The Cengar, crouching against the wall, wiped blood from his mouth. He slipped an iron dagger from a boot and sprang back into the battle. The *tellek bicha* raced at him, then plucked him from the air and hung on despite Kellach's sliding the dagger beneath scales on its forearm.

My mind sped through all I knew about Sepheri sorcery—a subject forbidden and hence much studied in every magick academy. In cases where imposture was planned, tightly linking the construct to the subject made the deception much easier to maintain. With Nitidean the switch had likely been made when he was a child, perhaps even an infant. And the best link would have been through flesh and blood, which meant the Sepheri had fed the child to the construct.

Pulling power through the Veils, I sharpened my sight. Black-veined as his father's had been, the infant's body lurked within the scaled creature's breast. His presence within that cyst would have rendered identification as the Duke's son magickally unimpeachable. Since he was born while Darikean was in my city, such verification certainly would have taken place.

The monster lifted Kellach high and squeezed. The dagger must have severed a nerve, for the thumb failed to punch through his breastbone. Kellach took the other thumb in both hands and pushed back. His muscles strained, and his face purpled. Veins stood out, but slowly the thumb inched toward his heart.

But it would never get there.

In discovering the creature's origin, I'd also located its

weakness. Though my skills at healing are not strong, I do know some spells. Gathering power in double handfuls, I funneled it into a spell that normally required only a tiny spark.

The magick, which I saw as a tiny, sizzling needle, drilled through the monster's armpit. Meant to lance simple boils, it burst the cyst around the infant corpse. The flux's ebon bile poured into the *tellek bicha*'s body.

Veins pulsed black throughout the creature's flesh. The *tellek bicha* shuddered and faltered. The right leg collapsed. Nitidean slammed to the ground, scattering stone. Kellach bounced from nerveless fingers.

The creature scrabbled weakly, clawing furrows through white marble. Its hisses grew shorter and weaker as blood dripped from its nostrils. A white membrane nictitated slowly over its black eyes.

Kellach climbed to his feet, and leaped over a weak grab. He approached its head, grasping the jaw and skull.

"Don't bother. It will be dead in another minute."

Kellach's muscles bunched. He wrenched. The neck snapped. "Why waste time?"

"I agree. Nitidean was a construct. He substituted the ring, but he didn't create it."

The Cengar nodded. "The sorceress?"

"I'm pretty sure." I stretched out on the ground. "I'm going for her. Wish me luck."

If he did, I don't know. I closed my eyes and pulled myself through the Third Veil before his words ever had a chance to reach me.

The realm beyond the Third Veil is a place of no set geography or climate. Some say it is the place where the gods dream. Others think it is the womb from which the gods sprang. I find neither idea comforting and consider both the musings of men who have too much spare time on their hands, none of which they've spent there.

I emerged into a black landscape lit with lurid crimson lightning. Steaming rivers flowed past. Bodies bobbed in blood, and half-hidden creatures dragged them to the depths. Barren black bushes festooned with thorns dotted the land-scape.

I smiled, and a flower blossomed a brilliant yellow. Such was the world past the Third Veil. Reality was mutable and decided upon by mutual consent. I'd painted lots of it black since Aviantis fell.

My flower wilted.

Someone was really angry.

I moved quickly, leaping the river with ease. As twisted and small as I am in the physical world, I stride through this realm like Kellach amid children. Such is the paradox of magick among men that, with a few exceptions, what you lack in the physical you gain in the magickal, leaving most people average in both realms and unable to pierce even a single Veil.

I found her Lair with ease, and called it a Lair not because she was Sepheri. Those of sufficient skill can fashion their own worlds within the realm, and hers hung as a bright, shiny apple on a cinder-armed tree. Her magickal essence waited within.

I reached up and let the apple rest in the palm of my hand. She stirred therein, a worm trapped in the fruit. She cultivated a sense of vulnerability to lure me in. To accept her invitation would be foolishness because whoever created the Lair governed the Lair. To fight her fairly I'd have to entice her to emerge.

Then I remembered her glamours. The apple was bait, something I'd been expected to see, and that meant I was already in the trap. I tried to pull back, but the apple stuck to my hand, then the thorny branches wrapped round me, piercing me, and drew me into the tree's heart.

She made no attempt to conceal her form. From the waist up she was fully human and female if I chose to ignore her scaled flesh. Below, where legs should have been, her body coiled like a snake's. She wore the sand gold she'd given Nitidean, though the speckles ran thicker on her neck, shoulders, and arms.

Her gold eyes narrowed. "You have vexed me. You've ruined plans long in the making."

I would have spread my arms, but they were already pulled wide. "You would rule through Nitidean, controlling lands that were once yours?"

"And will be mine again." She smiled, flashing fang. "I have traveled more swiftly than my kin."

"The Sepheri never arrive strong enough to reestablish control."

"Some of us anticipated the Scattering. We planned. Our plans bear fruit." She slithered forward and grabbed my jaw in a long, taloned hand. "You will help me."

Her claw raked through my neck. Energy spurted as if it were blood. I cast a spell to staunch the flow, and she opposed it, keeping the wound open. I moved to pinch off a vein. Though I had no veins there, if I visualized the rent in one, I could close it. She forced it back open.

A bulbous jar appeared in her other hand. She pressed it against my breastbone, slowly filling it with the energy leaking from me. Collecting it distracted her, so I plugged a hole. This gave me hope, but she crushed it, strangled it.

Then it grew anew as I fought back. I won, pushing hard, closing my throat. I smiled and almost laughed. In her realm I was winning, which should have been impossible.

And with another caress of a talon over my throat, I realized it was impossible. She toyed with me, torturing me, slowly draining my essence for future use. Hope could be incredibly powerful—able to work miracles among the magick-ignorant.

I stopped fighting.

She slapped me. "Do not give up now, little man." She came closer and pressed her lips to mine. "I want it all."

Repulsed, I wanted to fight, but she would win.

Her tongue flickered against my lips. She pulled me closer. A thumb on my chin pried my jaw open. Her feathery tongue slithered into my mouth.

Then she jolted, and her Lair imploded.

It felt as if her Lair had shattered into a million crystal shards. Every one of them blew through me. I gasped and coughed. I pushed up, but my hands slipped in blood. I rolled to the side and banged my head on a wall. Stars shimmered, then vision returned.

Kellach held Veneceana's severed head by the hair. Two servants lay dead, and four more cowered in a corner with a pair of the Duke's Wurmhounds holding them at bay. I pulled farther back, realizing my tingling feet still lay on her body, then pulled myself from the pallet.

I staggered and went to my knees.

Kellach buried a bloody short sword in a table, then hauled me to my feet. He stared at me.

I held up gory hands. "I need a moment. I should not be here."

"You are still welcome." He recovered the blade and wiped

it on her gown before sliding it into the scabbard. "We should not linger."

"No." I shook my head to clear it, then used a spell to check myself. None of the blood was mine. My throat wound was closed, though I'd carry a pair of scars for the rest of my life. Despite my legs' trembling and the overwhelming desire to lie down and sleep, I figured I would survive.

What I couldn't figure out was how I'd ended up there. Veneceana must have somehow dragged me physically through the Veils when she returned to her body. Such a thing was impossible, at least to my knowledge, but it had happened. She had suggested she had anticipated the Scattering. Was that ability part of it?

I leaned on a table and overturned a wine pitcher. I washed my bloody hands, then followed Kellach. I might not have made it, save one of the Wurmhounds let me hold on to its tail.

"The dogs found this place by the scent of your piss?"

The Cengar laughed, then emerged into a wider lane and crossed to a closed, horse-drawn carriage. Two hands slid through a curtained window and smeared Sepheri blood over themselves. The Bloodlock ring slipped off easily and shattered against the ground.

The carriage door opened and Duke Darikean stepped forth, still looking like a victim of the black flux. His pet sorcerer followed him and gestured, removing the glamour that had so effectively made him appear dead.

The Wurmhounds went to him but did not lick at his hands.

My eyes narrowed. "Kellach reported back to you that we'd met Veneceana and you recognized the name."

"Not the name, but the description. When I was a youth,

she seduced me. Though I kept her as a mistress for several years, I sent her away when I first married. I thought she had left the city."

"Then you went off to Aviantis. She poisoned your wife and child, then later replaced the child. You raised the viper in your own home." I shook my head. "You faked your death to precipitate her plans?"

He nodded.

"But that got your son killed. Your wife and daughter as well."

He cocked his head. "Though I knew she was involved, I did not know who had become her agent in my household."

"If you'd told me she was your enemy, I could have learned Nitidean's secret." I ran a hand over my jaw. "That would have required trust. You didn't trust me. You didn't trust your own family."

"I can always replace a family."

I closed my eyes, wishing no longer to peer into the soulless pits in his face. The carriage's springs squeaked as he got back in. The horse stamped. Something heavy bounced from my chest and clanked on the ground.

I looked. A bulging purse.

I almost did it. I almost reached back and gathered enough power to convert his carriage into the pyre he'd avoided.

The driver snapped the reins, and the carriage clattered from sight, the dogs trailing obediently.

Kellach knelt and hefted the purse. "A generous offering."

"I suppose." I rubbed my chest. "He's alive. That's all the Iron Duke cares about. It's all he *can* care about."

Kellach stood but said nothing.

"That man let my city die, and I just saved his life."

"He is mortal." The Cengar tossed the pouch up and caught it again. "He could die sooner than he expects."

I smiled at my friend's veiled offer of murder, then shook my head. "His home is a hall of the dead. He thinks he can replace a family. Maybe. But while he lay there pretending to be dead, he heard his family mourning his death. They loved him as he never could have loved them."

"Some men do not need that."

"Don't kid yourself, my friend, every man needs that, and those who think they don't need it even more." I plucked the money from his hand.

"In the cold hours before dawn, the Iron Duke will hear their wails repeated. He will never sleep well again."

The House of Seven Spirits

by Sharon Shinn

I had thought it would bother me to live in a haunted house, but in fact I grew fond of the ghosts in an amazingly short time.

The agent from whom I rented the property for the summer had been very clear about the amenities—three bedrooms, two bathrooms, renovated kitchen, wi-fi DSL, cable TV, a small backyard, weekly yard service, and seven unevictable tenants.

"Some people never see them," he told me, his dark eyes earnest and his pale face severe. He'd tried to talk me out of renting the place, but I couldn't pass up its dirt-cheap price. Writers just don't make that much money, and I had almost despaired of finding someplace I could afford for a few months while I put my life back together. "But everyone always reports a sense of being watched. Accompanied. I don't believe they'll harm you. But you might be—uncomfortable."

Uncomfortable was staying in the tiny New York apartment with Steve while we hammered out the terms of a divorce.

Could seven sad wraiths fill me with as much anger and despair? Hard to believe.

"How did they die?" I asked.

He reeled them off as if he'd given this particular speech too often to count. "Martin shot his wife, Suzanne, and her lover, Bradley, when he came home and found them together. Then he killed himself. That was fifteen years ago. A couple of years after that, two elderly women, Victoria and Charlotte, died of carbon monoxide poisoning—that's been taken care of, by the way. A middle-aged man named Edison fell down the stairs and broke his neck. Lizzie died of spinal meningitis when she was nine years old. Her mother thought she just had a bad case of the flu. That was three years ago. No one's died in the house since because no one's lived there very long."

"Who owns the place?"

"Family members. I deal most often with a niece who owns and rents out a number of properties in the area." He gave me another serious look. "You should think hard before you decide you want to live in this house."

"I'll chance it. I ain't afraid of no ghosts."

He didn't laugh. Maybe he didn't get the reference. I wrote out a check for my first month's rent, got a map, got a key, and set out for my new home.

I was met just inside the front door by an older woman with curly gray hair and a wide, hopeful smile. I'd always thought ghosts would be a misty white, floating from room to room like errant wisps of smoke. But this one was colorful in a pink-and-purple-patterned blouse and navy blue trousers. Insubstantial, though—she looked like a watercolor painted on a sheet of gauze. I could see straight through her to the polished taupe of the walls.

Despite the rental agent's warning, I was startled to see her, and I dropped my key. "Hello!" I said, feeling my heart beat suddenly harder. "Um—I'm the new tenant. Erica. I'm here for the summer. Hope that's all right."

She clapped her hands together, though they made no sound, and looked delighted. "You can *see* me!" she exclaimed. "Oh, I'm so glad. The couple who were here last—well—they clearly knew when one of us was in the room, but no matter how loud we were or how much we waved our arms, they just never seemed to be able to *focus*. They didn't stay long," she added sadly. "We didn't mean to frighten them. I hope you won't be afraid."

Indeed, my heart had already settled down to a normal pace. She looked like somebody's grandmother, just in from the kitchen after having made a batch of cookies. "Not afraid yet," I said. "Which one are you?"

She smiled again. "Victoria. So pleased to meet you."

I glanced around. "Maybe you can give me a tour of the house."

It was a lovely place, probably eighty years old, two stories of hardwood floors and hard plaster walls and shabby-chic furniture that someone had picked out with care. But my first walk-through was a little—unusual.

"Here's the kitchen, where Martin died," Victoria said, showing me the small but spotless black-and-white-tiled room. The dining room hadn't seen much action, but the living room was the place where "Charlotte and I were watching TV when we were overcome by carbon monoxide poisoning." She sighed. "We only got to see the first couple seasons of *The X-Files*. I always wanted to know what happened."

"There were a couple of movies, too," I said.

"I know! Never got to see them, either."

So they must have died before 1998. "Were you and Charlotte sisters?"

"Lifelong friends. Widows. We moved in together after her husband died." She headed toward the stairs, gesturing at a pretty rug placed beneath the very bottom step. "That's where Edison lay dying after he fell and broke his neck. He was alive for quite some time, but none of us could figure out how to use the phone and call for help. Very tragic."

I stepped gingerly on the floral pattern of the rug. "He just fell?"

She glanced over her shoulder at me, an impish look in her eye. "Well. He *says* that Martin pushed him. Impossible, of course. Martin *may* have appeared suddenly and frightened him, causing him to take a misstep, but he doesn't have any more strength than the rest of us."

I swallowed. Martin was the only one of the ghosts who had violence associated with his past, at least as far as I knew. "Would he—is Martin the kind of person who would *want* to shove someone down the stairs? Did he frighten Edison on purpose?"

"Martin *is* very angry," Victoria admitted. "It's my theory that no one who dies in this house will ever be permitted to leave as long as Martin's spirit is still tethered here. But did he try to kill Edison? I doubt it. He dislikes Edison even more than the rest of us do. I wouldn't think Martin would have wanted to be stuck with him for—well, forever."

I thought that over as Victoria showed me through the upstairs rooms. "Here's the bedroom where Bradley and Suzanne were killed. Some people say you can still see the blood on the floor, but *I've* never been able to make it out . . . This is the bedroom where Lizzie died. Poor thing. She was so *hot*. Charlotte and I stayed with her all night because, you know, a ghost can bring a chill to the air, and we hoped it would bring her fever down. But no such luck . . . Her body went still, then her spirit just sat up. She looked at us, and said, 'I guess I'm here with you two now.'"

Lizzie's room was smaller, for Bradley and Suzanne had been killed in the master bedroom, but I liked it better. More light streamed in through the two tall windows, and the view showed the small green backyard. And, OK, I was less unnerved by the idea of sleeping alongside the ghost of a girl who had died of illness than the thought of sharing a bed with the spirits of two murder victims.

"I think I'll make this my bedroom," I said.

Victoria gestured down the hall. "The third bedroom is quite nice, and no one died there," she said. Clearly I hadn't fooled her at all.

So I followed her into a room about the size of Lizzie's and prettily furnished, but it was instantly clear to me that it would be my last choice. For one thing, the sun had a hard time making its way through the single side window. For another, the room was significantly colder than any other room in the house.

For another, it really was haunted.

A thin, bony-faced woman sat on the bed, apparently reciting a story to a small blond girl who leaned against her, smiling sleepily. They had to be Charlotte and Lizzie. A dark-haired young woman stood at the window, looking out; I could only see her profile, but the twist of her mouth was bitter and dissatisfied. A few feet away from her stood a short, pudgy man who looked like he had once been ruddy and choleric. He was talking so loudly that I couldn't hear the tale Charlotte was spinning for Lizzie.

"If you'd only *ask* him to be more thoughtful. He'll listen to *you*. But, no, you're too selfish to think about anyone but yourself or anything but your own misery."

The woman at the window ignored him, but Charlotte gave him an icy stare. "For God's sake, Edison, no one has ever had any success at getting Martin to behave in any but the most abominable fashion, and your incessant complaining is about to drive every single one of us stark raving mad. Will you just *shut up*?"

I couldn't help it. I laughed. Instantly, they were all staring at me. I had the strange sensation that *they* hadn't seen *me* when I walked through the door—as if whatever plane ghosts existed on really didn't intersect with the ordinary world, at least all the time. I tried to smooth away my smile. "Sorry," I said. "I'm Erica. Victoria's showing me around."

Charlotte looked at Victoria with her eyebrows raised. "She sees *all* of us?"

"I see you and the little girl—Lizzie?—and Edison," I volunteered. "And someone at the window. Suzanne, I guess. I haven't seen Martin or—" For a moment I blanked on his name. "Or Bradley yet." I glanced at Victoria. "Did I miss them?"

She shook her head. "They must be in the yard. They can't go past the property boundaries, but both of them like to be outside of the house."

Charlotte stood up, urging Lizzie forward. I had the feeling that the older woman would have offered me her hand, except long experience had taught her it was useless for a ghost. "How very nice to meet you," she said, her voice more reserved than Victoria's but her pleasure just as genuine. "We hope you'll enjoy your stay."

Lizzie jumped up and down. "Will you play with me?

Will you read me stories? Charlotte tells me stories all the time, but she doesn't know any new ones. Will you go to the library and check out new books for me? And read them to me? Every night?"

I was charmed. "I will. What kinds of books do you like?"

Edison made a huffing sound. "Oh, sure, the cute little girl gets all the attention! It doesn't matter what anyone else wants. You could read *me* Tom Clancy books, but will you? I don't think so!"

"Shut up, Edison," Suzanne said. She had moved away from the window and was heading for the door. It seemed to me that she had less color than the others—she was a closer approximation of my idea of a ghost—that her very manner and expression were drenched in sadness. She gave me one unfathomable look and slipped out the door.

"Well, nobody cares about me," Edison muttered. "I'm the one everyone always forgets."

"I don't think I'll forget you, Edison," I said cheerfully. "I think we'll all be friends."

And oddly, we were. I mean, almost right away. As soon as I hauled all my stuff in from the car, I headed out to run errands. I picked up food at the grocery store, books at the library, and DVDs at Blockbuster. That very night, I set up entertainment zones in four separate rooms of the house. I'd rented a few seasons of *The X-Files* for Charlotte and Victoria, and I set up the first discs to play in the living room. Victoria told me that Bradley liked PBS shows, so I had the little TV in the kitchen tuned to the local public television station, even though Bradley still hadn't made an appearance. For

Edison, I'd rented a selection of Dean Koontz, Stephen King, and Tom Clancy books on CD, and I had one of them running on my laptop up in the third bedroom, where the ghosts seemed to like to congregate.

Lizzie and I settled into her room/my room, and I read her half of a Baby-Sitter's Club book. She leaned against me just as she had against Charlotte, listening happily. There was no weight to her body, but I felt a coolness against my skin, as if a curl of winter had blown through the window and come to rest companionably at my side.

Victoria had said there was no way to make Martin happy, so I didn't bother trying to figure out what I might do for him. The rest of us passed a very enjoyable evening, and I could feel the contentment radiating throughout the entire house. Indeed, when I finally turned out the light and went to bed, I fell asleep almost instantly and I didn't wake till dawn.

My first night in the haunted house was far more peaceful than my last hundred nights in the apartment I'd shared with my husband. Had my life held so many terrors lately that I had actually *upgraded* it by moving in with restless spirits? Had the world of the living proved so perilous that I was more at ease among the dead?

The following weeks quickly settled into a pattern. During the day, I worked on my novel, occasionally taking breaks to walk around the neighborhood, explore the town, or replenish supplies. In the evenings, I hung out with my new roommates. Now and then I was able to find a movie or program that everyone in the household could agree on—*Buffy* was a universal favorite, for instance, and even Edison enjoyed Pixar movies—but most of the time I activated the distinct enter-tainment zones that everyone preferred. Edison developed the habit of heading down to the kitchen to watch PBS with Bradley once the CD of the day had finished playing. I knew that, because he also developed the annoying habit of telling the rest of us the next day what he'd learned the night before about Mayan ruins or asteroid belts or creatures of the deep sea. It was preferable to his other favorite topic of conversa-tion, however, which was to claim that Martin had murdered him by pushing him down the stairs.

I didn't know what Bradley thought about sharing his TV viewing time with Edison. During those first two weeks, neither Bradley nor Martin made an appearance. I couldn't decide if I should be sorry or glad.

I did meet a few of my neighbors, though. The young couple on the right usually just waved as they left for work in the mornings, and the older woman on my left never wanted to talk about anything but how late the paperboy was, but the woman who lived behind me was gregarious and cheerful. A low tangle of honeysuckle separated our yards and perfumed our conversations as we stood on either side to talk.

That first day, she introduced herself as Janet and waved at me with a trowel. She was a fiftyish brown-haired woman dressed in shapeless gardening clothes and a big straw hat that partially obscured her face. "You're the new renter?" she asked. "How are you getting along with the ghosts?"

She said it in a playful way that made me think she was joking. So I gave a noncommittal answer and a big smile. "Very well, thank you. They don't trouble me at all."

She laughed. "Excellent! So perhaps you'll stay longer than the last few tenants. I think one of them decamped within a week."

"I'd like to stay," I admitted. "I'm falling in love with the house." I fanned myself with the magazine I'd been reading on the back porch before I spotted Janet. "How long have you lived here?"

"Oh, let's see—goodness, I think I moved in twenty years ago."

"So you must have been living here when the murders happened," I said.

She nodded. "It was terrible. I was very close to Suzanne. I kept telling her to leave Martin. He was so unstable, it was so *obvious* he would turn violent if he ever found out about Bradley. I'd had an abusive husband of my own, and so I knew—" Janet paused and shook her head. "But she wouldn't listen to me. And when that sweet girl was murdered, I wept for days."

"Were you here when it happened?"

She nodded. "I saw the police cars, and I ran over to see if I could help. I'm a nurse at the ER and—but they were all long dead."

I thought she might be weeping, all these years later, and I hastily changed the subject. "My other neighbors seem very nice," I said. "I haven't had very long conversations with them, though."

"Oh, I like them all," she said. "But I think Joan and Bruce might be moving soon. She wants a dog."

"And? She can't have a dog here?"

Janet shook her head. "It's your house. Animals don't like it. Last three or four times one of the near neighbors has tried to get a dog—any dog—the animal would just refuse to calm down. Would stand right there in the yard, facing your house, and bark its head off. Cats won't stay either. They run off the first time they can get out the door."

I was disappointed. I'd been thinking about getting a cat. "Maybe the house really *is* haunted," I said softly.

Janet smiled sadly. "Oh, I'm convinced it is."

I was working on my book one afternoon when a ghost I hadn't seen before stalked in and settled in the chair across from my desk. "I suppose you're not going to leave," he said in a dark voice.

He startled me. I believe an undignified "eek!" actually passed my lips, but I wasn't exactly afraid. I hit SAVE and closed my laptop so I could study him. A handsome man, I decided. I guessed Suzanne to be about thirty, and this man was maybe a year or two older. He had rumpled brown hair and an intense gaze that gave him a brooding air. Altogether, he cultivated a somewhat Byronic manner that suited my notions of ghosthood as much as Suzanne's die-away despair. "Which one are you?" I inquired.

He sneered. "You mean, am I the wronged husband or the doomed lover? The murderer or the fool?"

"Yes," I said calmly. "That's what I meant."

He didn't answer for a moment. I made sure to take in details of his face and clothing so that I could ask Victoria later whom I had had the pleasure of meeting, in case he never told me. But he shrugged, and said, "I'm the fool."

I propped my chin on my hand. "For loving a married woman?" I said. "Lot of people make that mistake."

He snorted. "For believing she was worth loving."

My eyebrows rose. This was a new twist. "You and Suzanne had a falling-out? Was this the night you were—were discovered?"

He looked away. "No. That night I loved her as much as I ever had. It was just—later—when I found out—" He shook his head. "How could I ever have loved someone like her?" he burst out.

My eyes went wide. "You discovered something—after you died? A secret about Suzanne?"

He watched me a moment with those dark eyes. Sexy. *Just a little more corporeal mass,* I found myself thinking, *and I'd want to sleep with you, too.* "Doesn't everyone have secrets?" he asked at last. "Don't you?"

I reviewed my own life. "Things I don't like to talk about, maybe," I allowed. "Not necessarily secrets."

"I have to wonder about someone who seems to be perfectly happy when she's living in a house that harbors seven ghosts and the memories of three murders."

"Three? Oh, you mean Edison?" I said, a little amused. "I haven't encountered Martin yet, but did he really push Edison down the steps?"

Bradley was sneering. Still attractive. "He talked about wanting to do it almost from the day the man moved in."

I almost laughed. "I'm sure the rest of you tried to dissuade him. To be stuck with Edison forever!"

Bradley didn't smile. Indeed, his gaze became even more intense as he hitched himself forward on the chair. "You must help me," he said. "Help all of us. We're trapped in this house together—for time everlasting—hating each other, unable to get away. For so long I wanted Martin dead, but once he died—he's the one who keeps us all here. Put him at rest, and all of us will be at peace."

"But how do I do that?" I asked, bewildered.

Bradley stood up. "Uncover the lie," he said. "Once a living person knows the truth, we will all be free." And, before my eyes, he vanished.

"I don't know what truth he means," Victoria said. She was helping me make dinner that night. I wasn't much of a cook, and of course Victoria couldn't eat, but apparently she'd been something of a chef in her day. We had gotten in the habit of meeting in the kitchen a couple of nights a week so she could walk me through one of her favorite recipes. "The truth is that Martin killed Bradley and Suzanne, then killed himself. No, dear, not *that* much garlic."

"But maybe that's *not* the truth," I said. "Maybe Suzanne is really the one who shot Bradley and herself. Maybe that's what Bradley meant. And Martin's been blamed all this time. Maybe that's why he's so mad. I'd be mad, too."

"She was shot in the back, so I don't think so," Victoria said. "But, you know, ever since I've been here, there's been some trouble between Bradley and Suzanne. You would think that lovers who had been murdered together would cling to each other in the afterlife, but that's never been the case. They're almost never in the same room, and if Suzanne comes in the kitchen while Brad is here, he simply walks out. You can tell that she's devastated, after all this time. She doesn't know why he no longer loves her. Because she loves him still."

I tasted the sauce I was creating for my pasta del mar. Victoria was right. Not *that* much garlic. "Is that why she seems so sad? I mean, even for a ghost, she seems—miserable. Inconsolable." I smiled at Victoria. "*You* seem quite happy."

"Well, I always was," she said comfortably. "No need to change now."

Edison wandered through and made a great show of holding his nose. "I hate the smell of fish. Makes me want to vomit."

"Shut up, Edison," Victoria said, and he *humphed* and stalked out.

Edison had also complained a couple nights ago when I ate some takeout crab rangoon. "I don't know, maybe I shouldn't eat seafood while I'm living here," I said with a sigh. "I hate for him to be offended."

Victoria was unimpressed. "If you're going to worry about all of *our* food preferences, you won't be able to eat a thing," she said. "Suzanne is a vegetarian, Lizzie hates broccoli, Bradley is allergic to tomatoes and blueberries, red wine gives Charlotte a migraine, and Martin is lactose intolerant."

"What about you?"

Victoria smiled. "I eat everything." She looked suddenly wistful. "Or I used to. Now, of course, I can't taste a thing."

"I still wonder what Bradley meant," I said. "I did a Google search about the murder—"

"A what?" Victoria repeated.

"Google. It's—it helps you find information on the Internet." She still looked mystified, so I shook my head. "Never mind. I think I'll have to go to the library and see if they have microfiche with newspaper coverage. Maybe that will give me some ideas."

"Oh, I have a scrapbook," Victoria said. "After we moved in, I looked up the stories about Brad and Suzanne and Martin. There wasn't much," she added. "It was such a very common and obvious crime."

After my meal (which was pretty good, if heavy on seasoning), Victoria led me to the living room, where a jumble of books and old magazines filled two built-in bookcases.

"All your stuff is still here?" I asked. "That's convenient."

Victoria nodded and settled on the floor to scan the bottom shelf. It was completely filled with scrapbooks and photo albums. A treasure trove for me to look through on some future date, I decided. She said, "We were only renting the house from Suzanne's sister, but we planned to live here a good long time. She let us decorate however we wished—and then she just kept everything in the house so she could rent it out furnished. I think she knew right then she would never have boarders who stayed very long. There, I think that's the book you want."

I pulled out the volume she indicated and began leafing through the pages. It wasn't a modern scrapbook with decorative papers and fancy borders. No, it was just a couple of sturdy covers wrapped around thick black pages. In it, Victoria had collected all sorts of news clippings related to events in this decade of her life—her husband's death, her son's Army heroics, her granddaughter's baptism.

Articles about the murder/suicide appeared late in the book, and I sat right there on the floor and read them. The first thing I found out was that Martin hadn't killed himself with a gun, as I'd always believed.

"He took morphine?" I said, looking up from the page to stare at Victoria. "He shot two people, but he couldn't stand to shoot himself?"

"It's harder to bear pain than it is to inflict it," Victoria said.

The second thing I learned was that Martin really was cold-blooded. Police theorized that Martin had come home unexpectedly, heard voices, retrieved his gun from the living room case where he always kept it, crept upstairs, and shot his wife and her lover. Then he'd come back downstairs, laid the gun on the kitchen table, opened a beer, eaten a bowl of leftover chili, and turned on the football game. (The television was still playing the next day when police came to investigate why his wife wasn't at work.) He appeared to have chased his second beer with a handful of morphine tablets, which took effect when he was back in the kitchen (looking for his third beer, they believed).

"Where'd he get the morphine?" I asked Victoria. "It doesn't say."

She pointed at the book. "Next article."

I turned the page and read another story that gave more detail about the troubled couple. A friend was speculating that their marriage had started to show signs of strain the year before, when his mother moved into their house as she was dying of cancer. "Probably some leftover morphine in the medicine cabinet," Victoria said. "Surely his mother had a prescription."

I nodded. "Makes sense. Still. This is even creepier than before."

"Now you know why the rest of us are just as happy when Martin keeps to himself."

But Martin made an unexpected, and not particularly welcome, appearance just the next day. I had gone to the third bedroom—the place I was most likely to find ghosts—and had been lucky enough to discover Suzanne alone. As usual, she stood at the single window, looking insubstantial enough to evaporate, but weighted in place by the heaviness of grief.

"I want to ask you some questions," I said, speaking fast. Suzanne never hung around for long, so it was best to skip any amenities and get straight to the point. "When you were married—why didn't you leave Martin?"

She didn't turn around to look at me. "I was afraid of him. I thought he'd kill me." She gave a small laugh. "And he did."

"Did Brad want you to run away with him?"

"Yes. Said we could change our names. Move to a different state. Move to a different country. Said he would always love me." She sniffed, as if holding back tears.

"But Brad is angry at you now. Why?"

She didn't answer for a moment. "He won't tell me," she said at last. "He just says I'm not worth loving anymore."

Well, *that* was unhelpful. "Do you have a guess?"

Even if she'd planned to answer, she didn't get a chance. "Don't ask a lying *bitch* for information!" a voice roared, and I jumped nearly a foot in the air. The room was suddenly ice-cold and dark with shadows. I could just make out a lumbering shape—big body, small head, fisted hands—an even-more-insubstantial spirit than Suzanne. "Goddamn *whore* would say anything she thought you would believe!"

Suzanne choked down a cry and hurried past him, out of the room. I didn't know if I should be glad for her or worried for myself that Martin didn't follow. Instead, he stayed facing me, panting heavily, swinging his little head from side to side. I wrapped my arms around myself and wished I had a sweater.

"I suppose you're Martin," I said.

"Get the hell out of my house!" he bellowed.

I stood my ground. "I'm just trying to help," I said calmly. "I want to understand what happened that night."

"What happened? What *happened*? I found my wife screwing another man, that's what happened! Should have strangled both of them with my bare hands. Bitch deserved to die staring me right in the face."

"Why didn't you shoot yourself?" I asked.

He took three quick steps closer, and I felt myself enveloped in menace and chill. Suddenly I believed Edison when he said Martin had deliberately forced him down the stairs. I was pretty sure Martin would have liked to shove me out the window. "Because I didn't want to give her the satisfaction," he spat. "Why don't *you* shoot yourself?"

Shooting, no; running, yes. I was shivering, and frightened, and trying to edge past him toward the door, when suddenly I felt a flurry in the air behind him. "Martin!" came Charlotte's stern voice. "You leave her alone *right this minute.* Such behavior! Out of the room—out, I say!"

He turned on her with a curse, but Bradley and Edison flanked her on either side. I wondered wildly whether ghosts could touch each other even if they couldn't touch living people and if that meant the other three could manhandle Martin out the door. But they didn't need to. He snarled something unintelligible at the three of them and stomped into the hall. Instantly, the room warmed by fifteen degrees.

"My heroes," I said faintly. "Thanks, guys."

That night I rented season two of *Buffy,* and all of us, minus Martin, gathered in the living room to watch. I worried that the story line might be a little violent at times for Lizzie, but she just curled up on Charlotte's lap and covered her eyes anytime there was too much blood. Suzanne and Bradley were both in the room, though in opposite corners, and her eyes were on him more often than they were on the screen. For the most part, he ignored her, but if ghosts could be said to have body language, I was sure he was highly aware of her.

What had gone wrong between the lovers?

After the first DVD, I was too tired to stay awake any longer. "Want me to set up the next disc or just turn the channel to TCM?" I asked through a yawn.

"TCM," Victoria and Charlotte said in unison. Victoria added, "There's a Barbara Stanwyck retrospective. I just love her movies."

"Then movies you shall have," I said, and flipped the necessary switches. *Double Indemnity* had already started before I was halfway up the stairs.

I woke at noon the next day and sat straight up in bed. Maybe if I'd stayed up to watch the movie, the revelation would have hit me the night before. It was certainly the stuff of cinema: Woman schemes to kill her husband, ensnaring an innocent man in her plan. Except Bradley hadn't had any idea what Suzanne planned to do. Easy enough for her to crush a few morphine tablets and slip them into a container of leftover chili, then wait for Martin to come home and eat it. All she had to do was not taste the doctored food.

I frowned and leaned back against the headboard. But unless she'd told Bradley not to eat the chili, how could she be sure *he* wouldn't accidentally take the drugs? And it was clear Bradley had had no idea Suzanne intended to do away with her husband. Once he'd found out, he was horrified. But how to warn him off without giving herself away?

I heard Victoria's voice in my head. *Suzanne is a vegetarian, Lizzie hates broccoli, Bradley is allergic to tomatoes and blueberries, red wine gives Charlotte a migraine, and Martin is lactose intolerant.*

Safe to leave poisoned chili in the fridge for Martin. The allergy-stricken Brad would never eat it.

I drew up my knees and thought hard. So. Martin hadn't killed himself after all. He came home, shot his wife and her lover, and *didn't* shoot himself because he didn't *plan* to kill himself. *I wouldn't give her the satisfaction.* Still, it didn't make it any less creepy that he'd gone back downstairs, opened a beer, microwaved the chili, and settled in to watch the game while Suzanne and Bradley lay dead upstairs.

I frowned again. Unless that hadn't been exactly how the story played out . . .

I jumped up, threw on some clothes, paused long enough to brush my teeth, and began hunting for Suzanne. She wasn't in the third bedroom with Charlotte and Lizzie, nor on the stairwell landing with Edison.

"Martin pushed me down the steps, you know," he said in his whiny voice as I hurried past.

"Shut up, Edison," I said automatically, and bounded down the stairs. Suzanne wasn't in the living room with Bradley (TCM was still on, playing John Wayne movies), and she wasn't in the kitchen with Victoria.

"Garden," Victoria said when I asked. "Why? Erica, you look so excited!"

"I think I've solved it," I said.

I heard Brad's voice behind me. He must have noticed my wild-eyed look, too, and followed me into the kitchen. "Solved what?" he asked.

I shook my head and pushed through the back door. Suzanne was sitting on a little bench set near the house, facing Janet's backyard. There was a woman working in the garden, but I didn't think it was Janet. At any rate, she didn't straighten up and wave, as Janet always did.

"Suzanne," I said as I strode toward the bench, trailed by Victoria and Bradley. "*You* did it. *You* killed Martin."

I heard Victoria's gasp and Bradley's little hiss of victory, but Suzanne jumped to her feet. "I did *not*!" she cried. "I know that's what Bradley thinks—how could you believe such a terrible thing about a woman you love?—but I didn't! I *didn't*!"

"You put the morphine in the chili," I persisted. "You knew Brad wouldn't touch it, because he was allergic to tomatoes. You just had to wait for Martin to come home and eat the chili, and you'd be rid of your husband. You tried to murder him before he tried to murder you!"

"Oh, my," Victoria said. "That *would* explain why Martin is so angry."

"But I didn't do that," Suzanne sobbed.

I ignored the obvious lie. "In fact," I said, "I'm guessing Martin was already half-dead before he pulled the trigger on you. He didn't come home, shoot you, then settle in for a little football and beer. He'd already eaten his poisoned dinner and was watching the game when he heard something upstairs. You killed him *first*."

"We had fallen asleep," Bradley said, sounding weary. He had moved around from behind me so I could see his face. He looked tired, too tired of holding on to secrets for so many years, maybe. "I woke up and heard the TV downstairs. I knew we had to get out of there before he found us, so I shook Suzanne. But she—" He shrugged. "I'd forgotten that it was a bad idea to wake her up suddenly. She had nightmares, and she always came out of a sound sleep screaming. That's what Martin heard. He was upstairs with the gun before we could get out of bed."

"And downstairs, already staggering, before he could leave the house," I said. "He had no intention of staying there with the two of you dead. But the morphine overtook him while he was in the kitchen, trying to get out the back door."

Bradley was staring at Suzanne. "How could you *do* that?" he whispered. "I would have taken you away from him. I would have kept you safe."

"How could you hate me so much?" she wailed. Weeping, she stumbled back into the house.

"Oh, dear," said Victoria. "Such a nasty thing to discover."

Bradley was looking after Suzanne with an expression of utter wretchedness on his face. "God. And I still love her," he muttered.

I said, "Maybe you—" But he cut me off.

"No," he said. "She killed a man." And he stalked around the side of the house to go pace back and forth across the front yard and frighten passersby.

"I'll go talk to her," Victoria said.

I looked at her curiously. I had discovered the truth, which was what Bradley had said Martin wanted. Did that mean Martin would be at peace? Did that mean all my ghosts would disappear? But Victoria looked the same as ever, brightly colored and almost fleshly. "You realize this might mean the end of Martin's hold on you," I said slowly. "You realize that, once he finds out what I've discovered, you might all dissipate."

I expected her to show a moment's sadness, but she nodded firmly. "Good. Time for us to move on. We'd all be glad of the rest. But as long as we're still here, I'm going to go comfort that girl."

I watched her go, wondering if I should join the conversation but not ready to hear Suzanne's protestations of innocence one more time. Before I could go back inside, the neighbor from Janet's yard waved me over.

"Hello!" she called. "Come introduce yourself. I'm Marianne."

I wondered if she had just noticed me having an excited conversation with my collection of wraiths—whom she probably couldn't see—and if that had led her to deduce that I was crazy. But as I strolled up to the tangled thicket separating our yards, I saw nothing but friendly interest on her face, which was tan and cheerful. She looked to be in her early thirties, with streaked blond hair and a trim figure. She was wearing gardening clothes at the moment, but it was easy to imagine that she spent most of her days in tailored suits. She had that sort of professional air.

"I'm Erica," I said. "I don't think I've seen you before. I've scarcely met any of the neighbors."

She gave a little sigh. "None of us gets to know our neighbors in these busy times," she said. "And I've been traveling. But I heard the haunted house had found a tenant for the summer, and I'm glad to see you're still here. Any trouble with ghosts?"

So happily worded! So easy to answer in the negative without admitting my affinity for the dead. "No trouble," I replied. "I love the house."

She rested her rake in the dirt and folded her arms on the handle. "So do I," she said. "I inherited four properties from my aunt, and these two are my favorites." She gestured at my house, then her own.

Ah, so Marianne was the niece who still owned the house that had once been Suzanne's. I supposed Janet had been renting all this time. "You must have been pretty young when the murders occurred," I said.

"Sixteen," she replied. "But my aunt Janet talked about them all the time. She just couldn't get over Suzanne's death."

"Aunt Janet," I repeated.

Marianne nodded. "She lived here right up until the day she died. Personally, I think I'd have moved away from a place where I was so tormented by tragedy, but that was Janet for you. A little obsessive."

Janet had *died*? Janet was *dead*? Wait a minute, wait a minute. "I'm confused," I said. "Who was Janet? And she used to own *both* these houses?"

Marianne shook her head. "No, she owned mine. Suzanne owned yours. They were sisters. Janet inherited yours when Suzanne died, and I got everything five years ago when Janet passed away."

I was staring at her. "Sisters . . ."

"I never knew Suzanne all that well, but Janet was strange. Jumpy. My mom said it was because her husband had beaten her up all the time and so any loud noise would scare her. He was killed in a car accident a year or two before Suzanne was murdered. Aunt Janet was never really sane after that. To be honest, it was something of a relief when she died."

I felt a moment's profound dizziness as my mind recalibrated everything I knew. Martin's chili had been poisoned by someone who had known Bradley wouldn't eat it because of his allergies—and that Suzanne wouldn't touch it because it contained meat. Surely a sister would know both those things. Janet had mentioned she was an ER nurse, so she could have had access to morphine even if there hadn't been leftover pills stashed in Martin's medicine cabinet. Janet still hated the husband who had abused her and didn't want to see Suzanne's life ruined in a similar way. *Janet* had killed Martin. Suzanne was innocent, just as she'd said.

"I'm sorry," I said to Marianne. "I've just remembered I

need to make a phone call. So good to talk to you!" And I left her staring after me as I ran to the house.

I started shouting as soon as I was in the kitchen. Victoria looked up in astonishment from the cookbook I had left open on the counter.

"Erica, what in the world—"

"It was Janet!" I called, racing past her. "She poisoned the chili!" I tripped up the stairway, where Edison was lying in wait.

"Martin killed me," he complained. "Just as surely as if he'd pushed me."

"Sorry about that," I panted, and kept going. "Martin!" I called as I dashed toward the third bedroom. "Martin! I know what happened!"

Suzanne was there, flung facedown on the bed, sobbing. Bradley stood over by the window, his hands balled into fists, his face filled with both fury and longing. "She didn't do it," I said breathlessly.

Bradley stared at me. "What?" Suzanne hiccuped and rolled over on her side to give me a drenched but hopeful glance.

I felt the air chill behind me, and I spun around to confront the half-formed darkness that was Martin. "You *were* murdered," I said, speaking very rapidly. "But not by Suzanne. Her sister, Janet, put the drugs in your soup."

Suzanne sat all the way up. "Janet?"

I nodded. "She loved you. She hated him."

Before anyone else could speak, Martin emitted a roar so terrifying that the house actually seemed to shake. It was suddenly zero in the room; for a moment I couldn't see. I shut my eyes and covered my ears and spent a moment shivering with unutterable cold.

Then the noise was gone. The room had warmed back to

its usual cool temperature. I opened my eyes, and not a shadow remained.

Bradley was sitting beside Suzanne on the bed. His arms were wrapped around her shoulders, and she was crying into his chest. "I'm so sorry," he murmured over and over. "So sorry. I love you so very much—"

I left them to their tearful confessions and went to look for the others. But Lizzie wasn't in my bedroom, and Edison wasn't on the stairs. Charlotte wasn't in the living room, and Victoria wasn't in the kitchen. I had the sudden conviction that, for the first time since I'd stepped inside the house, I was truly alone.

I ran up the stairs again, but Brad and Suzanne were no longer in the third bedroom. And the place actually felt as warm as a house ought to feel on a summer day.

I never saw any of the ghosts again, not even Janet. Now and then, just in case they were still nearby but out of my realm of vision, I would let PBS play all night long on the down-stairs television. Occasionally I borrowed a children's book from the library and read it out loud, just in case Lizzie was listening. I still left cookbooks open in the kitchen. But none of them came back to visit; the house was peaceful.

I signed the papers that turned my husband into my ex-husband. Much more civilized than slipping him poison.

I told Marianne I'd be interested in buying the house if she was willing to sell, and she had a price to me the next day. Well within my means, now that Steve and I had divided our property.

But I was lonely. The house was too big for me to live in alone. I decided it was time to get a cat.

Glamour

by Mike Doogan

"It ain't like being a peasant 'n the kingdom o' Tharp is a day at th' Harvest Faire ina first place," Alf said to a chorus of grunts and nods. He lowered his nose into his wooden mug of ale and drank, wiping his mouth with the back of a hand dirty enough to plant a crop on.

"You gotcher locusts," he said, extending a grimy finger for silence, "cher crows, cher rats, cher blight, cher root rot, cher floods 'n frosts, cher drafty mud huts wi' leaky roofs and smoky fireplaces, cher wife what loses interest in you-know-what th' minnit cher done jumpin' th' broom handle t'gether, cher nobility droolin' over cher daughter what's onny thirteen, cher barmaids what whacks you if'n you pinches 'em, cher dragons, cher trolls unner cher bridges and cher drug enforcement agents what's lookin' fer cher field o' kif what you're growin' owny fer personal consumshun."

The grunts of his listeners reached a crescendo at that, then subsided. The effort of all that talking and grunting led every peasant at the table to take a long pull from his mug.

"I had me all o' that," Alf said, " 'cept the dragons, o'course. Ain't nobody seed a dragon in Tharp since me gaffer's day. But all else, that was me. 'Specially thet oily majordomo always comin' by and saying me Brittney should go to th' castle for 'finishin' school.' I know what that no-good count be finishin' all right. And me old woman sayin' it'd be a good idear 'cause we want Brittney to have the same advan, advan, ad-van-ta-ges she did. Wimmin."

A wave of head nodding ran around the table of ill-fitting planks.

"But the gods mus' think even with all o' thet a poor peasant might have a mort o' happiness," Alf went on, "so las midweek, they sends imps. Cheeky little blighters. Killin' chickens. Scarin' cows so's they stops givin' milch. An t'day, when I got to the bottom o' me mornin' gruel, what's there but a imp, actin' all drowned an' bloated. Gave me a fair start, I don't mind sayin'."

Alf looked over his listeners. The usual after-sunset crowd at the Mangy Owl: Jeb Berry and his simpleton brother George, One-Eye Simmons, Three-Finger Brown, Lefty O'Doul. Peasants all, except for Cheney, who was always putting on airs because he had a government job. Of course, he never said it was shoveling horse crap up to the castle. They'd all arrived at the smoky, low-ceilinged pub just after sundown, exchanging "whotchers" and "how's the missuses" while Vera, the barmaid, filled their mugs with ale.

Vera was making another pass around the table, refilling mugs. Her long, raven hair was done up in a single braid and interesting parts of her anatomy peeked from the skimpy outfit that Wilf, the owner of the Mangy Owl, insisted she wear. Despite her abundant charms, not a hand reached for her as she poured the beer.

That had all changed from a few months before. One night all the customers were pawing Vera like usual, and Wilf was confiding to his regulars that as soon as his missus left to visit her mum, Vera was going to have to come across or he'd pitch her out into the street. The next, Alf found he wasn't interested in anything about Vera but the wooden pitcher in her hand, and from their actions neither were any of the other men in the pub. Oh, they all still agreed she was a goer, and said "huzzah, huzzah" and so forth, but they were just going through the motions in the hopes of a free mug of ale. Alf was baffled by the change, but didn't say anything to his cronies. Who wanted to admit to a lack of manliness? But he wasn't surprised that, when he asked Wilf if he'd done the deed, the landlord vaguely waved a hand and changed the subject.

Now, as he watched Vera from the corner of his eye, Alf thought he saw something hanging from her neck. But, as always, when he looked directly at her, there was nothing there.

An icy hand brushed his spine. Everyone knew magic was practiced in Tharp, but that wasn't the sort of business a self-respecting peasant like Alf wanted any part of. Nothing was free in life, and the cost of magic was said to be dear. What did the children's rhyme say? "Girls, cast ye a simple spell / And pay for it with a night in Hell."

Besides, kitchen magic was strictly the province of women. And high magic? Even thinking about that was dangerous.

"So these impses," George said, "where did they come from, Alf?"

Alf shrugged his big shoulders.

"Same place as th' trolls 'n' dragons, I reckon," Alf said. "Probably over to Spam way. They's odd, them Spamish."

Silence reigned as the peasant mulled the strange ways of the residents of the next-door kingdom of Spam. None of them had ever seen such a person, but they'd all heard stories.

"An' then, 'bout th' same time, me daughter, me sweet Brittney, up an' vanishes," Alf said. Breaths were taken sharply. More than one man in the village of Daughnting Underhill enjoyed running his eyes—or in Simmons's case, eye—over the girl's ripening figure.

"I reckon she's up th' castle getting finished," Alf said, shaking his head sadly. "Me old woman says she don't know nothin' 'bout it, but I suspects."

More nods greeted that statement.

"The ways o' wimmin pass unerstandin'," said Three-Finger Brown, who was second in status to Alf at these gatherings. He didn't have a cost-plus contract to deliver oats to the army like the one Alf's wife had brought from finishing school to their marriage, but nobody had healthier goats.

Alf reflected that, for once, Three-Finger had a point. Women were always doing foolish things, like chattering at one another and trying to get their men to bathe and suchlike. And they changed from one day to the next. Like Vera. Or his own Elspeth, now that he thought about it. There was a time he couldn't wait to have a go in their trundle bed next to the fireplace. And if she wasn't interested, well, Alf knew his rights and didn't scruple to enforce them with a clip on the ear. Then, not too long ago, he just lost interest. Strange. Elspeth was still as slim and saucy as the day he'd led her from her parents' hut, but for some reason he couldn't quite put a finger on, he no longer thought about demanding his marital rights.

"Did the girrl," a voice like a scythe on a whetstone said

from the shadows, "really vanish at the same time the imps arrived?"

Alf started at the sound of the voice. Like the other peasants, he'd sensed the stranger sitting next to the fire, but he couldn't exactly say when the fellow had arrived. It was more like one minute the figure wasn't there, and the next minute it was. The stranger wore a traveling cloak pulled tight around him and a slouch hat jammed down on his head so that only his eyes showed. The eyes glowed oddly in the firelight, while the rest of the figure seemed to gather darkness to it in a disquieting way.

The peasants all looked to Alf.

"She did thet, your honor," he said with a peasant's habitual deference. "I come home from th' fields one night, an' she was missin', and th' imps was there."

The figure made a noise like nails being shaken in a tin can.

"And was there anyone unusual in the neighborhood?" it asked.

"Not thet I could say," Alf said. He reached out and wrapped a big hand around his stout, thornwood walking stick. "Mebbe your honor could tell us why ye'd be wanting t' know."

Seeing Alf take his walking stick in hand, his cronies casually produced weapons of their own. Among them they had three cudgels, a dirk, a dagger, and a rusty cleaver, not to mention Alf's walking stick. No one walked around unarmed after sundown, not even in a place as civilized as Daughnting Underhill.

The same nails-in-a-tin-can noise issued from the figure.

"Now, now, gentlemen," it said. "There's no need for concern. My name is . . . call me Marlowe . . . and I've been dispatched from . . . Spam . . . to collect payment for various services and to return the creatures you call imps, who escaped from my master. And, of course, I'm willing to pay in gold for your help in this matter."

When they heard the word "gold," the peasants relaxed their grips on their weapons.

"I don't know as what we could help ye much," Three-Finger Brown said. "But fer gold . . ."

The figure rolled its head in a way that made the hair on Alf's neck stand up straight. No human neck could make such a motion, he thought.

"I believe I could usse the hhelp of Alf Worthy," the figure said. "And you gentlemenn could come alongg aass well. We'll meet tomorrow eveningg at his ffarm, just afterr ssunset."

"Shouldn't yer honor start in daylight?" George asked. "So as to see better?"

The peasants all looked at George as if he'd grown another head.

"That's the most intellergent thing I've ever heard 'im say," Jeb said to general nodding.

The figure made the nails-in-a-tin-can noise, and said, "I'm afraid nott. I don't llike the ssun, and I have some . . . collecting . . . to do thiss evening."

The statement was followed by a noise like the crack of doom, and something wet hit Alf in the side of the head. He turned quickly to see Vera standing over the tray containing their mugs and a widening puddle of beer.

"Whot's thet?" the landlord, Wilf, called from the back of the pub. Wilf could hear lost profits from a mile away.

"Never mmind," the figure called back. It seemed to be waving signs in the air with hands that, in the dim light, looked like they had too many fingers. "In ffact, why don't you ggentlemen go home, and I wwill hellp Vera cleann up?"

No one wanted to comply. The peasants were still nearly sober, and Wilf never left the pub before locking up to prevent pilferage. Vera, pale as a ghost, seemed to like the idea least of all. But she said nothing, and the men, Wilf included, soon found themselves outside the pub saying their "g'nights" and "go safely's" as if getting home was the most important thing in the world. Alf stood for a moment enjoying the cool night air as the others walked off. So he was the only one to hear, from inside the pub, what might have been a gasp, a cackle, and a muffled scream.

With a fearsome grunt, Alf shouldered the final burlap sack of oats onto his cart. Just past midday, and the load was ready for transport to the castle. The new seed the majordomo had delivered in the spring was performing even better than promised. Alf reckoned he might be able to get three full crops in the year instead of the three crops in two years the old seed had produced. And if, as some whispered, the improved yield was the work of the court magician, what of it? Alf hadn't done anything magical himself.

He picked up his whip and cracked it next to the ox's ear. With a low moan, the beast surged against the wooden yoke, and the cart creaked forward. As he walked, Alf reached into the big pocket of his tunic and removed the lunch Elspeth had prepared. Elspeth was usually a fine cook, but that day she'd burned both the bacon and biscuits she'd used to make his meal.

Maybe she was distracted by their daughter's disappearance, or the prospect of help from the Spamish Marlowe.

When he'd told her about the encounter in the pub the night before, she'd fingered her throat, as if something hung there, and spent the night tossing and turning.

Women, Alf thought. Who could figure them?

When Alf reached the high street to the castle, the first thing he saw was Elspeth, drinking tea with a group of women at a table in front of Rumsfeld's Dainties and Finery. Alf recognized Rumsfeld's wife, Mavis, who had, until the past year or so, borne the marks of regular beatings; Letty Stone, whose recent marriage put paid to the common opinion that she was too homely to find a husband, and the Bartholomew sisters, who no longer attracted the attention of loungers and layabouts as they once had.

Alf tipped his cap to his wife and her friends but didn't stop. He'd never get the ox going again amid all the distractions of the village. Among the people walking along the street he saw Vera, moving as slowly as an old woman toward the women seated at the table. As he watched, Vera sat and began talking rapidly. The other women put their hands to their mouths. Vera held her hands more than a foot apart. A gasp went up from her listeners. Still talking, Vera made a motion as if to simulate a tail, and Elspeth and the others began fanning themselves with their hands.

I wonder what that's about, Alf thought, as the women were lost from sight.

The rest of Alf's day was typical for a peasant of Tharp. The castle's quartermaster tried to give him short weight for the oats, and the blacksmith insisted that the new plow he'd ordered cost four florins and not the three they'd agreed to. He lost a half hour alongside the road, prying a stone from the ox's hoof, and when he finally reached his home, he found his farmyard boiling with imps mounted on rats, using tines from his best pitchfork to joust with one another and try to stick his pigs. The sight of him flailing away with a broom while the rat-mounted imps dodged and skittered made even the distracted Elspeth laugh.

Alf was just finishing his dinner of burned chicken and undercooked garden vegetables when his cronies began to arrive. They sat around his fireplace drinking his tea and listening to Cheney tell a story intended to impress his listeners with how important he was to the governing of Tharp.

"Where's thet curst Marlowe?" Alf asked, interrupting Cheney's tale.

"I am herre," the scythe-on-a-whetstone voice said from the darkest corner of the hut.

All of the peasants gave a start, and Elspeth squealed and put her hand over her mouth.

"Crom, man," Alf said, invoking Tharp's warrior god, "don't do thet. It's, it's unnacheral. You liked to scare th' wits out o' me wife."

"No, no," Elspeth said in a shaky voice, "it's all right."

"Yess," Marlowe grated, "it musst be, mussn't it?"

Alf started to ask the Spamiard what he meant, but before he could get a word out, Marlowe was standing at the door to the hut.

"If we are to find yourr daughter, we should be ggoing," he said.

The others passed through the low door, but Alf lingered.

"Is all well wi' you?" he asked his wife.

"Yes, yes," Elspeth said. "Find Brittney, and all will be well."

As he went through the door himself, Alf thought he

heard Elspeth whisper something. It sounded like, "Debts must be paid," but Alf couldn't be certain.

The group spent most of the night stumbling around the countryside. George was pursued by a pack of dogs and One-Eye Simmons fell into the creek. Alf was grateful that the nearly full moon shed enough light to prevent serious injury, but it illuminated nothing in the way of clues to his daughter's whereabouts.

"I'll never see me Brittney again," Alf said in despair, as they neared his farm once more. The promise of sunrise cast a pinkish glow over the bucolic scene of tidy huts and tidy farms. "I still suspect my Elspeth knows where the girl is. She's keepin' a secret of some sort, anyways."

The nails-in-a-tin-can noise issued from Marlowe.

"That'ss not her ssecret," he grated. "She hass other concerns . . ."

His voice trailed off and he stopped walking, turning to face a fenced paddock that held a pair of horses. One was a white stallion; the other as pretty a bay mare as Alf had ever seen.

"Are these yourr beastss?" Marlowe asked.

"No," Alf said.

"But this is yer field, Alf," Three-Finger said, "what you said you was lettin' lie fallow fer a season."

"True enough," Alf said, "but they's not me horses."

This occasioned a good deal of shrugging and head scratching among the peasants. Even Marlowe rubbed his chin, if that was what it was.

"Verry interesting," he said at last. He resumed walking, and the peasants followed.

"I'm certainn you gentlemenn hhave thingss to do," he said, as they reached Alf's gate. The other peasants nodded and mumbled and left amid a volley of "see yer's" and "best to the missuses."

"Now what will we do?" Alf asked as the odd pair trudged up his lane.

"I believe you shouldd spendd the day keeping watch on those horsess," Marlowe said, "while I will sstay here and interrogate yourr wife."

"Not on yer life," Alf said indignantly. "Nobody inter, inter, interrogates me missus but me."

Marlowe put a hand on Alf's arm. The fingers didn't feel exactly like fingers.

"It meanss to ask questionss," Marlowe said. "Iff I am to find yourr daughter, I must ask questionss. And ssomeone must watch the horsess to see who is interested in tthem."

Alf didn't like the plan but couldn't think of what else to do. He flung the door open and Elspeth sat up in bed.

"I need breakfuss, woman," Alf barked. "And this here Spamiard wants t' interrrogate you."

Elspeth put her hand to her mouth.

"Yes, dear," she said bravely. And although she looked pale, Alf couldn't help but notice as she rose from the bed that she had bathed and tied ribbons in her hair. Marlowe refused food and sat silently while Alf ate and Elspeth prepared a lunch.

"Keepp a close watchh," Marlowe told Alf, as the peasant stood at the door. "Returnn at duskk with any newss."

The door closed, and Alf thought he heard the bolt shoot home. And as he turned to walk down the lane, he could have sworn he heard Elspeth say, "Oh, my," in a very small voice.

Alf spent the morning sitting in a copse at the edge of the field, watching the horses gambol. The stallion seemed to have breeding on its mind, but the mare was having none of it, snapping and kicking up her heels every time the stallion approached. If someone had set them into his field to breed, Alf thought, they were going to be disappointed.

After he ate his lunch, Alf drowsed, wondering what, if anything, Marlowe was getting from his interrogation of Elspeth. The heat of the day and his lack of sleep combined to make him nod off, but he awakened with a start each time, determined to do his part to find his daughter.

Still, he wasn't really sure if he was awake or asleep when an old man in a white robe appeared out of nowhere at the edge of the field. The figure stood, running its hands through its long, white beard, and Alf could faintly hear it speaking.

"Oh, you fool, you young fool, what have you done?" the old man said.

The stallion seemed to toss its head at the man's voice and trotted off in pursuit of the mare. The figure stood there, dithering, then vanished as suddenly as it had appeared.

"Thet ain't nacheral," Alf said, and wondered if he should be off to tell Marlowe what he had seen. But the Spamiard had said to wait until dusk, and Alf did, slogging home with the setting sun at his back.

He found Elspeth sitting at the table in their hut, her ribbons askew and a dreamy smile on her face.

"Where's th' Spamiard?" he asked.

"Hmm?" Elspeth said.

"The Spamiard," Alf said. "The odd feller wi' too many fingers?"

"Oh, yes," Elspeth said, shaking herself as if awakening from a dream. "He said he had to report and that he would be back later. You should wait."

All through dinner, Alf caught his wife staring into space,

"actin' all loony goony," as he explained it to his cronies later. But she insisted that nothing was wrong, and the arrival of Marlowe, suddenly there in the same, dark corner, cut off his questions.

"Do you hhave anythingg to reportt?" Marlow rasped.

Alf told him about the behavior of the horses and the appearance and disappearance of the old man.

"Sso," Marlowe said as Alf finished, "it is justt sso. Under . . . questioning . . . your wife rememberss a well-dressed youngg man spendingg much time chatting with yourr daughter."

"Elspeth?" Alf said.

"I had forgotten, Alf, truly," his wife said. "Master Marlowe helped me remember."

She gave the figure a smile that might have made Alf wonder if he hadn't been so intent on trying to make sense of what had happened to his daughter.

"Do nott blame yourr wife," Marlowe grated. "I am afraidd there iss magic involved."

The word made Alf shiver, but he squared his shoulders when the Spamiard said, "I must to the castle, thenn, to see if thiss unfortunate business cann be rrepaired."

"I'll be goin' wi' yer honor," Alf said, surprising everyone, himself included, with the words.

"Oh, Alf, no," Elspeth said.

"She's me daughter," Alf said stubbornly.

Marlowe and Elspeth exchanged a look Alf couldn't interpret.

"Verry welll," the Spamiard said. "I mustt travel differently than I hadd anticipated, but you may have some purpose to serve in this matter yett."

So Alf found himself walking along the road, through the

silent village and into the castle. For some reason, no guards challenged the pair and, within the castle, people hurried past them in the hall as if they weren't there.

The apartments they entered were austere and smelled of sulfur and other things Alf couldn't identify. Their darkness was relieved only by a faint light from the far end. Marlowe led Alf across the room, navigating around obstacles the peasant couldn't even see. What they reached was another door, open just a crack, from which spilled the light and the sound of a man's voice chanting sonorously.

"Be carefull," Marlowe said, and led Alf into the next room.

The old man Alf had seen in the field sat facing them, nose buried in a book. Beakers and tumblers sizzled and smoked, and what might have been an owl seemed to be boiling in a pot on a brazier. He continued chanting, as if unaware of the presence of others.

"A little late forr that spelll, is it nott?" Marlowe said.

The old man started and stared at the intruders.

"Well, well," he said pleasantly. "An afrit, if I'm not mistaken. A minor enough demon. And this fantastic creature with you is . . . ?"

It took Alf a moment to realize that the old man was referring to him.

"I'm a peasant," he said indignantly. "Name's Alf Worthy. I delivers oats t' this here castle."

The old man waved a hand dismissively.

"A peasant," he said. "How boring. But what brings this afrit from the domain of Ali Ben Salim?"

Marlowe made his nails-in-a-tin-can noise, and Alf realized the . . . whatever he was . . . thought that was what a laugh sounded like.

"Right directionn," Marlowe said, "wrong dimensionn. But no matter. It appearss your educational effortss have gone amiss. Or is that nott your apprentice capering aroundd in Alf Worthy's field."

Alf made a noise of astonishment.

"There's naught but horses in thet field," he said.

The old man and Marlowe looked at each other.

"Aren't very bright, are they?" the old man said.

Marlowe laid a hand on Alf's arm.

"Thiss will go fasterr if you are silentt," he said. Then, to the old man, "Unless I amm much mistakenn, there is a substantial paymentt to be made if this error is to be rectifiedd."

The old man cocked his head to one side and smiled.

"I'm surprised that your master, whoever he might be, didn't send a more powerful representative," he said. "This is a bit above your pay grade, isn't it?"

Marlowe laughed again

"I wass in the neighborhood," he said, "on business."

"Really?" the old man said. He looked thoughtful. "Collecting for kitchen magic, perhaps?" His voice contained what sounded to Alf like a sneer. "Well, lust was always the weakness of the afriti, wasn't it? Still, a wise demon would have chosen a better collector for high magic."

Marlowe rotated his shoulders, if that was what they were, in a shrug.

"Itt was only a matter of some dozenss of impss, until now," he said. "I'm sure that when my master learnss high magic is involvedd, he will sendd someone more appropriate to collect payment."

The old man leaned back in his chair.

"And what do you suppose that payment might be?" he asked.

Marlowe shrugged again.

"I tthink we both know whatt iss traditional in a case where someone borrowss power without permission," he said.

The old man ran his hand through his beard.

"A soul?" he said. "Does it have to be a particular soul? Could I interest your master in the girl, perhaps. Certainly she bears some responsibility for this problem, if only that she made my apprentice lose his senses. No? Then how about this oaf? No one will miss him."

Marlowe rolled his head around in what Alf hoped was a negative motion.

"We know who hass to pay," Marlowe said. "And we know who hass to pay iff, somehow, the rresponsible one cannot."

The old man nodded and played with his beard some more.

"Then I'm afraid we have a problem," he said, "since the responsible party is my patron's wife's sister's son. She'll make his life a living hell, you should excuse the expression, if anything happens to the boy. And my patron, in turn, will wonder why he so lavishly supports a mage who cannot protect the members of his family from demons. I can't have that. Sorry."

He sat stroking his beard.

"You could returnn the powerr," Marlowe said. "With interestt, of course. Then all would be well."

The old man nodded vigorously at that.

"I could do that," he said, "but it would take all the power I possess. Perhaps more. And, again, the count would wonder why he is supporting an old man who is, without any magical power, just an old man."

Silence stretched out until the old man said, "No, I'm

afraid I'll just have to kill you, find a way to bring the boy back, and pretend all this never happened."

He picked up a scroll.

"This should do the trick for an afrit," he said.

Marlowe made a noise.

"Oh, yes," the old man said. "This room is warded. No teleporting out of here." He pointed the scroll at Marlowe. "Now, if you'll just raise your hands, or whatever those things are, I'll take you somewhere tidier for what comes next."

The afrit raised his arms.

"What about my Brittney?" Alf said. "You'll be bringing her back, too, won't you?"

The old man looked at Alf and laughed.

"My dear fellow," he said. "How droll. Waste power on a peasant girl? I think not."

Marlowe moved then, faster than anything Alf had ever seen. Something shot from the scroll and whistled past the afrit's ear, hit the stone wall, and ricocheted back into the room, blowing a pair of beakers to dust. Marlowe dove and came to his feet next to the old man's chair. But he was looking right down the tube of the rolled scroll.

"Nice try," the old man said. He leveled the scroll. "Good-bye, afrit," he said, just as Alf hit him over the head with his thornwood walking stick with a noise like a five-pound hailstone hitting a melon. The old man slumped in his chair.

"Not bringing my Brittney back, eh?" Alf said. "Won't waste power on a peasant girl? We'll see about that."

Alf, Elspeth, and Brittney were just finishing dinner a few nights later when Marlowe appeared in the corner.

"Do nott lett me disturb yourr meal," he said. "I have come to say good-bye."

"Then your business here is finished?" Elspeth asked with what sounded like sadness in her voice.

"Until nextt time," Marlowe said. "Magic mustt be paid forr."

"What does thet mean, exactly?" Alf asked.

"I suppose I can tell you thiss," Marlowe said. "Magic changess the nature of reality. Doing this requiress power. There is much powerr in the universess, butt all belongs to someone or something. If you are strong enough, like the count's mage once wass, you can justt take itt. Few are thatt strong. Mostt must pay for itt. If itt is simple magic, kitchen magic, the paymentt is not much and can evenn be pleasantt."

Elspeth nodded at this and smiled.

"But," the afrit went on, "serious magic, high magic, requires big paymentt."

They were all silent for a moment.

"This, what happened to Brittney, it was high magic?" Alf asked.

"It wass," Marlowe said. "The mage's apprentice did nott know whatt he wass doingg. So instead of casting a simple glamour, which would have made all humanss think he and your daughter were horsess, he cast a transmogrification spell. Very expensive, that spell, and not cheapp to undo. And since he was nott an establishedd magic wielderr, he had no arangementt to purchase the powerr. His spell stole it from my masterr, and in such a clumsy fashion that the impss leaked through into yourr world as well."

"That's right, the imps," Alf said. "What about them? The last I saw they was tryin' to set th' barn cat afire."

From the farmyard came a series of pops.

"That's themm now," Marlowe said, "returning to where they came fromm."

"And what about the other?" Elspeth asked. "Who paid?"

"Why, the mage, of course," Marlowe said. "The boy hadd no powerr. My master simply had me take all knowledge of magic from his mindd. Unfortunately, it sweptt all other knowledge as well, but he is of noble bloodd so few will notice he iss a simpleton. But someone hadd to pay, because magic isn't free. And the mage was supposed to be the boy'ss teacher."

"Did he have enough power to pay?" Alf asked.

"No," Marlowe said, "but he made upp the balance in the usual wayy."

"How is that?" Elspeth asked.

"Why, with hiss soul," Marlowe said.

The three humans and the afrit sat in silence until Marlowe spoke again.

"That's the problemm with menn gaining knowledge of magic," he said. "Women use gentle magic for protectionn. Butt men are aggressive magic userss. They are dangerouss. We cannot stop themm from gainingg knowledge through studyy, but we cann prevent the easy spreadd of such knowledge."

The afrit wove its fingers, if that was what they were, in front of Alf's eyes.

"He will rememberr nothing of magic, now," Marlowe said, shooting Elspeth a look. "High magic or kitchen magic. He will be happierr thiss way. I owe himm that, for he saved . . . I guess you couldd call itt my life."

With that, Marlowe vanished. Mother and daughter sat looking at each other until Alf suddenly came to his senses.

"I really think Brittney should go to the castle for finishing school," Elspeth said, as if continuing a conversation already in progress.

"Oh, yes, father, please," Brittney pleaded, batting her eyes.

Alf set his fork on the table and stood.

"I'll hear no more of sech talk," he said, even though he knew this was an argument he would lose. "This comin' an' going' an' strangers an' such, it just ain't nacherul. But I'll tell you what is."

"What's that, Alf dear?" Elspeth asked.

"Goin' t' the pub," Alf said, and stalked toward the door.

Spellbound

by Donna Andrews

Gwynn stopped outside Master Justinian's study. She knew she hadn't left the door hanging wide open. That was the first thing she'd learned as an apprentice: the importance of keeping the Maestro's door closed. Although it wasn't Justinian but Headmaster Radolphus who found it so important.

"We don't want anything just wandering in or out, my dear," the headmaster had said. "Especially not out," he added, looking disapprovingly at some of the Maestro's more unusual pets.

Indeed, everyone at the Westmarch College of Magical Studies knew better than to wander uninvited into Justinian's study. But since it was the first day of the college's annual conference, the halls were overflowing with strangers who wouldn't know any better.

Surely that's all it was. Someone who didn't know any better. Not someone deliberately causing trouble. Though Gwynn knew Radolphus was worried about the possibility.

"Mark my words, Jus, we'll have some kind of trouble,"

Gwynn had overheard the headmaster saying a few nights ago.

"From old Horatio?" Justinian had asked. "Surely even a reactionary like him wouldn't embarrass the college publicly."

"I wouldn't put it past him. And if he doesn't cause trouble, odds are one of his allies will."

"Or one of his enemies," Justinian had said. "He's got enough of them."

Gwynn didn't know what kind of trouble the headmaster expected—only that everyone was on edge. She took a deep breath, tiptoed up to the study door, and looked in. The gremlins were not in their usual place. At that hour, they would normally have been lying on the windowsill taking their after-breakfast nap, sunning their round little bellies and belching softly from time to time. But they were nowhere to be seen. Instead, the sill contained Master Justinian's cat, Asmodeus, who would normally have been sleeping in the Maestro's chair. Asmodeus was washing himself with great fury and glancing from time to time with narrowed eyes at the back of the chair.

Gwynn sighed. She would have to evict whoever had appropriated the Maestro's chair, then inventory the entire study to see if any creatures had wandered off and make sure none of them had eaten anything or anyone they shouldn't have. She walked in, closing the door carefully behind her.

And was overcome with a fit of sneezing.

It was the smell. The Maestro's study had been home to many odors in her time, not all of them pleasant. But she'd never encountered such a strong, cloying, sickly-sweet smell before, like rotting tropical flowers, with a nasty undertone of stale musk.

She steeled herself, walked farther into the study, and started with surprise to see a woman sitting in the Maestro's chair. A beautiful and relatively young woman, wearing a red silk dress and rather too many rings, charms, and amulets. You didn't see many women at the college, apart from the servants, and none of them would dare invade the Maestro's study.

So obviously their visitor was a witch, come for the conference, though the woman was a lot younger than any of the other witches Gwynn had seen arriving at the guesthouse.

A traveling cloak was draped over the nearby table, but Gwynn doubted that their visitor could have traveled far in that spotless, low-cut silk gown. She glanced involuntarily down at her own worn homespun apprentice's tunic and hose. The woman's legs were crossed in a way that showed more of her bright red stockings than was considered quite proper for a respectable lady—although Gwynn wasn't sure witches cared about such niceties.

The woman was leaning over a book, in a pose that showed both her bosom and her profile to advantage. She held the pose a second longer than was believable, then looked up, her face assuming a look of pleased surprise. Then she glowered at Gwynn, who clearly wasn't her intended audience.

"Well, don't just stand there, you silly girl," she snapped. "Go and fetch Master Justinian."

"Yes, ma'am," Gwynn said, curtsying. "May I tell him who's calling?"

"Carima," the woman said, rolling the R slightly, and making the name sound slightly suggestive.

Gwynn noticed, with dismay, that Carima was reading one of the Maestro's rare books. A book of Chthonian poetry.

Pretending to read it, Gwynn realized, hiding a smile. Apparently Carima had no idea that because of the peculiarities of their anatomy, the Chthonians wrote diagonally, rather than horizontally, and bound their books on the bottom, which meant that Carima was holding the volume sideways.

"I'll go and fetch him right away," she said, with another curtsy.

As Gwynn turned to leave, she heard Asmodeus sneezing delicately.

Of course, fetching Justinian would be a lot easier if she had any notion where he was. She had to search through the college halls, which were teeming with every imaginable kind of magic user—not only mages from other colleges and witches like Carima, but also contingents of astrologers, alchemists, necromancers, shamans, illusionists, seers, mediums, theurgists, thaumaturgists, soothsayers, sigilists, amulet-makers, ring-wrights, and practitioners of magical arts so obscure they hadn't actually been named yet.

Not many women, though, except for a few witches, most considerably older than Carima.

When she finally found Justinian, having tea in the headmaster's study, he didn't seem overjoyed to hear that Carima had arrived.

"What in blue blazes is she doing here?" he asked.

"Here for the conference, obviously," Radolphus said.

Justinian snorted.

"Now, now," Radolphus said. "She's our guest. And one of the official witch delegates. Not, of course, one of the speakers."

"Well, I should think not, since this year's theme is magical ethics—not precisely Carima's forte, is it?"

"Now, Jus. You're starting to sound like old Horatio."

"I am not," Justinian said. "I don't think the conference is an abomination, and I'm not signing his petition to the duke to outlaw it. We can learn a lot from the allied branches."

"Even the witches," Radolphus said.

"Especially the witches," Justinian agreed. "We know almost nothing about how their magic works. I'm particularly looking forward to Mistress Hecate's classes. I support the conference, you know that. But Carima!"

"Is our guest, for the time being," Radolphus said. "Perhaps for the last time, if Master Horatio's efforts succeed. But in the meantime—"

"Yes," Justinian said, gulping the rest of his tea and standing up. "Be hospitable. I'd better go see what she wants."

As Justinian stalked out, trailed by Gwynn, Radolphus sighed.

"As if there were any doubt what she wants," Gwynn heard him murmur.

Master Justinian didn't say anything on the way back to his study, and he walked so fast Gwynn could hardly keep up—though she had no trouble keeping his tall, gaunt frame in view as he plowed through the crowded halls. Gwynn felt reassured by the Maestro's reaction. No doubt he'd find out what Carima wanted and toss her out of his study as quickly as possible.

"Justinian!" Carima cried, as he strode into the study. "I'm so glad to see you."

"Carima," the Maestro said. "I—achoo!"

Master Justinian sneezed with great vigor, startling some of the fledgling bats into flight.

"Your study is rather dusty," Carima said, frowning at Gwynn. "It can be so difficult to get the servants to clean properly."

"Oh, a little dust never hurt anyone," Justinian said. "And I don't let the servants in. They could do untold damage, bustling about in my things."

"Then what—" Carima began, looking at Gwynn.

"Gwynn's a student. And my apprentice," Justinian said. "Very promising young mage. Sit down, if you like."

Gwynn began to feel alarmed. Carima's expression suggested that she wasn't at all happy to learn that Gwynn was a fellow magic user. And the Maestro was being remarkably polite. He wasn't usually so polite to visitors. What if his show of annoyance in Radolphus's study was only that—a show?

What if he liked Carima?

Carima resumed her seat in Justinian's chair. Instead of taking the other large chair beside it, Justinian pulled a stool in from the workroom and perched on it at a safe distance from Carima. Gwynn slipped into the workroom and tried to appear busy while maintaining absolute silence, in the hope they'd forget she was there.

"Oh, I brought you this," Carima said, picking up a box from the table beside her.

"What is it?" Justinian said.

"Come and see," she said, with a sidelong glance. After a moment, Justinian slid off the stool and went over to peer into the box.

"Candy?" he asked.

"Not just candy!" Carima said. She selected a piece, bit into it, uttered a small ecstatic sigh, and began chewing it with half-closed eyes.

Justinian watched the performance over the top of his spectacles, his face expressionless.

Carima swallowed, licked her lips suggestively, and offered the box to Justinian.

"You've never tasted such delicious marzipan," she said.

"Marzipan? Too sticky-sweet, for me, I'm afraid," Justinian said, with a grimace. He returned to his perch on the stool.

"Oh," Carima said, closing the box. "Well, perhaps you can offer it to your guests."

As Carima placed the box back on the table, Gwynn saw a small gremlin head peek out from under the tablecloth, following the motion of the witch's hand. Then the gremlin sneezed several times and used the hem of the tablecloth as a handkerchief.

"Gwynn," Justinian said, turning, "open a few windows in here. It smells . . . rather stuffy."

"I really must be going now," Carima said, rising from the chair. "But I do hope you'll invite me back for tea."

"Yes, of course," Justinian said, "although I suppose you'll be very busy with the conference."

"Oh, I'm free in the afternoons," Carima said. "We shall have plenty of time to get reacquainted."

Justinian stood, watching her departure.

Gwynn took several deep breaths. Amazing how much easier it was to breathe all of a sudden. And it wasn't just Carima's overpowering perfume. The scent, she realized, also carried some kind of spell. Neatly camouflaged, as perhaps Carima had intended, by all the other magical auras and residues that permeated the Maestro's study. Had Justinian noticed?

Yes, almost certainly. He was still frowning at the door. Then he sighed, shook himself, and turned to Gwynn.

"Let some air in, and do something with that stuff, will you?" he said, waving his hand at the marzipan. "Take it down to the dormitories if you like." Then he strode out.

Gwynn stared at the marzipan for a few minutes. Then she picked up the box, took the top off, and slid it gently underneath the tablecloth.

A flurry of squeaking and scrabbling noises erupted from beneath the table. Several hours later, after she had finished dusting the entire study and washing the windows, Gwynn reached back under the table, gently nudged several of the sleeping gremlins out of the box, and put it back on top of the table.

Carima was not completely stupid, though, Gwynn found. She showed up again after lunch, trailing only a faint and rather pleasant odor of rosewater. And carrying another present for the Maestro.

"What is it?" Justinian asked, holding the package as if he expected it to explode.

"You'll have to open it," Carima said.

After a pause—was he casting a masterfully unobtrusive spell of detection, Gwynn wondered?—Justinian tore off the paper to reveal a small toy brass dragon. He looked puzzled.

"Here, hold it away from you like this," Carima said, coming closer to Justinian than seemed quite necessary and putting her small, red-nailed hands over his long, ink-stained fingers. "And press this little catch."

The toy dragon's jaws opened with a tiny roar—more like gremlin's squeak, really—and a jet of flame shot out.

"How ingenious," Justinian said. He pressed the little catch again and imitated the dragon's squeak as the flame shot out.

The gremlins, who had poked their heads out from under various pieces of furniture when they heard the squeak, dived back under cover when they saw the flame. Carima sat smiling as she watched Justinian roaming around his workroom, lighting candles and incinerating unwanted odds and ends.

"How does it work?" he asked finally.

Carima shrugged.

"Probably something mechanical," Justinian said, pushing up his spectacles and peering more intently at the little toy. Over the next few minutes, he singed quite a bit of his hair, trying to peer down the dragon's throat while it was flaming. Carima didn't seem to enjoy this turn of events nearly as much. She kept grabbing at his elbow and imploring him to be careful, which was bound to irritate him. Gwynn readied a fire-extinguishing spell and watched his investigations with silent interest.

"Radolphus should see this," Justinian said finally. He trotted off, with an anxious Carima trailing behind him. Gwynn followed at a more leisurely pace.

The dragon was an enormous hit with everybody who saw it. At least until it ran out of flame an hour later, during a mock battle with some of Master Kilian's yearling salamanders. Carima had no idea how the thing worked or how to fix it, which Gwynn hoped would cancel out at least some of the goodwill the witch had gained by bringing such an entertaining present in the first place.

"That's no problem," Justinian said, holding the little dragon to his ear and shaking it. "I'll just take it apart and see what's wrong with it."

He trotted off to his study. Carima, to Gwynn's satisfaction, retired to the guesthouse with a headache.

"Well," murmured Master Radolphus, "so much for the

poor little dragon." Justinian's complete lack of mechanical ability was legendary.

Gwynn, who was slipping out the door, smiled. And then stopped at the next words she heard.

"It's an unnatural device, that's what it is," Master Horatio said. "No better than the she-devil who brought it. You mark my words, it'll lead to trouble, having her here. Especially the way she's hanging around that young whippersnapper."

"Whippersnapper?" Radolphus repeated.

"Justinian!"

"He's nearly thirty and a master mage," Radolphus said.

"Too young to be trusted around a baggage like that," Horatio said. "It's bad enough bringing in every hedge wizard and potion-dauber to this infernal conclave of yours—did you have to invite the inhabitants of the brothels as well?"

"I'll thank you to be civil to the witches when you meet them at dinner tonight," Radolphus said, with more anger in his voice than Gwynn had ever heard. "Or you can stay in your chambers and sulk for all I care."

"When I'm running this college—" Horatio began.

"If you succeed in replacing me, you can run the college as you wish, but until then, you will follow my orders!"

Horatio snorted and stormed out. Gwynn, too startled to hide, stood looking after him with her mouth open.

Radolphus swore softly, and Gwynn heard several thumps, like books being thrown. She tiptoed away.

Was Horatio really going to be the new headmaster? If that happened, Gwynn realized, it would be the end of her studies. Horatio didn't approve of teaching women to read and write, much less cast spells.

And he didn't approve of Master Justinian either.

Back in her room, Gwynn tried to study, but no matter how hard she tried to focus on the pages of her book, she kept seeing Master Horatio's face, or Carima's, or—enough! She slammed the book closed and headed back to the Maestro's study. Most of the time, she did only enough cleaning to meet the Maestro's far-from-exacting standards, but when she was unhappy, as she was then, cleaning made her feel better.

It usually made her feel better, but when she entered, she found the table littered with pieces of the little mechanical dragon. She stared down at them, feeling both a fierce satisfaction that Carima's wonderful gift was no more and a curious sadness. After all, it wasn't the little dragon's fault Carima had brought him. She knew the pieces would stay there, eventually mingling with all the other clutter on the worktable. Justinian would use the flat pieces as bookmarks, and the cat or the gremlins would play with others, and eventually there would be nothing left of the ingenious little thing.

On an impulse, she took the discarded marzipan box and used it to gather all the pieces of the dragon and put them aside. Perhaps someone else could fix it.

When she'd finished that, she decided she'd done enough tidying for the time being.

But the next morning, she was busy sorting out the amulet drawer when Carima reappeared, in yet another expensive and revealing gown. Gwynn was relieved to see that at least she hadn't brought any more presents. The Maestro was busy with some new chemical experiments and greeted Carima with absentminded politeness. Although he did send Gwynn down to fetch midmorning tea for them.

"And some more gingerbread, if Cook has any," he said,

glancing at a large glass cookie jar that was empty except for a few crumbs.

"Bless the boy," Cook said, when Gwynn arrived in the kitchens. "As if I'd run out of his gingerbread. I think he likes it as much now as when he were an apprentice."

"You knew Master Justinian when he was an apprentice?" Gwynn asked, in surprise.

"Dearie me, yes," Cook said, laughing as she led Gwynn into the pantry and began filling a bowl with cookies. "Quite a handful he were. Bright, of course, but always up to some mischief. Some things never change, do they?" she added.

Gwynn smiled. But Cook's face fell suddenly.

"Except everything's changing now," she said, in an undertone. "I don't know what we'll do if they make that horrid old Horatio headmaster. He don't approve of women servants in college. He'll replace us all with a bunch of ham-handed men. Throw us out in the cold. I came here as a kitchen maid. Eight years old. I've spent my whole life here and—"

Cook suddenly stopped and whirled toward the doorway.

"Who's there?" she asked.

Gwynn cast a quick spell of detection.

"No one," she said.

"Not now, but someone could have been a minute ago. Too many strange faces around, between all the servants who came with them foreign magicians and the extra help we took on for the duration. Here."

Cook thrust the dish of cookies into Gwynn's hands and hurried back into the kitchen.

Gwynn followed more slowly, glancing around. At least a dozen maids and manservants were busy in the kitchen. Several smiled at her, but more than half the faces were unfamiliar. But why was Cook so anxious? None of the newcomers looked sinister. The boy turning the spit and the three pink-cheeked girls peeling vegetables were probably extra help hired from the village for the duration of the conference. No doubt so were the plump woman mending a brown mage's robe and the hump-shouldered crone ironing and folding linens. The man loading up a tray was probably the servant of one of the visiting mages, but he looked perfectly ordinary. And even if one of them had tried to eavesdrop, what Cook said wasn't that awful. Why was she so worried?

Probably it was just the strain of the conference, and her worry over what would happen if Master Horatio prevailed.

"Off with ye," Cook said, bustling back with the tea tray. "Don't hang about here," she added, in an undertone. "You should be keeping an eye on that wicked witch. I can't for the life of me see why Master Radolphus allows it, her hanging about here. Ought to throw the baggage out. No better than she should be, I warrant. I'd throw the whole lot of them out."

It was probably the one subject Cook and Master Horatio agreed about, Gwynn thought, as she made her way back to the study.

Carima was having an uphill battle gaining Justinian's attention. Although he roused himself long enough to devour much of the gingerbread, he quickly returned to his retorts and beakers. Carima eventually gave up trying to talk to him and merely hung about, no doubt waiting for his preoccupation with his chemicals to wane. She amused herself with folding little bits of paper into animals.

Gwynn watched, fascinated, as the little bits of paper were slowly transformed, in Carima's hands, into birds, fish, cats, deer—a dozen intricate miniature animals.

"What do you think of this one, Justinian?" she would ask, when she had finished one.

"Mmmm," Justinian would say, barely glancing up.

"Origami," she said, noticing Gwynn's attention and visibly torn between being annoyed at Justinian's preoccupation and pleased that someone, at least, was paying attention to her. "It's an old art form from the East. From Cathay."

Justinian finally gave up pottering with his chemicals in time for luncheon. Gwynn watched them cross the quadrangle, Carima half-running to keep up with Justinian's stride, hanging on his arm, chattering breathlessly.

Gwynn breathed a sigh of relief when they'd gone. She cleared a place on the table to put her bread, cheese, and ham, pulled up one high stool, and sat down to eat with one hand while paging through one of the books Master Justinian had assigned her that week with the other. With Carima gone, the gremlins emerged and began scouring the place for crumbs and licking up any spills.

Gwynn's eye fell on a little origami bird, standing next to her plate with its head down, as if pecking the table. She eyed the little thing with distaste. As with the dragon, it was something she would have enjoyed but for the association with Carima.

She would throw the little things in the fire, she decided, and reached over to pick up the bird. But when her fingers touched the paper, she felt a small spark, then an overwhelming flood of sensation.

She jerked her hand back and took a deep breath to steady herself. There had been a spell on the origami bird; that was obvious. But it hadn't harmed her, as far as she could tell. Apparently the spell's only purpose was to trigger those seconds of sensation in the mind of its target. Like a dream that slips away when the sleeper wakes, the spell eluded her attempts to define it. She had a vague impression of fingers, touching her with featherlight strokes in sensitive places. A feeling of languid heat. A suggestion of a pair of eyes gazing into hers. It wasn't unpleasant, really. More unsettling. Except that the whole thing was somehow associated with Carima. That was unpleasant. Were those supposed to be Carima's eyes and fingers? Even more unpleasant.

She steeled herself, and touched the little bird again. It was only paper. Evidently she had triggered a onetime spell. She flicked the little paper toy into the fire.

A love spell, she realized, or more likely an aphrodisiac one, doubtless intended for the Maestro. And carelessly designed—the spell had affected her, even though she was not only the wrong person but the wrong sex. But if Master Justinian had picked up the little bird—

She felt a sudden surge of fear and anger. She hopped off the stool and looked around, seeing a half dozen of the little folded animals in various parts of the study. She wasn't going to let the Maestro touch a single one of them, she thought, reaching for the nearest one.

The little spark again and the brief but overwhelming flood of sensation. Gwynn found herself staring down into her hand, at the tiny paper cat she was holding. Touching one of the little animals with her thoughts focused on Justinian was a rather different experience, she reflected. Not at all unpleasant. But considerably more unsettling.

She picked up a box, and the silver pelican-shaped sugar tongs that kept finding their way from Master Radolphus's study into Justinian's. She carefully picked up another little animal with the tongs. She felt no effect, so she placed it in the box and gathered the remaining origami animals, one by one, being careful to touch them only with the tongs.

Back in her room, she chalked a small magic circle on the

floor—a small circle being all there was room for—and used the handle of her candlesnuffer to snag a paper animal from the box and place it in the circle. Then, for the next several hours, she used every technique she knew, trying to tease out as much information as she could about the spell on the paper toy. And about the spell's creator.

Finally, she sat down cross-legged beside the circle and scrubbed at her aching eyes with tired fingers. She hadn't learned much, certainly not enough to unenchant the little animals. It was as if Carima's spells were at odd angles to the way she expected them to be, like Chthonian script. But she felt a renewed respect for witch magic. It might be very different from the magic she was learning, but it was powerful.

Perhaps it was a good thing if, as Master Radolphus had often told the apprentices, witch magic rather narrowly focused on love spells and healings. And sex, she added, recalling the effects of touching the little animals. Radolphus must have thought the students were too young to know about that.

But what should she do with the little animals? She could keep them around and study them some more, but she didn't think there was any more she could learn from them, at least not at her present level of magical skill. And she was afraid that if she left them in anywhere about the college, someone would find them; perhaps someone who shouldn't. Carima was still around, she thought ruefully. If she wanted to study the spell some more, she was sure Carima would provide some more samples. So she should dispose of these. Burn them. Or deactivate them and put them back in the Maestro's study.

Deactivating them was probably the best thing, she

thought. Carima might notice if the little animals all disappeared. And if she was careful how she did it, setting off the little spells didn't need to be unpleasant. Quite the contrary.

No, she thought, angrily. They're Carima's tricks. She poked her tiny fire until it burned its brightest and, one by one, fed the little animals into it.

She was careless with the last one, and it brushed her arm on the way down. Again she felt the overwhelming rush of sensation, stronger than before and very far from unpleasant. She sat for a long while, thinking, her face flaming with a heat that had nothing to do with her tiny fire.

The sound of the tower bells ringing to signal dinner startled her out of her thoughts, and she hurried to throw on a clean tunic and race down to the dining hall.

Normally, the inhabitants of the college could all fit in one end of the cavernous dining hall, with plenty of room in the corners and alcoves for misanthropes to hide and students cramming for classes to lurk quietly with their books. The conference crowd filled the hall to overflowing.

Gwynn found a seat at the corner of a table stuck up in the minstrels' gallery. The food, though plentiful, was usually cold by the time it arrived so far from the kitchen, and she shared her table with a trio of taciturn dwarfs and a group of apothecaries' apprentices who seemed more than half-convinced that she was a kitchen maid sneaking into the banquet.

But she'd chosen the place on purpose. The minstrels' gallery was designed to give the guests of honor an unimpeded view of the performers, which meant that it gave her an equally good view of the head table. She could even catch the occasional snippet of conversation.

Most of the occupants of the head table were elderly, even
the two women seated near one end. Gwynn assumed they
were the senior members of the witches' delegation. Master
Justinian's dark head stood out among the gray and the
white.

As did Carima's emerald green dress among the black,
brown, and gray mages' robes. Not that Carima was officially
seated at the head table. But shortly after the dinner began,
she flitted up onto the dais and perched on the arm of the
chair next to Justinian. The aged astrologer who was supposed to be occupying the chair had drawn himself as far
away from Carima as possible and appeared to be making a
desperate attempt to pretend she wasn't there.

In fact, everyone was deliberately ignoring Carima except
Justinian, who acted as if nothing out of the ordinary were
happening.

And Master Horatio, seated at the other end of the table,
as far as possible from the two elderly witches. He spent so
much time glaring at Carima that he barely ate.

"No business being here," Gwynn heard him mutter during a lull in the conversation.

"What's old Thunder Brows so upset about?" one of the
young apothecaries asked.

"He disapproves of the conference," Gwynn said.

"Why?"

"Brings in the riffraff," one of the dwarfs rumbled. "Like
us. Not big on nonhumans, old Master Horatio is."

"Or women practitioners," Gwynn added.

"How's he feel about apothecaries?" the apprentice asked.

"Lesser form of the art," the dwarf said. "Mere tradesmen
who should be sent to the back door."

"Stupid old fogy," the apprentice said.

"Old fogy's got the duke's ear," the dwarf said. "Way I hear it, this could be the last year for the conference if they make him headmaster."

It wasn't just college gossip, Gwynn realized. Everyone had heard about the possibility that Horatio might take over as headmaster.

Gwynn stared down at Master Horatio. He was chewing away steadily, while frowning at Carima. A wave of anger swept over Gwynn and she fought hard to keep from wishing him harm. You never knew, with so many mages around, who might sense a wish like that or what ill use they could make of it.

Suddenly, Master Horatio stopped chewing and looked straight up at Gwynn. She quickly dropped her eyes to her plate and tried to think of nothing but the food she was eating. But every bite seemed drier than the last, and she wished she had stayed in her own quiet room, eating bread and cheese.

Maybe Master Horatio was wishing the same thing. When Gwynn stole another glance at him, she saw him reaching for a platter of food, then pausing for a split second to make a slight gesture—a poison-sniffing spell.

Evidently Master Horatio knew how little liked he was.

Finally, the banquet came to an end. A servant tossed one last dish on their table—a bowl filled with steaming-hot linen towels. Down at the head table, two servants were circulating with the fancier version—instead of the communal bowl, a platter with individual towels, neatly folded into flower shapes. Pretty, but all separate like that, probably lukewarm by the time they got around to everyone, Gwynn thought, as she buried her face in the comforting warmth of her own towel.

"Disgraceful!" she heard Master Horatio say. Gwynn frowned and pulled away the towel to glance down. Did he have something against cleanliness? Evidently not. He was scowling at Master Radolphus, not the hot towels.

"I won't stand for it," Master Horatio said. He was absently reaching out for the towel platter with one hand and shaking the forefinger of the other at Radolphus. "If you won't take any action, then I'll—"

He froze, suddenly, holding the towel in one hand, his other forefinger still pointing at Radolphus. And then he vanished with noise like a peal of thunder and a flash of light so bright Gwynn was temporarily blinded.

Before the purple afterimages had cleared from her eyes, Gwynn was up and running for the Maestro's study to fetch the battered carpetbag in which he kept his traveling magic kit. Justinian would want to investigate this strange happening. And while he wouldn't necessarily need his carpetbag—he was fond of saying that true mages relied on the contents of their skulls, not their spellbooks—carrying the bag let Gwynn make her way to the Maestro's side unchallenged.

In her brief absence, the hall had become a beehive of magical activity. The alchemists, potion-makers, and apothecaries had seized every bit of food and drink on the head table and were testing, sampling, and squabbling. Every window held an astrologer, pointing his traveling scope at the sky and scribbling diagrams. Tarot spreads jostled with crystal balls and scatterings of runes or bones. One mage was pouring colored sand into intricate patterns. Another was throwing powders into a small brazier, sending up puffs of variously colored smoke.

The college mages seemed to be focused less on the food

and more on the remaining linen towels. Everywhere you looked, you saw one of them studying a towel with a magnifying glass, holding one up to the light, or making magical gestures over one. Gwynn thought this seemed more sensible than what most of the other practitioners were doing—she couldn't shake from her mind the image of Master Horatio with one hand pointing at Radolphus and the other holding the towel. But from the mages' expressions, they didn't seem to be learning much from the damp linens.

"Good work," the Maestro said, when Gwynn appeared at his side with the bag. "I don't need it yet, but keep it handy. Sooner or later this lot will calm down, and we can get something done."

"Surely with so many mages trying, they'll figure out what happened soon," Gwynn said.

"Not likely," Justinian said. "The problem is there's too bloody much magic in this room already. Odds are the attack was a magical one, so anything that could possibly have been used to trigger it will show a certain amount of magical residue—but that's about as helpful as finding flour in the kitchen on baking day. Anything that's been in the hall for more than five minutes will have some degree of magical residue. We've had adepts in here all day doing demonstrations. Apprentices practicing their homework. The cleaning staff using spelled brooms and dustcloths to ensure the hall was spotless for the banquet. So even if the evidence didn't go up in smoke with Horatio, good luck separating traces of the crime from all those other traces—and that's before all these amateur forensic wizards began cluttering up the atmosphere with their efforts."

"We don't even know for sure the killer used magic," Radolphus said. "Could have been poison. Or a knife in the ribs. No matter what he used, odds are it disappeared with Horatio."

"Yes," Justinian said. "The old goat would have to be a banger."

"A what?" Gwynn asked.

"A banger. He didn't approve of necromancy."

"He didn't approve of much," Gwynn said.

"No, but he was especially down on necromancy," Justinian said. "A banger's someone who casts a spell to ensure that when he dies, his body will explode and incinerate. Remember that even the best necromancer needs at least a tiny bit of the remains to work with. But whatever's left of Horatio's all blown to dust and spread all over the hall."

"Couldn't we dust the hall and let the necromancers use that?"

"Too mixed up. For every bit of Horatio, you'd have a hundred bits of somebody else. Fingernail parings, bits of dead skin, cat dander—you could aim to call up Horatio and find yourself trying to interrogate that old one-eared ginger tom Cook used to have in the kitchen to keep down the mice."

Though some of the necromancers were sweeping up piles of dust and sifting them into bags—hoping, Gwynn supposed, to hit on a pile that contained a sufficiently high percentage of Horatio to be useful.

"You've got to admire the killer's nerve," Radolphus said.

"And his skill," Justinian added. "Whoever did this knew that the best magicians in the duchy would all be here, and that they'd all insist on investigating. But look at it!"

The more traditional magicians from the college faculty had apparently despaired of finding a corner quiet enough to hear themselves chant and were packing up and relocating. But their departure did little to calm the chaos in the hall. A quarrel had broken out between a dervish and a tarot reader whose cards had been scattered and torn by the dervish's dance, and it looked likely to escalate into a full-scale brawl as more and more guests took sides.

"I fear we won't be solving anything here," Justinian said, with a sweeping gesture to the hall.

"You think it's unsolvable?" Radolphus asked. His face looked drawn and anxious.

"No, but we'll be solving it here," Justinian said, tapping one temple. "Let's go back to my study, Gwynn. You had a front-row seat for this, up in the musicians' gallery. I want to hear what you saw."

"I'll come too, if I may," Radolphus said. "Since I'm one of the prime suspects, I've put the seneschal in charge."

Back in the study, Justinian and Radolphus settled down, and Gwynn described everything she'd seen and heard from the balcony. To no avail.

"Still puzzling," Radolphus sighed.

"Still an utter bloody bafflement," Justinian said. He got up, stirred the fire with the poker in an irritated manner, and strode over to the cabinet where he kept the wine and glasses.

Gwynn hurried to fetch another log. To her dismay, she discovered another little folded paper animal balanced on top of the woodpile. Anyone reaching for another log would almost automatically pick up the tiny cat to put it aside. And when Justinian opened the cabinet, Gwynn saw little angular paper birds peeking out of every goblet. Had Gwynn missed them earlier, or had Carima been skulking around again?

Master Justinian simply tipped the little paper toys out

onto the shelf. He appeared oblivious to them, but Gwynn noticed he had been careful not to touch them all the same. Had he set off one of the spells, she wondered? Or did he know what they were beforehand? And if he knew, why didn't he do something? Get rid of the dangerous things?

Silly question, she told herself; this was the man who had once let a wounded viper stay in his study because it was too cold outside. He wouldn't care about the danger of a few small bespelled objects. He was probably going to take the origami figures apart and study them when he got around to it.

"Blast," Radolphus said. "This couldn't have come at a worse time, what with all the rumors that the duke was going to put Horatio in my place. The duke's bound to wonder if I had anything to do with it. And the longer it takes us to find a solution, the more convinced he'll be."

"Nonsense," Justinian said. "Why would you kill Horatio at the banquet, with so many inconvenient witnesses around, when you could have knocked him off quietly at any time?"

"Thank you," Radolphus said. "Though I'd find it more reassuring to hear that you can't possibly imagine me a murderer."

"Reassuring and irrelevant. You know very well I can't, but that won't convince anyone in Horatio's camp. We'll just have to figure out what other mage did kill him."

"Doesn't have to be a mage," Radolphus said. "If it was poison, anyone could have done it. We'll know soon enough. We've got adepts scouring the kitchen as well as the dining hall. Someone's bound to find something."

"If someone used poison, we'd find it, which is why a clever murderer wouldn't use poison," Justinian said.

"Besides, he was scanning everything for poison," Gwynn said.

"Except the towels," Justinian said. "And they're not telling much."

He reached into his pocket, pulled out a damp wad of linen, and frowned at it.

"Is that Master Horatio's towel?" Gwynn asked.

"No, that would have gone up in smoke with him," Justinian said. "This one's mine. But if it was a spell that did Horatio in, it would have to have been cast on all the towels—there would be no way anyone could ensure he'd get one particular towel from the platter."

"Besides, if the towels were bespelled, wouldn't Master Horatio have noticed?" Gwynn asked. "For that matter, wouldn't everyone at the head table?"

"No, because we were all expecting bespelled towels," Horatio said. "The duty mage in the kitchen would have cast a stasis spell to keep them hot until they reached the tables—just as he did with all the food."

"Your food, maybe," Gwynn muttered.

Justinian was gesturing over the towel and frowning.

"Nothing, I assume," Radolphus said.

"Too much. Remnants of the stasis spell. Faint signs of other kinds of magic that would have been in the air at the banquet, most of them relatively harmless—light spells, poison sniffings, beauty spells. None of them dangerous. Also traces of bleach from the laundry, and the rosewater they scented the water with."

"Rosewater?" Gwynn said. "Could that be significant? We didn't get rosewater up in the minstrels' gallery. Of course, we just got big bowls of hot towels, not those fancy folded ones."

"If he had a reaction to the rosewater, you mean?" Justinian asked. "The way Master Killian breaks out in hives and has trouble breathing when he eats a crayfish by mistake? It's a thought. Could also have been something he ate that his body reacted to."

"Of course, you'd have to know Master Horatio rather well to know he couldn't tolerate rosewater or crayfish or whatever," Radolphus said. He got up and strolled over to the cabinet with his empty wineglass in his hand. "And he's never shown the slightest anxiety over what's in his dinner, as long as there's plenty of it. No, my money's on a spell of some sort, targeted to Horatio."

"Then why can't we find any traces of it?" Justinian said, frowning at the rectangle of linen. "I wouldn't expect it to be easy, but we should be able to find some faint trace . . ."

Gwynn suddenly realized that Radolphus had spotted the little origami birds lying on the shelf and was reaching to touch one.

"Don't touch that!" she shouted.

They shouted. She and the Maestro had uttered the very same words, in unison.

"Don't touch what?" Radolphus said. He had frozen, one foot about to take a step, one hand hovering between the wine bottle and the little folded creatures.

"The little paper birds," Gwynn said. "They're bespelled."

"With what I thought was a relatively tailored spell," Justinian added.

"Tailored to what?" Gwynn asked.

"Not you, certainly," Justinian said. "If I'd known—go ahead and touch one," he said, turning to Radolphus. "They're annoying, not dangerous."

Rather hesitantly, Radolphus picked up a bird. He blinked in surprise, then he dropped the bird and his face assumed a bemused expression.

"How interesting," he murmured. "And rather ingenious. But quite unscrupulous. Am I correct in assuming that Carima is behind this?"

"Yes, and I have no idea how it's done," Justinian said. "I spent several hours this afternoon trying to find out, with no luck. I didn't even pick up the fact that they were completely indiscriminate spells. If I had—"

He glanced at Gwynn and shook his head.

Gwynn felt better at her own lack of success with the paper animals.

"No trace left behind," Radolphus said, peering down at the bird. "Just the ordinary residue you'd get from anything that had been in an atmosphere with so much magic."

He was leaning close to the bird, but with his hands clasped behind his back, as if afraid to touch it.

"You can pick it up if you like," she said. Radolphus continued to stare at the bird, so Gwynn reached over and picked it up herself. "Only paper now," she said. She undid a few of the folds and shook the entire paper out flat. A few crumbs of gingerbread fell out of the folds and onto the table.

"That's it!" Justinian exclaimed. "That's how it was done!"

Gwynn noticed that he was staring not at the paper but at the gingerbread crumbs.

Radolphus was gesturing over another of the little paper birds.

"You can tell they're bespelled, if you bother to check," he said. "But it's so faint that you might not notice it if you weren't looking for it. Especially in the banquet hall, with so much magic swirling around. The stasis spell alone would pretty much drown it out. Still—however depraved he would have found these, I doubt if the shock would have killed him. More likely set him off on a rant, and wouldn't someone have noticed if Carima handed him one?"

"But it wasn't a paper bird," Gwynn said. "It was the linen towel."

"Precisely," Justinian said. "And there's a good reason we found no trace of a deadly spell in the towel. The spell was never in the towel—it was caught up in the folds."

"And Master Horatio was at the far end of the table—by the time he got his towel, everyone else had touched theirs," Gwynn added.

"Thereby dissipating the spell harmlessly," Justinian said, with a nod.

"They weren't that elaborately folded," Radolphus said.

"I imagine once you've mastered the technique, you can accomplish a lot more with much less folding," Justinian said. "And the spell that killed Horatio must have been a lot more accomplished than these silly birds. For one thing, it was tailored to him, or we'd have seen a lot more casualties."

"You don't think Carima did it, then?" Radolphus asked.

"I think she's still learning the technique."

"Yes," Gwynn said. "Remember the way she kept folding things, over and over, all day—it's what we're always taught to do when we're first learning a technique. Do it over and over until we don't even have to think about it."

"Rather alarming that she could do it right in the room without either of you noticing she was spellcasting," Radolphus said.

"Of course, these little toys don't really do that much," Justinian said.

"They do enough," Radolphus muttered. Gwynn noticed that his face had turned bright red. "Absolutely unprincipled, leaving those things around where impressionable young minds could find them."

"But consider what she could have done if she were better at this folding magic, whatever it is," Justinian said. "And someone is. That's the person we want."

"The witches," Radolphus said.

"One of the witches. I doubt if it was an official plan. This smacks more of the act of a single fanatic."

"All the same, they're not going to react well if we start asking them which of their number is a murderess. And if we show too much interest in this paper-folding spell technique, whoever did it will get the wind up."

They both frowned and stared at the little paper birds.

How maddening to know how it was done and still not know who did it, Gwynn thought. She brushed the gingerbread crumbs off the table and found herself thinking that if, no, when the Maestro identified the killer, Cook might enjoy hearing that her gingerbread had played an important part in solving the puzzle.

"Cook," she said aloud. "She was complaining yesterday about all the extra people underfoot in the kitchen, temporary help from the village, servants of the visiting delegates. And there was an old woman I'd never seen before sitting in the kitchen, folding laundry. At least, that's what I thought she was doing. I bet she was bespelling the towels. If we didn't spot the folding as spellcasting, there's no way Cook would—but if she saw the old woman again, Cook would recognize her."

Justinian and Radolphus looked at each other.

"Worth a try," Justinian said. "Let's go find Cook. No, you stay here, sprout," he added, as Gwynn got up to follow them. "If this gets unpleasant, Radolphus and I can take care of ourselves."

It's not fair, Gwynn thought as she watched the study door close behind them. I did as much as anyone to figure it out.

The door opened again, and Justinian stuck his head back in.

"Besides, if the direct approach fails, you're the only one of us qualified to infiltrate the witches' ranks."

He winked and closed the door.

Alas, Gwynn's espionage skills proved unnecessary. Early the next morning, Master Radolphus summoned the entire college and all the visiting magicians to the dining hall. One of the two elderly witches Gwynn had seen at the banquet stood beside him, her face frowning sternly as the headmaster announced that thanks to the timely assistance of Mistress Hecate and the rest of the witch delegation, the culprit who had infiltrated their ranks and killed Master Horatio had been discovered and handed over to the duke for appropriate punishment.

The other witch who had been at the head table was conspicuously absent.

Radolphus revealed no details about how the murder was committed, and the look on his face discouraged anyone who might have been inclined to ask.

Gwynn's next visit to Cook, ostensibly to replenish the gingerbread supply, proved more enlightening.

"Sitting up there at the head table with that other witch, just as snooty as you please," Cook said. "I recognized her at once. Hadn't she just spent two days hanging around in my kitchen? Looking for a way to cause trouble. Well, at least she only went after Master Horatio and not someone anyone would miss. And everyone's saying how clever it was of Master Radolphus and Master Justinian to catch her."

"Everyone" presumably included the duke, who reportedly sent a letter of thanks and congratulations to Master Radolphus.

And the conference would end tomorrow, Gwynn thought, as she climbed the stairs carrying a tea tray and the new bowl of gingerbread cookies. Surely that meant Carima would be leaving?

She entered and knocked aside a little origami frog to put the tray down on the tea table. She took the plate of gingerbread and went over to the cookie jar.

Which was already full. It hadn't been a few hours ago. She knew that. So she'd gone down right after her last class of the day, waited until Cook's first batch of cookies came out, and brought up the best.

Come to think of it, those didn't really look like Cook's gingerbread. The color was a little darker than the rich, golden brown of the cookies in the bowl she'd brought from the kitchen. The edges were slightly ragged, and the size was a little more irregular.

Carima. She had no idea how the witch managed it, but she was sure Carima had baked the cookies. And had done something to them, if the little origami animals were anything to judge by. Carima, making one last desperate attempt to ensnare the Maestro in her love spells.

She heard Justinian's voice in the quadrangle. He hadn't stayed, talking with students, or strayed off to have tea with Master Radolphus. In a few minutes he would be in the study. Would he believe her if she tried to warn him? What if he cast a spell of detection on the gingerbread? Would it show traces of a spell? Or was all witch magic, like the little paper birds, impervious to the detection spells they taught at the college? And if he didn't believe her—or if he did believe her but decided it would be interesting to eat a cookie anyway—

She had to do something. But what?

"Well, it looks as if my gremlins have deserted me for good," Master Justinian said the next afternoon.

He and Master Radolphus were gazing down at the quadrangle. Gwynn looked up from where she was setting the tea table and peeked over their shoulders. Carima was walking down the path to her carriage, following the porters who carried her luggage. She was trying hard to ignore the half dozen adoring gremlins scuttling after her. They gazed up at her with looks of abject adoration on their wizened little faces; they scrabbled at her dress with their muddy paws, leaving long, dirty streaks; and often they stepped on the heels of her shoes in their eagerness to be near her.

"Oh, well," Justinian said. "They were rather getting in the way here. But it is odd behavior for gremlins."

"Makes me wonder if she tested some new love potion on them," Radolphus suggested.

"If so, it rather backfired on her, don't you think?"

"Definitely," Radolphus said. "Yes, that's probably it," he went on. "Witches will fool around with love potions. Ought to be outlawed. They're almost impossible to detect, and as for counteracting them—well, I wish her luck. Very careless, if you ask me."

"Yes, she's often careless, isn't she?" Justinian said, glancing briefly at Gwynn. "Do you suppose Mistress Hecate knows how much of a help Carima was to us in solving Horatio's murder?"

"I hope not," Radolphus said. "That would be bad for Carima's career—and possibly her health. I know I didn't tell, though I suppose Hecate might have guessed. Still, not our problem. Let's have the tea now."

The two mages settled by the table, and Gwynn began pouring tea.

"Oh, Gwynn, did you bring the gingerbread?" Justinian asked.

Radolphus frowned as if he thought that rather an odd question—probably because Justinian had paused on the verge of sinking his teeth into one of the cookies in question to ask it.

"Yes," Gwynn said, glancing up. "And the scones for Master Radolphus."

"Good," said Justinian, completing his bite. And then through a mouthful of gingerbread, he added. "Light a few candles, tadpole. It's getting dim in here."

Gwynn smiled. She produced the little brass dragon from her pocket, aimed it at a candle, and pressed the catch.

"Grrroarrr!" squeaked the dragon, as the little flame from its snout lit the candle.

"The dragon!" Justinian said, reaching for it. "It's all together again? How did that happen?"

"I put it together last night," Gwynn said.

"You did? How?"

Gwynn shrugged. How could she possibly explain? The pieces just fit a certain way, that was all. She could no more explain to the Maestro how she had reassembled the dragon than she could explain casting a mage-light spell to Cook, but she could do either trick with ease. So far she hadn't figured out how to fold the little paper birds and animals, much less endow them with spells—useful spells, of course, not nasty, silly ones like Carima's. But she had collected another whole box of them to experiment with, when time permitted. One way or another, she'd learned a lot from the conference.

"Amazing!" Justinian exclaimed, pressing the catch and watching with delight as the plume of fire shot out. Asmodeus, about to jump into the Maestro's lap, was alarmed and sat down on the floor beside Gwynn instead.

Gwynn took a bite of her scone. The cat looked up at her in a hopeful manner—not exactly begging, but indicating his willingness to dispose of any unwanted little bits she might happen to have lying about. She smiled, recalling the eager faces of the gremlins as she'd fed them every last crumb of Carima's gingerbread. She fed Asmodeus a bit of buttered scone.

"But how on earth did you get it to work again?" With the dragon, Justinian took aim at several of the little origami animals that were still lying around.

"It was just out of oil," Gwynn said, offering the cat another bit of scone. "I filled it again after I reassembled it."

"That's marvelous!" Justinian said. "Look, Radolphus, isn't this marvelous!"

"Yes," said Radolphus, folding his hands contentedly in his lap as he watched Justinian incinerating another little paper figure. "I rather think it is."

The Duh Vice

by Michael Armstrong

"If you're smart, you'll just ignore me and walk away," Novak said right before I arrested him on six counts of resource-allocation waste in the first degree.

Months later, when I was warming my ass over a little nub of what he called the Duh Vice up there in my suck-ass little shack near Boundary, I realized he had been right. What the heck did I know last winter, when I got a call out to Novak's place to check out a citizen tip of resource waste?

I'm a cop, a Rawhide, the petty little bureaucrats who hassle good citizens about keeping their thermostat set too high. Yeah, I get grief for doing my job. OK, here's the deal: when the United States government figures out how not to piss off the world so we can get some of its spare energy, I'll retire. Until then, I'm the guy who knocks on your door at 2 a.m. because you're using more than your fair share of energy. You don't like it? Move to Canada.

Which was how I got called out to Novak's place that

crisp winter day. Not that I told Novak that, but his neighbor, a real dickhead named Stark, had ratted him out. Stark was one of those reserve-police-officer wannabe cops who had taken fifteen hours of training and become dangerous enough with a remote thermal sensor to fink on his neighbors. If Stark hadn't said Novak was leaking over 1,000 BTUs an hour, I wouldn't have bothered. We Rawhides don't get out of bed for anything less than 500.

Stark had come by the Resource Allocation Department station with his little readouts, an infrared video, and even a cheap-ass blurry digital photo of Novak sitting in his living room in T-shirt and shorts. I could tell by his smarmy little smile he thought he'd nailed the guy, and if his tip resulted in a conviction, he'd get the reward of one hundred resource-allocation points.

Good citizen, my ass. Stark was looking to be able to jack up his thermostat another two degrees.

"So, you gonna check it out, huh?" Stark asked me.

I was investigating a major violation of the 2017 Resource Allocation Act, some guy who'd found a stash of honest-to-goodness gasoline and had been seen running a snow machine out in the Caribou Hills—I mean, a two-stroke, internal-combustion sled, not one of those electric snow coaches. I didn't really have time for penny-ante crap. But Stark knew someone in the department, I never could figure out who, and his tip had landed in my in-box with a note from the chief, "Check this out."

I didn't know Novak. He'd moved to Della on the ass end of Alaska a year ago, got himself an approved one-bedroom, nine-hundred-square-foot cabin for him and his son. "His retard son," Stark told me, but I'd pulled the APSIN records on the Novaks, and his son checked out as having Williams

Syndrome, kind of a rare developmental disability—only we were supposed to say "differentability"—that meant the kid was high end in some abilities, low in others. You know, like most of us, only more so.

I let Stark tell me all sorts of gossip about Novak he couldn't have known unless he had a password into the Alaska Public Safety Information Network, then I shooed him out of my office and told him I'd get back in touch with him later. I ran a 10-97 and Novak came through clear, no wants, no warrants. Just for kicks, I ran his court history.

Six arrests for RAW 6 to RAW 2. No one had ever gotten him on RAW 1, but he'd been arrested for resource-allocation waste in three states over the past eight years. No convictions, and on one of the cases, he got a civil settlement for false arrest.

Now that was peculiar. I should have listened to the little voices in my head that said something was hinky. Only when I got out to Novak's place and stopped at the top of his clean-shoveled path, I didn't listen to the voices. No, I just stared at the screen on my little handheld monitor and saw all the dials going off the charts.

A Marine likes to say his KA-BAR knife is his best friend. A state trooper swears by his little buddy, the Glock 27, with its random-burst fléchette rounds. We Rawhides keep a handheld strapped to one hip, keep the batteries charged, and upgrade the software every thirty days.

My handheld told me I had a real solid case of RAW 1. In my fifteen years with the RAD, I'd only gotten two RAW 1 convictions, and with good reason. People like Stark think it's real easy to steal resources, but the truth is, the system is so ironclad, you have to be either smart, sneaky, or bold to grab more than your fair share of resources.

You get calories based on size, physical need—like if you were a manual laborer—and age. Every calorie you bought got tracked against your monthly allotment, and if you went over, tough. You couldn't buy food. After a month or two of going hungry at the end of the month, most people figured it out. Same thing with energy. The grid fed your allocation, and if you used too much, the power shut off.

Most RAW charges came about when someone tried to tinker with the system, either jigger the power meter or try to get extra calories on a stolen or hacked account. The 2017 Act allowed for individual initiative, on the idea that maybe some entrepreneur or inventor could come up with the Holy Grail, unlimited cheap energy, so just being warm, fat, and happy wasn't enough for a RAW charge. You had to catch someone stealing resources.

Except what most people didn't know was that there was a maximum cap to what anyone could have, I mean, outside the ration. That's how I nailed Novak. See, the law figured someone might get clever, might put in a few inches of insulation, keep up on weather-stripping, maybe jigger a personal vehicle's electric motor to get 15 percent more juice out of it. That was the cap: 15 percent. Someone could be 15 percent overweight, or 15 percent warmer, or go 15 percent faster or farther, but anything over that was de facto waste.

When I came up to Novak's house, my handheld showed he had an energy leakage of 33 percent. That's leakage, not overuse. His walk not only had been shoveled clean of the previous week's three feet of snow, but the concrete was bare—steaming, in fact. When I knocked on his door and Novak opened it enough for me to get a quick read on the interior, his inside temperature was a toasty seventy-five degrees, 22 percent above the thermal allocation. I looked down at my handheld's readout, downloaded the readings to dispatch, and smiled.

"Mr. Novak?" I asked.

Novak stood there in shorts, no shoes or socks, and a light cotton T-shirt. There was a little drop of sweat on his forehead. Inside. In winter.

"You want me or my son?" Novak waved over at his kid, no more than thirteen, snacking away on a huge bowl of cornflakes. It had been a long time since I'd seen a pudgy kid, but there he was, a genuine potbelly and little puffy fat cheeks. The kid wasn't even wearing a T-shirt, just shorts.

"You, sir." I showed him my badge and identification.

Novak nodded. "I wondered when that schmuck Stark would rat me out. Well, come on in, do your investigation." He grinned. "You might want to take your coat off. It's a little toasty inside."

Novak led me through the arctic entryway—the inside door to the house standing wide open—and into the great room. I could see it had the standard design of a nine-hundred-footer: main room, kitchen off to one side, a door to a bathroom, and a bedroom at the other end. Only the center of the room had been dug out, down into the crawl space and into a basement, so the middle was like a big cathedral ceiling. Not that you saw those anymore, two-story inside rooms, but I'd read about them in books. There was a tiny pond, big bright lights shining down from the ceiling, and all sorts of tropical plants—even palm trees—growing inside the house.

Once for a vacation I'd saved up five years of travel points and taken two weeks in Florida. Walking into that room was like walking outside from the airport into a tropical night.

This big waft of warm, humid air hit you. I quickly took off my coat, my sweater, my boots and socks, and was down to an undershirt and pants. And I was still sweating.

The place was off the charts. Forget about going over 15 percent. If my readout was right, Novak was using 250 percent of his monthly energy allocation. He had to be damn clever to steal that much energy—either damn clever or outright bold. He leaned forward and looked at my readout.

"You might want to get that checked out," he said. "I've got the latest upgrade on a handheld—a Rawhide gave it to me in that little civil suit you no doubt have read up on—and mine says I'm actually at 267 percent." He grinned, that same smarmy grin he'd given me before. He actually looked like he was enjoying this.

"I've got you on RAW 1," I said. "Slam dunk. You're looking at an unclassified felony. Every day is a count, so if I record you for the next month, that's enough counts to put you away for life."

"Uh-huh," Novak said.

"You don't seem concerned." I waved over at his lard-ass son. "What about chubby there? How's he going to find cornflakes if you're in federal prison?"

"Probably the same way he does now," Novak said. "Trade them for carp." He waved at the pond, and I could see little orange fins swimming through the water. The guy was growing fish inside the house. Tropical fish! I did a readout on the water and got back a temperature of eighty-five degrees. The water was warmer than the house.

I shook my head. "Novak, I don't think you get it. I've got you busted. I'm gonna call it in. You're in big trouble. Really big trouble."

"That's what the last six Rawhides said." Novak got up,

waved at a little box humming away in the corner of the room. "Why don't I show you the Duh Vice?"

"Yeah, sure," I said.

Later, I thought I should have just left it at that, but what did I know?

"The Duh Vice," Novak said. He opened up a cabinet the size of a washing machine, and I saw a dull silver globe about the size of a basketball. Copper tubing ran around it, one line coming up from the bottom of the box, swirling around the globe, and the other end going down. "The Device, we'd say, but I like how Tim says it." He waved at his son, who'd now finished his cornflakes and watched us with big huge pale blue eyes. "It's Tim's invention, or rather, discovery."

"What does it do?" I asked. Stupid me. I should have shut up.

"It gives off heat."

I ran a probe over the globe, and got a reading . . . well, part of the globe was six hundred degrees, and another part of it was even hotter. I mean, hot, like the inside of a blast furnace.

"But how?" I could see it gave off heat like a mutha, but where did the heat come from?

"It comes from another dimension," the kid said.

I looked up. Tim Novak stood there staring at the cabinet. He had a big grin on his face, like father, like son. "I found it one day when I was, uh, playing with some toys. There was a leak between null spaces and I just grabbed it and pulled it into our dimension." Tim looked down at his right thumb and forefinger. "It burned! It did. I shoulda used pliers."

"Uh-huh." I looked over at the Novaks, and the way Dad looked at his little boy, I could see that the old man believed what the kid said. Not me, though.

"Sure is hot," I said.

"If I didn't pipe heat off of it, it would melt into the ground," Novak said. "When it was smaller, that's how I excavated the basement." He waved at the walls, the floor. "I have heat coils running through all the walls, through the floor, even the roof. You might have noticed there wasn't any snow on the roof? On the walkway? Heating coils there, too. The walls are R-3, basically the insulation of Sheetrock and wood."

Novak opened another little cabinet, with all sorts of dials and wiring. "There's a little steam turbine in there. I generate my own energy, trade it to some people for, well, stuff." He pointed at my handheld. "Go ahead, call your dispatch, ask them to check with the power company. I'm sending energy back into the grid, fifteen times my monthly allocation. That's positive energy, in excess of my ration." Novak crossed his hands over his chest. "Still think I'm violating the law?"

"Something's not right," I said. "Something's just not right."

Novak shrugged. "So arrest me. That's what six of you bozos did. And ten of you didn't. Those ten are the smarter ones."

In the end, though, it wasn't my call. I transmitted my report, bumped it up to the chief, and I don't know, Stark must have been in really good with the chief, because a few minutes later, the order came back.

Arrest the bastard.

Yeah, and even though it was the chief's call, guess who's now sitting in a guard shack at Boundary, checking visas of

Canadians coming into the States for a little of that fast and easy American nooky? Yeah, it's the cardinal rule of bureaucracy: the bosses get all the glory, the grunts get all the blame.

So, I called in backup, got almost the whole department, forensics and engineering and the chief himself, even Stark along as a reserve office to sign people in as they came and went. They tore up Novak's floor. They punched holes in his walls. They tore up his steam turbine, disconnected the cooling pipes—because that was what they were, really—and would have taken the Duh Vice, except it got so hot no one could handle it, and it started to melt through its stand.

Even though I was the investigating officer, I got shoved aside as more and more big-shot cops came in to take over the case, then bigger-shot cops came in to take over the case from them, until after three days of this, with me standing guard by then, and no one allowed to enter or leave without federal clearance, by God, federal clearance, well, eventually the black ops guys showed up.

We all knew about them. The suits. The guys in the crisp white shirts, the dark glasses, little Bluetooth ear sets so tiny you could hardly see them. Those guys. Spooks and dark agents, people so weird and funky and mysterious I couldn't even sign them in by name, just checkoff codes, Agent 1, Agent 2, Agent 3, and the big cheese, Agent 4, who everybody called Mr. Smith.

OK, what was really hinky was that Novak knew them. They came in and bantered with him, joked around with the kid, called them Jim and Tim. After a while they shut the door on me, and I stood out there in the arctic entryway, sitting on a rough bench, the front door open since it was still so damn hot. I got hotter and hotter, the heat blowing through that flimsy little inside door, blowing over me and making the subzero air outside steam. I realized then what had happened. Our cops had disassembled the Duh Vice, and the black ops guys were putting it back together. After a while they all came out, said good-bye to Novak, and escorted me to my patrol van.

Well, they let me have the dignity of walking with them, but I knew what the little taps on the shoulder meant, the little push on the elbow. They were escorting me.

Back at the station, the chain of command unfolded in reverse. The director of the Resource Allocation Department took over the chief's office, then he called in his deputy director, and she called in the director of enforcement, and he called in the chief, and he called in the lieutenant. The lieutenant called in the sergeants, all three of them, then they called in the senior officer, then they called in me, the junior senior officer and the investigating officer, until we were all crammed in there, with Mr. Smith standing behind all my superior officers, and everyone staring at me, the investigating officer.

They made a point of telling me that—the directors, the colonel, the chief, the LT, sarges 1, 2, and 3. "He's the investigating officer," as if I was the one who called in trouble, as if I was the one the who made the command decision to arrest Novak.

OK, I got it. I was the arresting officer of record. Which was how I wound up there in the office with the whole organizational chart lining up to grind me into the carpet. One by one they chewed out my ass, and when they were all done, the chief handed me my transfer papers for a post I for damn sure didn't remember putting in for, but there it was: Boundary.

After I looked at my papers, after I saw my career fade away like steam rolling off Novak's Duh Vice, Mr. Smith excused everyone, took over the chief's office, and sat me down, "officer to officer," he put it, so I would understand.

Oh, I understood by then. I had figured it out. But Mr. Smith had to explain it to me anyway.

"You should have just let Mr. Novak be," he said. He shook his head. "I guess it's our fault, really. When he moved here, we should have warned you. The RAD."

"Warned us?"

"To leave him alone. To pretend like the Duh Vice never existed."

"What device?" I asked.

"You're learning fast," he said. "Too late."

"Yeah, too late." I looked at him. "But why?" I knew why, but Mr. Smith had to tell me. I wanted a senior agent of the United States government to tell me why I was to shut up about the energy source that could save our country, that could give us unlimited cheap energy, that could restore our rightful power in the world, and maybe, just maybe, kick some Canadian butt.

"Because we don't need it. The Duh Vice."

"Don't need it? While people are shivering in houses set at fifty-eight degrees? While the U.S. gross national product has declined 750 percent since 2010? While people are going without good medical care—"

"Oh, shut up, you little ninny," Smith said. "Yeah, we're poorer—poorer, but not poor. Yeah, we aren't the Top Dog in the world anymore, like it's 2008. Yeah, we've had our trade cut off because the world hates America. So what? No one is trying to blow us up. No one is trying to pick a fight with us. Europe and China get to be the world's policemen, and Americans don't have to die trying to bring democracy and freedom to suck-ass little countries who'd rather be told what to do by priests and mullahs and dictators anyway."

"But—"

"But," Smith raised a finger. "It's taken us decades to convince Americans not to be the wasteful assholes we once were. We're not a nation of fat slobs. We walk and exercise and eat right and live longer. Healthier. Happier . . . yes, *happier*. We don't waste food, waste resources. Our rivers and lakes and oceans are clean again, you can breathe fresh air, you don't risk death in high-speed car accidents. It's a better world. Think about it. If we gave America cheap energy, what would happen?"

I thought about it. I could sleep warm at night. I could eat a full meal every day and not just at Thanksgiving and Christmas. I could travel outside of Alaska. I could go someplace warm. I stayed quiet, though. I couldn't argue with Smith, not with his guns and his power and the mysterious black ops. I knew the system.

Someone had to be hosed. That someone was me.

"Yes, sir," was all I could say. "I understand."

So here I am in my shack, trying to keep warm. Actually, doing a damn good job of it. Novak further explained the Duh Vice to me, at least in a way I could understand. He said it was like a hernia between dimensions or worlds of folds of worlds, I never did quite get it. The Duh Vice slipped from one world to another, and where it slipped, it protruded like the inside of the sun, white-hot and warm and with unlimited energy. Little Timmy, the guy with the spooky eyes, had poked open the hole and pulled the Duh Vice out. No one figured out how he did it, but it didn't matter. The Novaks had all the power they needed.

And so did I. See, that was what I got for my silence, for sucking up my assignment to Boundary. I got the little shack. I got the day-in and day-out duty of checking passports. I got the job and the pension and the godforsaken loneliness. But I also got the Duh Vice.

Or part of it, anyway. Sometimes it got too big, Novak said, and he'd figured out a way to pinch off a little bit of it, like sourdough starter. It would get bigger and bigger with time, and when that happened, there was a number I should call and either Novak or Smith or someone would come and pinch off another little part of the Duh Vice and take it away. I don't know where. There was talk the U.S. had this super-secret project to build a star drive, but that was just talk.

All I know was, there in my little shack, with the big basement hollowed out under the trapdoor, and the little tropical paradise with the fish pond and the palm trees and the orange trees, there inside, for once, I was nice and warm.

Nice and warm, indeed.

Weight of the World

by John Straley

The fat man rubbed his belly in the sun. He was happy, after his long night of work, feeling the warmth easing out over the Tasman Sea.

A black dwarf with Maori tattoos covering his torso walked up to the fat man with a frosted glass of beer.

"Congratulations, sir," the little man said without looking up into his face.

"Thank you, Clive," the big man said without taking his eyes off the rising sun. "It goes without saying that I'm grateful to you and the crew. Heck of a job this year. Top rate, really."

"Too kind, sir," he said, and backed away, with a stiff, half-bent bow.

As he watched the little Maori go, the fat man recognized his nagging irritation with his little employees: their fingers wriggling like link sausages at the end of their arms, and the constant tinkle of bells . . . and even though the little buggers sometimes made his skin crawl, he had to admit they were his family. "We are all freaks here," the fat man had often thought while working at his bench, surrounded by hard-scrabbling little men with their wheezy voices, "and there is nothing any of us can do about that."

The delivery team always ended their long night's work there, at Young Nick's Head, along the coast of New Zealand. By a fine trick of geography and the arbitrary date line, it was one of the first pieces of land to greet the new day. Of any sunrise over dry land, it was the closest to the first. He leaned his head back and took a long drink of beer, wiping his mustache with the back of his hand.

They would rest on the beach for a few weeks. The crew would take care of the equipment and the stock. He would sleep and settle his frayed nerves, then the preparations would begin again, as they always did . . . returning as relentlessly as this promised sunrise. He was tired, he had to admit it. The responsibility, the millions of intricate moves and judgments he had to make in pulling it off year after year, were beginning to take their toll.

"Let it go . . ." he said aloud to no one but the surf birds skimming the edges of the waves. Then he heard bells frantically cackling up the trail behind him.

"Sir . . ." the Maori dwarf said, clearly out of breath, "I think you better come . . . no . . . I'm sure of it, sir." Then he turned and ran off, leaving behind only a puff of dust like a bad odor.

The fat man let out a long sigh and lingered for a moment. Clive's tone of voice worried him, and the fat man was tired and wanted to stretch out his feeling of satisfaction for another year done.

"Sir?" the little voice called out from down the hill.

"Coming," he mumbled as he filled his beer glass.

He walked down the trail and reached a grassy flat. A smaller man lay sprawled at Clive's feet. His legs and arms were splayed out like a broken marionette that had fallen from the sky. The fat man slowed down, but the bulk of his great belly kept him moving toward the scene.

"I just found him like this, sir," Clive said, his cartoonish voice scratchy and pitched higher than normal. "I didn't touch a thing. I swear."

The big man knelt and looked at the head of the tiny sprawled creature. The back of his skull was soft and pulpy red. A bloody rock sparkled like a ruby in the middle of the trail, where someone with tiny blood-spattered feet had run through the dust.

"Holy Moly," Santa Claus said, "this elf is dead!"

"It appears so," Clive said.

Santa Claus didn't speak for several moments. "Well," he said as he drained off his beer in three gulps, "put something around the body to keep everyone away from him, then gather the others down by the water."

Clive was choking back his tears. "What should I use for perimeter tape, sir?" the distraught dwarf said.

"It doesn't matter, Clive," Santa said softly. "I suppose we have some ribbon left over. Get James to help you."

The dwarf wandered off, still stunned. The fat man stood up and took one last look at the sun easing over the water. It was a fine cool morning of what promised to be a warm day.

"Dear Lord," he said aloud. "Little Cletus . . ." And he put his empty beer glass into the massive pocket of his sweat-stained red pants, stood up, and walked down to the water's edge.

The delivery team was made up of six: four elves and two

dwarfs, who traveled with him on the night. Each had his job: navigation, gift preparation, list minding, and engineering. Cletus had been the gift-preparation elf. He rode with the sack. The dwarfs both sat second chair. One was a navigator, and the other was a wrangler, who looked after the stock. The fat man drove and did the deliveries. It was a busy night, of course, and all of them were tired. In a normal year they would spend the weeks on the beach in New Zealand, sleeping mostly, eating what they brought with them, and watching the reindeer wander the hillside, feeding and rolling in the dust, their harnesses off but for a garland of bells around their necks so they could be easily found when it was time to go north.

It was one of the most pleasant moments of their brief hiatus, walking out to the beach on that first morning of that new year. All of the elves and dwarfs stripped down to their shorts and the fat man himself without his shirt on, the sun blasting down on them, the rush of the waves, the smell of the warm sea, and the sound of the bells tinkling high up on the hillside. It was the moment he looked forward to all year.

That moment would be cut short by all the messiness. "Poor murdered elf," the fat man said aloud as he lumbered down the warm sand. "Poor . . . poor thing." Then he stopped short in front of the small gathering.

"Everyone here, Clive?" Santa Claus asked the young Maori dwarf.

"Well, sir . . . Cletus . . . of course . . . Cletus . . . is, well . . ."

"Dead, Clive. I wasn't really expecting him to be in the muster. Anyone else?"

"I cannot find Young Bob, sir." Clive could not bring his eyes to meet the fat man's. Young Bob was the list-minder elf. He was called "Young" Bob because of his advanced age. He might, in fact, have been the oldest living creature on the crew. There were probably bristlecone pines that were as old as the list minder.

"And the list?"

"Gone, as well, I'm afraid, sir."

The fat man rubbed his beard and looked around at the rest of the crew. They looked all the more frail for their fear, and their worry. There they stood with their plump little limbs to the sunshine, their faces feeling the first real warmth of the year, and all of them looked to him with their faith and loyalty intact. He felt a twinge of guilt at his earlier irritation.

"The list is blank now, isn't it, sir? What could anyone possibly want with a blank list?"

"I don't know, Bunny," the fat man said to the Jamaican wrangler dwarf with the red-and-green ribbon entwined in his dreads. "Just get the stock together now. There will be one missing, but that's all right. Don't waste time looking."

He looked at the others. "Make all preparations, and load poor Cletus into the sleigh. We'll rest on the ice and feed the stock on grain for a few weeks." They started to walk slowly up the beach, leaving the meandering tracks of creatures who didn't really want to go anywhere. "I promise you, boys, we will have a proper vacation after we get this all sorted out. And double rations of beer for the trip home . . . for all but the navigator."

A halfhearted cheer rose from the beach fringe, and the little men wandered toward the harness pile.

Like many things surrounding Christmas, not even Santa understood everything. The physics of compressed speed and time, how he managed to travel so far and so fast in the given time, was a mystery, and he was at a loss to explain his ability to travel up and down through narrow chimneys and sections of ducting. He did not know the mechanics of such things. Much like faith itself, the magic of their lives was too exquisite to question. It was simply possible and he did it.

But the list was a much more troubling mystery. There were not two lists of children in the sleigh. That had long ago become too cumbersome. For the last hundred years all children were assumed to be good, so a census was taken. It had been a wonderful change when it was first introduced to Santa Claus, who didn't like the thought of the naughty children being slighted on Christmas morning. It had weighed on him for centuries. It seemed punitive and unloving to exclude a child from the rewards of the birth day of the Savior. Santa had even begged to be able to deliver gifts to children of different faiths, but that was met with disapproval from the old guard. Children of different faiths were not added to the naughty list, they were simply ignored. No, the naughty list had been reserved for children of the faith who were somehow not deemed worthy of a gift.

That had always bothered him, and at times it had even tested his own faith. As the sun rose over Young Nick's Head in New Zealand the day after Christmas, the list would be blank, a slim binder whose paper glistened like arctic snow. Then, within seconds, names would begin to appear. The fat man could not bear to watch as the names of the naughty, the neglected, the shunned, lined up row after row. The list keeper, Young Bob, a staunch member of the old guard, watched them and subtracted their names from

the census with thick black pencil before the sleigh ever rose
from the ice.

Once when the fat man had asked the old elf how he felt
crossing the names off, all Young Bob would say was, "We
didn't put them on the naughty list, Boss, they did it themselves. That's free will. What's the point of being good if you
don't choose it on your own?"

The fact that Bob's free-will argument had some philosophical weight added to Santa's consternation. He wasn't a
philosopher. All he had ever wanted to do was give gifts of
celebration to every single creature on earth. It should have
been universal, like the gift of the sun which continued to
rise over the sea. But somehow the idea had not caught on.

They rigged the sleigh. The deer were restive and cranky, tired
like the others after their work. They fought their harnesses,
and a couple of them lay down in their traces. "I know I am
asking a lot of you," Santa said, "but believe me I wouldn't do
this if it weren't important. We must be home at once, for the
list is missing and one of our own has become horribly lost.
Please. You will have my gratitude and the gratitude of everyone who works with us." With that the reindeer stood up and,
after a few tentative hops, rose into the air pulling the fat man
and the drunken elves up into the morning light.

Flying behind the reindeer was one of the things he still
loved about the job. The creaking of the leather just under
the rhythmic pulsing of the bells. The musty smell of their
sweat-soaked hides as they warmed to their work. The tropical air was damp and full of scent as he rose higher and
higher, up into the thinner atmosphere. As the island nation

shrank away beneath them, he inhaled one long lungful of humid air, then left its fragrance behind.

The animals were tired, but still they were able to push north and west in a steady long arc toward the northern darkness that curved over the world. Stars winked alive in the purple sky as farther north they ran, and the fat man regretted whatever irritation he had held against his absent helper. The beauty of the northern sky had a calming effect on him. Its cold purity made him remember the blessings of his warm home, resting as it did in the coldest place on earth.

Cletus had been a fine, sweet elf, fussing over each package to be delivered. Young Bob would check the list, and Cletus would dig into the sack and find the correct present, fluffing the ribbon and repairing any nicks in the wrapping.

Like the names on the list and the mechanics of his travel, Santa did not understand the nature of the sack. It wasn't big enough to contain all the gifts at once. It appeared to be some kind of cornucopia. The correct presents were always there. He did not know why, and neither was he terribly curious as to how. They simply were there in Cletus's hands, and he would put them in the fat man's smaller delivery pouch.

They would stop. Bunny would steady the stock. The engineering elf would check the harnesses. Young Bob would be working on the next list, and Cletus would stand watching Santa disappear into the house, until Young Bob would yell at him to stop daydreaming and get back to work.

Cletus had been a truly generous soul. Others were industrious and some were reliable, but Cletus, unlike most of the others, was enraptured by the spirit of the season.

The blue of the night sky seared and flashed with aurora, the ion particles shimmering on the harnesses and hides of the stock. The whole outfit glowed with St. Elmo's fire as they pushed up past the Bering Sea, where waves frothed up phosphorescence to match the sparkle of the stars. The old man pulled on his hood and tightened its fur ruff around his face.

"Generous . . . generous . . . generous . . ." the fat man said aloud to himself.

They landed on the ice, the tired animals bending their necks down against their harnesses. Jets of hot breath pushed from their muzzles and rose to mingle with the steam rising from their hides. The elves and dwarfs hopped off the sleigh to help Bunny unhook the harnesses and get blankets fastened around the reindeer's necks so that they might not cool down too fast.

"Pardon me, sir," Clive said, "but do you know what you are going to do about"—the little Maori stammered with discomfort—"whoever did this to Cletus?"

"Take care of the stock, boys. And again, you all did a fine job this winter. Take care of the stock, then get yourselves something good to eat. Try not to wake the others. I'm sure they're all asleep yet."

So the little men wiped down the reindeer and led them to the fine dry barn. The fat man himself personally gave each of the deer a cube of sugar and smoothed their hide where they had sweated against the harness collars. Then he walked down to the shop floor and made his way to the office where Young Bob had kept the list.

The old elf was sitting with his head in his hands.

"This is not a mystery story, old friend." Santa Claus said.

"I know, sir," Young Bob said, without startling at the sound of the big man's voice.

"I don't know why you ran," the fat man said in the same kindly voice he used for all the children of the world.

"He was giving gifts that should have rightfully gone to others. He was giving gifts to those on the excluded list."

"I know," the fat man said, smiling with sympathy at the old elf.

"I didn't mean to hurt him," he said into his leathery palms.

"I know that too."

"We got in a fight. He said that it shouldn't matter. That everyone deserved something no matter what they had done. And I said even if they had done something really terrible, and he said yes. And I said even if you hurt someone, even if you hurt someone who didn't deserve it, and he said yes, then . . ."

"Open the book," the fat man said, and the old elf reached around behind him and opened the book to the first page. He grunted and shook his head, then turned it around for Santa to read.

And, of course, there on the first page was Young Bob's name. The first entry in the book for the new year.

"I feel awful," the old elf said. "Will I ever be forgiven?"

"You are already forgiven, Bob. But still, you must go."

"Yes," he said. "I know." He got up.

The fat man put his hand on the thin and shivering shoulder. "Bob?"

"Yes, sir?"

"Why don't you take this with you." He handed the little man the list, which was gaining names as quickly as stock quotes in a Wall Street office.

"All right," Young Bob said as he walked out onto the glowing ice of the long, arctic night.

Death was rare enough that some of the elves had to consult with the old books on how to bury Cletus. They prepared his clothes and sang the songs required by ritual. They gathered and ate afterward. They told stories and gave support to those who grieved him most.

And then, of course, they got back to work.

Young Bob was taken to the corner of the Canadian arctic, where he walked into a small village. He eventually found work in a traveling magic show that featured a talking dog and a woman who could eat broken glass and razor blades.

The next year, of course, you all remember. It was the year that everyone got a gift. Men and women in prison for the first time woke up to a small package of socks or a candy cane. Politicians who had lied to their constituents and stolen money found kittens in their stockings. Even the most hardheaded military dictators for whom Christmas had no meaning found something sweet on their breakfast tables, and even if they ignored it or threatened to behead their household staffs for putting it there, a certain generous sweetness nagged at them the rest of the day.

And in a trash-strewn lot in Saskatchewan, where the roustabouts smoked their first cigarette of the day while still in bed, and the talking dog trotted out of the caravan to take an urgent pee, Young Bob opened up his lovingly wrapped Christmas gift and felt the weight of the world settle on his tiny, still-beating heart.

Illumination

by Laura Anne Gilman

The boat was long and lean, and so was the guy pulling the oar. I leaned out so far over the bridge, I probably would have fallen if Joseph hadn't grabbed the back of my belt.

"Darling, the water level is high enough. No need to add your drool to it."

"But . . . pretty!"

Joseph has known me since I was eight. He was there when my hormones kicked in, there when I went through the "boys or girls?" agita. He was there for all of my not-too-stellar high school career, and he was there when I settled into semiresponsible adulthood. I don't think he's blinked once.

Well, maybe when I got into Amherst. I think he blinked then. He wouldn't admit to crying.

"Your mind on the crisis at hand, please?" he said without too much hope.

The crisis was my dad. As usual.

J. held the letter in his hand. It had come a few days

before, but I hadn't gotten around to opening it until the previous night. I'd read it halfway, and pinged J. In every way that counted, he was my real father. Zaki Torres was just my genetic donor and occasional pain in the posterior.

"I think he's dead this time," I told J. I wasn't sure, but it felt probable.

"Is that gut instinct, or something else?"

I had to think about that for a minute. "I don't know. Maybe both."

Gut instinct was the normal everyday "I got a bad feeling about this" sort of thing. Something else was, well, something else. And it had a lot less to do with feeling than knowing. Or, as J. put it, with kenning.

Magic worked like that, sometimes.

I cast a longing look after the sculler, by then halfway down the river, and sighed. J. hadn't brought me there for the scenery, more's the pity. There'd be time for that later, if I was lucky. If not, well, there were always new boys all over the place.

"Bonnie . . ."

"Right." I leaned against the stonework of the bridge and tried to soak up the cool spring sunlight into my skin. I'm pale like skim milk, with the annoyingly white-blond hair to match, but I keep hoping that some melanin will sneak into my epidermis, somehow.

"Let's review the facts. My father, also known as Zaki the King of the Shiftless Losers . . ."

J. made an inarticulate sound of protest, but it was mainly a formality. He's known my dad since I was eight, too. Zaki's Talent was slight enough to make him almost a Null, so he'd known he had to get someone else to mentor me. Thank God for great favors. Unfortunately, Zaki's idea of an acceptable mentor for his rather—modesty aside—strongly Talented eight-year-old daughter would probably make a slumlord blush. J. had been walking by on the street below the apartment when Dad tried to make the introductions, and I had been a pretty good judge of character even then. Desperate to find an alternative—any alternative—I had let out what J. later described as a mental all-points bulletin, asking for a mentor who didn't suck. My exact wording, apparently.

J. had been upstairs and talking to my dad before either of them knew what was happening. Which was how a back-street lonejack kid got a hoity-toity Council mentor, and don't think that didn't raise a few eyebrows and almost as many hackles on both sides.

But it worked. For us, anyway.

"He is, J. No use candy-coating it. He has, according to this letter, managed to get himself once again in debt to not only a loan shark, but a loan shark who would think nothing of roasting him over the coals for a human BBQ. What the hell possessed him to borrow from a cave dragon, anyway?"

"Because cave dragons always have money, and they take a long view. Usually."

"Yeah. Usually." Cave dragons, from what J. had gotten around to telling me, weren't all that much like their older cousins in Europe and Asia. They were small—only around ten feet long—and sort of dingy looking, and generally didn't hold with the eating of maidens, razing of homesteads, or stealing of livestock.

They did like their pretties, though, and stuffed their mattresses with cash, just like all misers. And they liked a nice return on their investments.

Only an idiot did a runner on a debt owed to them.

An idiot, apparently, like my genetic donor.

A dutiful daughter probably would have rushed out into the mountains and demanded an answer—or at least the personal effects and whatever was left of the body. But it was spring, and the mountains were damned cold and muddy just then. And J. didn't raise a dummy.

I went to the source, instead.

"Bonnie! Baby!"

I dodged the attempted embrace, and sidestepped my way into the apartment. Claire, my dad's girlfriend, wasn't bad, as they went—she was clean, sober, and actually cared about him. She was also intent on turning me into the daughter she'd never gotten around to raising, and at nineteen, I wasn't interested in suddenly having a mommy.

"Where is he? Where is the moron?"

"Baby, I don't know."

I stopped, turned and looked back at her. Claire's baby blue eyes were rimmed with red, and her long red hair—Pippi Longstocking hair, I called it—was done in a single messy plait, not her usual Medusa's crown of cornrows.

I'm not what you'd call a dispassionate person. In fact, J. says I throw my heart over the hedgerow, whatever the hell a hedgerow is, more often than any steeplechaser he's ever met. Whatever a steeplechaser is. But when something goes hinky in my world, I don't freak. Just the opposite.

Remember what I said earlier about magic? It's not something everyone gets. Just some of us: Talents. Humans who have the little extra kick of whatsis, lets us do . . . Stuff. It's called current these days, not magic, and according to the lectures J. sat me through, it's directly related to but not exactly like normal electricity. You feel it, inside you, in your gut, like a personal power generator.

J. says, and so does every other Talent I've talked to about it, which isn't, admittedly, many, that they feel current like this whirling, swirling mess of energy inside them, and the more agitated they get, the harder it is to control.

Not me. I get upset, I get agitated, or I get worried, and my current goes cold and calm. Instead of panic, I get planning.

"All right. When did you last see him?"

"Tuesday."

It was Friday now.

"The fourteenth."

The Tuesday before last. The idiot had been missing for over a week. And Claire hadn't been worried?

Scratch that. Obviously, she had.

"He had been fine up until then. Happy, even. He had been whistling. You know how he does that."

God, did I. Zaki the wonder whistler. Off-key and under his breath. Maybe someone with good hearing and perfect pitch had killed him.

"No worries, then?"

She shrugged, a flailing of arms that looked more Italian than Irish. "When did your father ever worry about anything?"

When he did, it was too late, anyway.

"Tell me everything you know." I tried to keep the request polite. She didn't seem to mind the edge in my words, thankfully.

"You'll find him?"

She didn't even ask how I knew that he was gone. Either

she had mailed the letter I got, which implied that she knew what was in it, or she believed more of my dad's stories about being able to use magic than she'd ever let on.

I steered her toward the sofa, and pushed her on the shoulder until she sat down on the nubby brown upholstery. "Tell me what you know, and I'll see what I can do."

Three hours and a plate of crappy bakery cookies later, I escaped with a pretty good idea that Claire didn't know shit. Feeling restless and annoyed, and trying to put my brain onto what little I had been able to learn, I reached inside and started braiding lines of current: blue for thought, red for inspiration, green for energy. Not that the colors actually meant anything, but it helped me focus. And focus was what it was all about, in the end.

The subway took me out of Brooklyn, and dumped me into midtown Manhattan, about ten blocks from where we were staying.

I could have gone back to the hotel, but the weather was nice, and I had missed being in the city, so I decided to take a walk instead. The feel of the city surrounded me, soaking back into my bones like a warm blanket on a cold night.

I loved going to school in Massachusetts, loved the slower pace and the whole academic immersion thing, but for a Talent, a big city was like a candy store—all that electricity zipping around, making an easy road for current to travel alongside. Current came naturally—lightning storms and ley lines—and it came artificially—neon signs and electrical wires. It didn't care, and artificial forms were easy to piggyback on, so hey presto, a ready-made pool of current every time you turned on a power switch.

There was a downside to it, though.

"Hey, what the hell?"

I had been so busy braiding current I hadn't realized how thick the string had gotten. It crackled and sizzled under my mental touch, and one of those crackles jumped outside of me, touching the overhead marquees and shorting them out, one after another after another, all the way down Forty-sixth Street.

Oops.

That was the payoff, for magic. Not that it didn't like technology, but that it *loved* it. So much that it always wanted to go where it was, and make best buddies with it. Hang with it.

But like two cats in a single household, electricity wanted not much to do with current. It could tag along so long as it didn't interfere, but the moment electricity got annoyed— bam. Sparks, and ugliness, and you had to go out and buy a new computer. Or cell phone. Or anything else that got caught in the cross fire.

Talents didn't make great electricians, generally, although we knew theory inside and out.

Bonnie?

The familiar mental ping was like mashed potatoes: comfort food.

On my way back to the hotel. J. had been good, staying out of my space, but I knew that he was worried, too.

"He was working," I told him twenty minutes later. We were sitting in the lounge of the hotel, which was pretty decent without being wildly overpriced, and they didn't ask for ID when I ordered a vodka martini. I had ID, of course, but it was always easier to just project "legal drinking age" at them, and not worry about an ex-cop being behind the bar. J. had settled in with a beer. He might have been Council, which is sort of the equivalent of being the country-club set of Talents, but he never did seem like it.

"Claire said it was a job with a construction guy, over in Staten Island. He was doing some detail work."

That was one thing Zaki *was* good at, no question. Give him a chunk of wood and his tools, and he'd hand over a banister, or a mantel, or some other bit of house that you could point to decades later and say, "Yeah, we had this handmade, and it was worth every penny."

He made a decent living at it. Only he kept insisting he knew how to play poker, too. As a gambler? Zaki made a damned good carpenter.

"The job was set to go on for another couple of weeks. Sometimes he'd stay out there, stay in a hotel room overnight rather than lug back to Brooklyn. She had a couple of trips"—Claire was a flight attendant for Air Cheapo—"so she didn't think anything of it when he wasn't home when she got back. But then she went to pay the rent"—the apartment was hers, not his, which was the smartest thing both of them had ever done—"and the money he was supposed to have left for her was gone. She got suspicious, because she does know Zaki, and went to look—and her stash was gone, too."

"How much?"

"Twenty thousand. And no, I don't know why she kept that much in the apartment. I guess dragons aren't the only ones who like to be able to fondle their hoards. Anyway, that's when she went looking for him. Only the guy who hired him said he hadn't been there all week, had asked for time off to, and I quote, 'deal with some family shit.'"

I was the only family he had, far as anyone knew. Zaki would be the type to rush off and embrace a new alleged offspring, but he'd be busting to tell someone—me—about it, first.

I actually would have liked a kid brother or sister. Claire had never seemed interested in producing, though, and they'd been together for almost ten years, so . . .

"Bonita, you are not focusing."

J.'s reprimand got me back on track.

I pulled the letter out of my backpack. It was a little rumpled from being shoved into my psych textbook, but it wasn't like I'd ever gotten points for neatness. "'I'm going to take care of this,'" I read, "'and then I swear, never again. And I won't ever trust a dragon to hold my marker again, even if it swears up and down I can have a full decade to re-pay.'" I folded the letter and stared at J., thinking hard.

"You still know people who know people?" J. had worked for the state before he retired early at fifty-eight, about the same time he took me on. And yes, the two events were probably connected.

"I might. What do you want me to do?"

"Get them to pull his records. Credit reports, stuff like that. Maybe we jumped to the wrong conclusion for all the right reasons. See if he took out any loans, or had been bouncing checks, stuff like that."

"Not a problem." J. had friends who had friends who had friends all the way down, I sometimes suspected. He was the kind of guy who collected people. And it was something he could do sitting in the hotel bar, sipping his beer, which was where I wanted him. He might still be rough and tough mentally, but he was pushing seventy, even if he didn't want to admit it, and I worried like any dutiful mentee.

"And in the meantime, you will be doing what?" he asked, waving the waitress over for a refill.

"His tools and stuff are still on the job site. I think I need to go sniff at them."

Ask anyone in the tristate area what that smell is, and more than half the time you'll get back the wiseass response of "Staten Island." Unless the speaker is from Manhattan, in which case it's a toss-up between Staten Island and New Jersey. But the truth is that the little borough gets very little respect. And with good reason: it's the kind of place you grow up in, and get the hell out of, as soon as possible. Why? Because it's boring.

The ferry over was kind of fun, though. I liked the feel of the wind on my face, and the fact that it was off-hour meant there weren't many people crowding the bright orange deck—the old ladies and older men with their shopping bags and snot-nosed grandchildren were inside, glomming the molded-plastic seats.

The job site was a reasonably ordinary-looking house. I don't know much about architecture—I grew up in a series of apartments, until I got to college and dorm housing—but it seemed pretty nice without standing out. In other words, classic suburbia.

Inside, though, I could see why they'd hired Zaki. Wood everywhere. And not just wood, but WOOD. The kind that has texture, and almost glows from within. Wood like current, actually, the more I looked at it.

Zaki must've loved this job. He wouldn't have just walked out on it.

"Can I help you?"

Guy, big. *Foreman,* my brain whispered to me.

"Hi. I'm Bonita Torres. Zaki's daughter? I called, about his kit?"

Foreman guy melted. He must be a dad, too. You can always tell. "Right, right. Damnedest thing. I hope everything's okay."

"Me, too," I said.

The guy showed me where Zaki stashed his stuff, and looked like he was going to hover. I plucked a thread of current like a harp string and listened to it resonate. *Go. Deal with something important. This isn't important. I'm trustworthy.*

"Okay, I gotta deal with some stuff—you'll be okay?"

"Oh, yeah, sure." I gave him my very best virtuous-daughter look. "I'm good. Don't let me distract you." *Really. Don't let me distract you.*

He left, and I turned my attention to the tools Zaki had left behind. A metal locker, which my occasionally not-so-useless dad had lined with a cushion of foam padding. Even when you weren't using current, you tended to leak, and using tools with metal—good conductors—meant you ran the risk of transferring it. Metal to metal, with current? Could be bad.

That was the stuff you learned from your mentor. My dad never told me anything about his mentor, so I guess I'd figured he didn't know much.

Live and learn. Revise impressions. If Zaki was still with us, I was going to have to apologize. After I kicked his ass for putting us through hell.

I looked, first. Two hammers, each a different size. A plastic case that, when opened, revealed a series of chisels, each of a different size. One of them had a fleck of something on it that looked like rust.

Zaki would never let rust get on his tools. Never.

A chamois cloth wrapped around a larger chisel that had some kind of carving in the wooden handle.

One pair of work gloves, dirty, and another pair, clean. A small bottle of hand lotion—unscented, half-empty.

My brain felt like it was going at half speed, taking in the details, but at the same time really revved up, like everything was flooding in all at once, giving me all these impressions and ideas, most of which didn't seem to make any sense.

Slow down. Let them come. Don't push.

J.?

The voice went away when I pinged at it. It hadn't felt like J., but who else would be hovering around my brain?

Dad?

No response.

Right, then. I looked at the tools, and didn't touch anything, letting my impressions filter in without distraction.

"Tell me something, guys," I said, then lifted my hand and placed it inside the locker, palm down, about six inches over the tools.

"Tell me something."

Love.

That was first. The absolute love that only comes from joy, and the joy that builds out of love.

If I hadn't already known that Zaki totally followed his bliss, his tools would have told me. In that instant, I think I probably forgave him almost every horrible un-dadlike thing he'd ever done to me. Not that he deserved forgiving, but because I understood that he couldn't help it. He loved me, but he was always going to be dragged in another direction, too.

I wondered if Claire knew that, too. She probably did.

Never love an artist.

I moved my hand slightly, so that it was over the chisels. The current-hum intensified.

Exasperation.

Huh. That was different. I cast my memory back over the site, what little I had seen of it. The banister had looked like it was almost done—they had installed it and were doing some kind of treatment on it; it had smelled like varnish or something. The mantel over the fireplace had looked done, too. Was it prefab? Probably not, in that house. But that didn't seem right.

Think, Bonnie. What else? There had been wooden doors leading into the room with the fireplace, hadn't there? Sliding doors, with some kind of pattern carved into them. I let my finger dip down just enough to touch the plastic case, and thought about the quick glimpse of the doors I had gotten.

Zaki's current-signature reacted to my memory, an irritable growl rising from the tools.

It wasn't anything that would stand up to even a sympathetic Talent's questioning, but I was convinced. Zaki had been working on those doors when he disappeared, and there had been something about them that had bothered him.

"Where are you, Dad?"

I dipped my finger again, and touched the chisel with the rust stain on it.

Wings. Teeth. Thick leathery skin, and heat and brimstone. Red, red eye in the darkness, and a snarl that would and did scare the piss out of a cougar, and make a bear back up and apologize.

I clenched my finger and pulled my hand out of the locker, sweating slightly.

Dragon blood. There was dragon blood on my dad's work chisel.

I pulled on the clean gloves and bundled everything in the foam padding, and shoved it into my backpack. It made it heavier than hell, but I didn't want to leave anything behind.

Look at the door.

That voice again, tapping at my brain. I grabbed at it, trying to get a taste of who was trying to instruct me, but it danced away and disappeared.

Good advice, though.

The site was busy, but everyone had seen me with the foreman, so they assumed I had the right to be there, so long as I didn't bother anyone. Maybe he'd told them I was Zaki's daughter, but if so, they declined to stop work long enough to say hi or ask after my old man. That worked for me.

The door was absolutely Zaki's work, and equally as obviously unfinished. The pattern at first looked like some kind of leaves falling, but when you looked at it carefully, you saw there was a face in the leaves. At first I thought Zaki had gone all Celtic and done the Green Man, but no, it was a woman's face, delicate and fey.

I checked: no pointed ears, no antennae, and no wings. Not any of the fatae species that I knew, anyway. Zaki was just feckless enough to have used one of the nonhuman species as a model, thinking that nobody would ever notice.

Was the owner of the house a Talent? The *Cosa Nostradamus* wasn't all poor, far from it, and they would know about Zaki's skills . . .

But no. From what I'd seen of the wiring going into the

walls, this place was going to be high-tech. Not a *cosa* household, then.

Zaki! I didn't expect a different response than I'd gotten before, but I was frustrated enough to try it. *Zaki, you stupid son of a bitch, where are you?*

No answer.

"You sure about this?"

"Hell, no."

I was sitting in the passenger seat of a tough little SUV, staring at a thirty-foot-high wall of stone. Becky, my room-mate, could probably have told me exactly what the stone was, and how old it was, and what kind of critters roamed the earth when it got folded and shoved up from the crust, but all I was thinking about was what waited above it.

"Here." Steve was in his forties, maybe. A good guy, if a little skeevy and one of the people whom J. knew. He had met me at the Albany airport and loaded me into the SUV, checked my gear, and given me the bag he was shoving into my arms.

"You know what to do?"

"Yeah." No.

"Just be polite. But not unctuous. Act like you would with a grandmother you really liked."

That was helpful. Not.

"Right. Let me get this done."

I got out of the car, the bag slung over my shoulder. I was wearing jeans and work boots, a heavy sweatshirt and a hoodie over that. It might be spring, but it was damned cold up here in the Adirondacks, colder even than it had been in Boston. Trust Zaki to find a cave dragon in the boonies.

I stepped and squelched. Cold, and muddy. "Nice," I said in disgust, and Steve, still behind the steering wheel, laughed. "A little wet dirt won't hurt you," he said.

No. Mud wouldn't hurt. Not like screwing this up might.

"Stay here. I'll be back soon."

There was a path, if you could call anything that narrow a path. In drier weather the stones would have been a footing hazard, but the mud kept them in place, and all I had to worry about was not stepping off the trail and falling off the side of the cliff.

"Zaki actually dragged himself up here?" My father was a lazy SOB, and his love of woods was restricted to dead and polished ones, not things with bark and leaves. I made sure my footing was secure and tested the current in the air.

"Oh yeah." The swirls and swoops in the air ahead matched the signature I'd gotten off the blood on the chisel. The dragon that had bled lived there.

Probably, from that letter, the same dragon who had given him the loan he needed to get out of the trouble that he was in, whatever that was.

Which meant that, not knowing who he had been in trouble with, the dragon was probably the last to see Zaki before he disappeared. And, therefore, was the most likely suspect for causing that disappearance. Especially considering the blood.

"The things I do for you, Zaki, you don't know . . ."

Some part of me still hoped that he was alive. That I'd track down the pieces and rush in just in time to save him. But dragon's blood didn't suggest anything good.

"Were you moron enough to attack a dragon?"

I'd know, soon enough.

The cave was nice, as caves went. Maybe ten feet wide, and six feet high, dry and well cleared. The inside was smooth, like someone had sanded it for a long time . . . or hit it consistently with really hot breath.

"You're psyching yourself out. Stop it. Cave dragons don't eat people."

Usually.

"Think of something else. Like, who's been pinging you with suggestions, and where are they now when you could use the helpfulness?"

There. That was a nicely unanswerable question to annoy myself with while I walked.

I adjusted the bag over my shoulder, turned on the flashlight, and walked into the cave.

Ten paces in, and it made a sharp left turn. Wind baffle. Smart. The ground underneath had been smoothed the same way the walls were, and was slightly rounded, like something had dragged itself back and forth across it for a very long time.

The beam from the flashlight reflected off the walls, catching bits of stuff in the stone.

"Pretty."

"I'm so glad you approve."

I am not ashamed to admit that I yelp like a girl. There's a biologic reason for that.

Fucking dragon was behind me!

"What did you do, hold your breath?" There hadn't been

any warning, not even the faintest whiff of heat or brimstone.

The voice was deep, sweet, and not at all what I had expected.

"Yep."

It was also almost sinfully proud of itself. I was in love.

I turned, trying hard not to move in any way that might be considered even remotely aggressive. Or disrespectful. Or sniveling.

Cave dragons weren't big. But "not big" when you're talking about dragons? Trust me, that's not like saying "not big" when talking about cars.

The body blocked out the entire cave behind us, his belly low to the ground like a cat skulking through the grass. The wings were furled close to the body. Thick legs tapered into clawed paws the size of hubcaps. But the body was totally secondary to the head, which loomed barely a foot away from my face.

It looked like the head of a snake, with wide nostrils at the pointed end rising to two wide red eyes that stared without blinking. If you could imagine an arrowhead two feet across and three feet long. And the neck . . . only a few feet, and not sinewy like I'd expected, but thick and muscular, like a python's body. Wasn't that a lovely thought, being crushed to death by a dragon's neck. It might, I suppose, be better than being eaten. Or torn apart by those claws. Or burning to death in its breath . . .

"And I really need to stop thinking about those things," I said out loud, somewhat desperately.

"What do you want, *cosa*-cousin?"

"An exchange."

Dragons, even cave dragons, didn't have eyebrows. But if

they did, this one would have raised them. "Please." The head moved slightly, as though to invite me to continue. "Let us take this into my office."

I swear to God, I don't know why that invitation made me feel better. But it did.

I walked forward, the dragon directly behind me. Once I knew what to listen for, I could hear his breathing, like the sound of the ocean, or rain. Which was weird, a creature that breathed fire sounding like water, but there it was.

"What is your name?"

"Bonita." I hated my full name, but Steve's words came back to me, and I figured formality was better. "Bonita Berg Torres."

"And you came here to see me, Bonita Berg Torres. To make an exchange. For what you carry in that sack?"

"Don't all the best fairy tales begin that way?"

A snort of laughter, the sulfur smell hit the back of my neck, and every single atavistic impulse I had rose and screamed at me to Get. The. Hell. Out. Of. There.

The cave opened in front of us, and we were in his—I couldn't call it an office. His lair. Because there, in the middle of the space, was a pile of greenbacks. Literally. Old cash, crumpled and dirty, the dark green of old-style bills. The pile was at least four feet high, and about ten feet in diameter, and had a depression in the middle that looked exactly like the shape my head left in my pillow every morning.

"So. What is it you want from me?"

"Don't you want to see what I have to offer?"

"You're a smart human. You will have done your homework."

God, I hoped so. "A man came to see you. A human. A *cosa*-cousin."

"Many do." The dragon passed me, crawling into the pile and curling up, exactly like a cat. Its eyes stared at me. I had no desire whatsoever to pet it.

"This one . . ." What the hell did I say now? I didn't know what Zaki might have said, or asked, or anything. "You loaned him money. Or something of value. His name is Zaki Torres. My father. You took his marker, and told him he could have a decade to repay."

The dragon rose, the wings that had been furled until then spreading like the shadow of doom. I stumbled back, landing hard on my ass.

The stone might have been smoothed, but it sure as hell wasn't soft.

"He stole from me!"

"What?" That was not Zaki. Clueless and useless, yeah, but never a thief.

"He stole from me!" the dragon insisted, its full fifteen-foot length rising in the air over me but not—thank God—doing anything more threatening than looming.

I straightened my spine and stared up into red eyes.

"Back. Off." I waited, then repeated myself, really really proud that my voice sounded so uber-bitchy. "Back off, *cousin*. Or theft will be the least of your worries." I strummed the threads of current, building it up into a crescendo, letting it fill my body. God, I hadn't thought to recharge before I came out, because I was an idiot, but there hadn't been much call for it at college, so it was relatively easy to pull current out of my own body without too much stress. I'd feel it the next day, though. Assuming I felt anything.

"This man?"

An image, of Zaki the last time I had seen him. His head back, teeth showing as he laughed, his shaggy brown hair a little too long on the back of his neck, his black eyes filled with mischief, his face totally without any remorse, conniving, or treachery.

"No." The dragon backed down, settled down. "Not that human. But that was the name he gave me." His eyes were red, and angry, but somehow less unnerving. "Why did this human lie to me, *cosa*-cousin?"

It was a shame that the fatae, as a rule, couldn't use current, or he could show me what the human who had used my father's name had looked like. I couldn't go in and take it out of his head, either. Someone else, maybe, but I didn't have the juice or the training. Especially not a dragon's head. He might talk, and react in a way so he could communicate, but he was a dragon. Humans who went into dragon brains didn't come out the same, if they came out at all.

"I don't know," I told him. "But I will find out." I remembered my manners then and extended the sack. "Here."

One huge paw took the bag and opened it with a surprisingly delicate claw. Bright, brand-new pennies fell out, a copper waterfall.

"Lovely. Truly lovely." He sounded enchanted. I was, too, for a moment—they were so bright and pretty, and the sound they made wasn't.

He scooped his paw through them, creating the waterfall effect again. "But I did not give you the information you came here for."

"You gave me information that contradicted what was established. That makes it better than what I came for. But the price remains the same."

Did cave dragons laugh? That one did. "You are a wise kit, cousin. And brave."

No, just desperate, I thought.

Steve took one look at me and didn't say a word all the way back to the airport. I don't remember much of the flight home. I could feel the thoughts running like salmon upstream in my head, but nothing went anywhere.

Except, if I was going to run with that metaphor, there was a bear waiting to chow down on my thoughts.

"I really need to stop thinking."

The woman sitting next to me looked pointedly out the window, shifting her body so that there was no risk of my actually touching her.

Hey, great, more space for me.

The flight was too short to allow them more than drinks service. I grabbed a Diet Coke and watched the ice melt.

The temptation to reach out with current was almost overwhelming, like the need to hug a teddy bear or stuff your face with chocolate. Tossing current in the middle of a plane held up entirely by electronics and faith, though? Next to the word "suicidal" in the damned dictionary.

What the hell happened, Zaki? What the hell happened?

The cab from Logan was where it hit me. He was dead. My father was dead. I knew that, somehow, now. No way to hope. Only to discover what happened. I needed to know what happened.

Traffic was mercifully light, and I had the right amount of cash on hand. I paid the cabbie off and slogged through the lobby, barely falling in through the apartment door when

J. was in my face. "Steve called. He said you were a disaster. What the hell happened?"

"I've got no idea," I said, too tired to take offense at his total lack of respect for my personal space. He was worried. "But I need to look at the tools again."

J. pulled back and was cool. He nodded, and I went into the guest room where I stayed when I was visiting, and pulled out the bag with Zaki's tools. I took them into the living room, where J. was seated in his chair, a huge leather monstrosity with a hassock that had seen better decades. His English sheepdog, Rupe, was sprawled by the chair. Rupe lifted his head when I came out, let his tongue loll in his own form of greeting, then went back to contemplating his paws.

Rupe had known me since I was eight, too. He wasn't much impressed, although I think he liked me okay.

There was a bottle of white wine open on the low glass table and two glasses poured. I ignored it for the moment and unrolled the tools out on the table.

"This." I put my hand over the chisel with the blood. "Dragon's blood."

J. nodded; he knew that already.

"But Zaki never went to see the dragon."

"His letter . . ."

"Yeah. I'm getting to that."

I wasn't going to get distracted. Anyway, having been nose to nose with that snout, picking up his echoes in the blood wasn't quite as overwhelming.

It was still pretty damn impressive, though.

"I've never seen a dragon in person," J. said thoughtfully.

"I'll introduce you sometime," I said. "In about a decade

or so. But this is too much. He's annoyed but not hurt. Not really."

"Annoyed?"

"Not like someone stabbed him with a chisel. More like . . ."

"A scratch?"

"Stealing enough blood to dip the point of a chisel in. Enough to leave a current residue that would trigger the memory of an angry dragon on it if anyone were to look."

"A Talent?"

"Or someone who knew about Talent. And knew enough to go to a dragon, and what would be a likely reason why Zaki would have gone to a dragon."

My head hurt.

Motive and means.

There was that voice again! Annoying, intrusive bastard. I didn't even bother chasing it down, because it was right. I knew the how—whoever had done whatever they had done to Zaki had set the scene to lead anyone investigating to assume that a dragon had killed him.

"But then how would the tools have gotten back to the locker?" The answer came to me even as I asked the question. "Who would have wondered? Seriously, who would even have gone this far, and once they saw the dragon . . ."

"Whoever did this was smart, but not clever," J. said.

"Yeah. And even if someone did, who would they go to? Not like we have a police force you can call, or anything." The *Cosa* tended to settle things one-on-one. You didn't need proof, but you'd damn well better be certain. And you had to be sure you were willing to bear the cost of making enemies who might be more powerful—or have friends who were more powerful—than you.

So. Means. Someone who had access to Zaki. To his tools, which meant the job site. And someone who had access to the dragon, and knew that Zaki would have debts, and knew that Zaki had a daughter who would get the letter and connect the dots.

But they hadn't counted on my being clever.

"Motive. Who has means, and motive?"

J. shook his head and reached for the wineglass. "To murder, and to murder a person you know, that is a strong crime. It requires a strong emotion. Who would Zaki inspire that sort of strong emotion in?"

Zaki had been a good guy. Not a great person, but a good guy. Seeing him as a man, not my father, was easy enough for me. And the answer to who he could piss off that much came pretty fast, but I wasn't sure. Not yet.

I needed to be sure.

Another long trip down to New York City on the Chinatown Express bus, me and twenty-four of my closest friends and all their worldly belongings. But it was cheap, and fast. The ferry over wasn't much fun. It was raining, and I stayed inside, huddled in my molded-plastic seat, ignoring the masses of commuters all trying to stay dry and just make it home.

The site was deserted. I snuck through the fence and into the house. Lucky for me none of the alarms had been turned on yet.

The door called to me. I could feel it, practically singing in the rain-filled dusk. My flashlight beam skittered cross the floor, allowing me to pick my way around piles of trash and debris. No tools left out. The carpenter's daughter approved.

"Hello, beauty," I said to the door. In the darkness, in the beam of light, she was nakedly apparent, a sweet-eyed woman who gazed out into the bare bones of the room with approval and fondness.

"Who are you, then? That's the key to all this. Who are you?"

The door, not too surprisingly, didn't answer. But I knew how to make it talk.

Or I thought I did, anyway.

It was all instinct, but J. had always told me that instinct was the way most new things were discovered—instinct and panic.

I held my hand over the door the way I had with the tools, carefully not touching it, and felt for the lightest levels of current, like alto bells.

The woman's hair stirred in a breeze, and her face seemed softer, rounder, then she disappeared behind the leaves again.

Zaki really had been an artist, the bastard. I could feel him in the work. But I didn't know, yet, what he had been feeling.

Evidence doesn't lie.

Shut up, I told the voice. I'm working.

I touched a deeper level of current, bringing it out with a firm hand and splaying it gently across the door so that it landed easily, smoothly.

Oh how I love her, such a bad woman, such a wrong woman, and I cannot have her, but I will show her my love . . .

Zaki, melancholy and impassioned, his hand steady on the chisel, his eyes on the wood, sensing even through his distraction how to chip here, cut there, to make the most of the grain. He was concentrating, thinking of his object of affection, the muse who inspired him. So focused, the way all

Talent learned to be, that he never saw the man coming up behind him, the man who had already seen the work in progress, and recognized, the way a man might, the face growing out of the wood.

The blow was sudden and sharp, and the vision faded.

No, I told my current. *More.*

It surged, searched, and found nothing. No emotions from the killer. No residue of his actions.

"Damn it." My flashlight's beam dropped off the door; I was unwilling to look at the face of the woman who had cost my father his life.

There is always evidence.

The voice was back. And probably right. I let the beam play on the floor, unsure what I was looking for. Scan, step, scan. I repeated the process all the way up to the door, then turned around and looked the way I had come.

"There."

On the floor, about two feet away. A spot where the hardwood floor shone differently. That meant that it had been refinished more recently than the rest of the floor, or been treated somehow. Zaki would have known. All I knew was that it was a clue.

I touched it with current, as lightly as I could. Something warned me that a gentle touch would reveal more than demanding ever would.

"The killer's actions, I beg you wood, reveal."

J.'s influence. Treat current the way you would a horse, control it through its natural instincts. Current, like electricity, illuminated.

A dent in the floor, sanded down and covered up. The point of a chisel stained with blood? No. The harder end, sticking out of a body as it landed, falling backward . . .

Oh, Zaki, you idiot was all I could find inside myself, following the arc of the body. *For a woman? For another man's woman when you had Claire at home?*

And then I saw it, the shadow figure of the killer, indistinct even in his own mind—shading himself. That meant the killer was a Talent, if of even less skill than Zaki. Had that been a factor? The man—the foreman, I knew now—jealous not only of the carpenter's attraction to his wife but of his skill to display it, driven to murder?

The chisel was removed, wiped down, and . . .

The blood alone flared bright in the pictorial, a shine of wet rubies in the shadows as the foreman dipped the chisel into a cloth still damp with the blood, laying the trace for me to find, a week later.

The picture faded, rubies and shadows into full, rainy dark. I might be able to regain it if I used more current, but with two men on the crew Talented, others might be as well. I dared not linger.

"So that's it, I guess." A long ferry ride, and I couldn't face the bus ride back to Boston that night. I was tired, and cold, and I had a class in the morning I hadn't done any of the reading for. I supposed the death of one's father was reason enough to skip a chapter, but it didn't feel right to me, somehow.

So I ended up at Claire's apartment, wrapped in a gold-and-brown afghan she had knitted, telling her—and J., who had the oomph to Translocate down for the night—what I knew.

"He knew Zaki, had hired him. So he knew about the gambling, figured we'd believe a story about debts, and assume he'd screw up the repayment enough to get him-self killed. Masqueraded as Zaki and went and offered his—Zaki's—marker to the dragon, stole the blood from a scratch, planted it . . ."

"And the letter?" Claire asked.

"When was the last time you saw Zaki's handwriting, J.?"

J. had to think about that for a while, which was answer enough.

"Yeah." I figured as much. "Me? I got to see a signature on a check every now and then. Genghis Khan could have forged that letter, and I'd have no way to know."

Zaki hadn't been a deadbeat dad, financially. Not even emotionally. He just hadn't been the dad I needed. To be fair, I hadn't exactly been the kid he was looking for, either, me and my Talent and my brains and my desire to actually get out there and *do* something.

"What now?"

J. asked a reasonable question. I had no idea. I could es-tablish cause, means, and motive, but who would listen? Who would care?

"A good daughter would take revenge," I said. Part of me liked that idea. I could prove I had loved him that way, right?

"Zaki would be horrified by the thought," J. said. He was right.

"Let it go, honey."

I looked at Claire. "How can you say that? You loved him, and he was dicking around on you."

Claire had a wistful smile on her face, like she'd said her good-byes already. "He came home to me. He always came home to me. His dick wandered, but his heart never did. Zaki was a gentle man, baby. Hopeless, but gentle. The last thing he would ever want would be for you to have blood on your hands. Even for him. Especially for him."

She had known my father. She had known him right.

J. forced the issue and Translocated me back to college. It's a decent way to travel, if you've got the skills. Sure as hell beat the Chinatown bus. So I got to curl up in my own bed that night, listening to my roommate's barely there snore, and the ticking of the alarm clock that was usually a surefire soporific. I should have been fast asleep, or so wracked with loss that I couldn't close my eyes. Instead, all I felt was too tired to sleep.

It's normal, the voice said. *After a case.*

"What case?" Across the room, Nancy stirred, but didn't wake.

An investigation. You did well.

"Who the hell are you?" A reasonable question, I thought. Talent, obviously. Strong—very damn strong, to ping me like this. I should have been nervous, if not outright scared. I wasn't.

Nobody you need to know yet. Take your classes. Finish your degree. Stay out of trouble. We'll talk soon.

And then he was gone.

I stared at the ceiling, mulling over the words. Male. Older. The voice of someone who knew how to mentor.

I already had a mentor.

But from the sound of it, maybe, I had—would have—a boss, too.

Investigation. A lifetime of finding answers, figuring out the why of things. Bringing people to justice. Yeah.

I fell asleep with a smile on my face.

The House

by Laurie R. King

"All I'm saying is that names are important. You know, if you're Bruce or Marvin or something, you're really stuck with that, like, forever."

We were outside the Weirdman House, looking at it. Which felt stupid but, you know, going inside, that wasn't something you did without thinking.

Not that there wasn't a lot to look at anyway. The house was big, and had turrets and towers jutting out from all the corners and that wooden lacy stuff they call gingerbread (I don't know why) from all the roofs and around all the windows.

It was probably the oldest building for miles, maybe in the whole county. It had been standing there in its field, falling to pieces, for longer than anyone could remember. My granddad said that it had been haunted when he was a kid, and that was like a hundred years ago, because he died when I was little, and he was really old then.

It wasn't haunted, exactly, just . . . weird. Which is why we were talking about names.

It was really named the Weildman House, anyway that's
what the paper called it when they had articles about the
people trying to raise money to restore it, and that's the name
on the old photographs in the local museum, where our class
was going next month. Back in September, Bee had dragged
me through the museum, which was one of her favorite
places, so I knew about the photos. Except that maybe there
was a typo somewhere, or maybe it was only logical, that one
letter changed it and gave it a different name.

Bee shook her head, disagreeing with me like usual. "That
place would be weird even if it had been called the Smith
Place, or Casa Thingummy. Weirdman comes from the place;
the place's vibes don't come from it."

Bee is in love with the past, the clothes and the people
and especially words like "vibes" and "far out" that you never
hear except from people like my mother, who's never recovered from the sixties. Bee uses lots of words no one else
knows, except maybe me, only I never use them in the open,
and she does. And even I wouldn't choose to sneak out of the
county fair to go to a historical museum—I mean, you've got
to be a little nuts to prefer a dusty collection of old stuff to
the pig races and the Tilt-A-Whirl.

Can you guess we're the geek squad at Henrietta Shore?
Can you guess who is still hanging around the computer lab
when the last bus pulls out of the driveway?

Yeah: Bee, and me—I'm Brad—and AJ always, and the
Kim twins sometimes if they don't have music lessons or
something. And some others, but mostly us. I'm the new
guy—we moved here over the summer, me and Mom, back to
the town she'd grown up in and moved away from when she
went to college. And because we lived miles from anyplace
where kids went, I had to start a new school without knowing

anyone, which just sucks, really. But the first day when I sort of sidled into the cafeteria trying to be invisible, Bee saw me and marched up to me and asked me about the book she'd seen in my backpack during third-period English.

Which led to Bee and AJ and me, on a cold-but-sunny February day, sitting just inside the bushes that make a square wall around Weirdman House (what was, once upon a time when actual people lived in the place, a garden—sometimes one of the wild bushes bursts into flower, and you realize that it's a rose or a daffodil or something). AJ had brought food, I'd brought drinks, and Bee had brought herself.

"So why Weirdman?" AJ asked. He had a mouthful of some disgusting candy called Snapquick. He always brought gross food but never seemed to gain an ounce.

"You don't know the story?" Bee asked. Half our conversations had Bee using that phrase at some point, at the beginning or the end, because she also liked old stories. Sometimes I thought she liked the past because it gave her a kind of escape, but I would never tell her that.

"Which story?" I said.

"Is there more than one?"

"I know three," I said, which was an exaggeration, but not much. "You tell the one you know."

"Well, the place has been deserted, like forever," she began. "The last Weildman just up and disappeared in the fifties or something. The mail wasn't picked up, the dog began to howl, finally somebody called the cops and asked them to check up on the old lady. And they never found her."

"Yeah they did," I told her. "She had Alzheimer's and wandered off, and they found her down in Monterey and put her in a home."

"Really?"

"That's what my mom says."

"Yeah, but your mom probably wants to reassure little Braddy so he doesn't have bad dreams."

I would have punched Bee then if she'd been a boy, but she wasn't, and besides, she hit harder than most boys. And she was probably right, anyway. My mom was always trying to keep what she called my imagination under control. Maybe all single mothers did that—when you were working two jobs at once, it was easiest if your kid was no trouble. So I tried.

Anyway, there we were, and there was Weirdman House looking at us looking at it. Our excuse was that we were researching the house for our class's local history project.

"You want to go in?" AJ asked.

"Nah, not right now," I said. "It's nicer out here."

"How do you know?"

"I been in there," I told him. "Lots of times."

"Twice," Bee said. Really, I was going to hit her. Except I wouldn't, because her father did, and there was no way I was going to be like him in her life, no way at all.

"So let's make it three times," I said loudly, and I stood up and walked toward the house.

Weirdman House really was just plain weird. Like I said, it sat by itself out in the middle of nowhere, in the middle of fields no one farmed even though it was farming land, surrounded by roads that didn't seem to have any view of it. Mom and I were about the closest neighbors, half a mile away, and the fact that, although I'd been in the garden a lot, I'd only been inside the house itself twice tells you something about its . . . well, its vibes.

I'm not a nervous kind of a person. I read a lot, sure, but my imagination pretty much shuts off when it's on its own, unlike AJ, who lives in a dream most of the time. And so in the summer, one day when Mom was off shopping or something, I wandered down the road and sort of pushed my way in through what had once been the front gate.

A place like that, you'd think a thousand teenagers a week would find their way inside, older kids with bottles and girlfriends, younger kids with cigarettes, all sorts with things to hide. But even though the doors didn't look very sturdy and I could see one of the windows open from where I stood, it didn't look to me like anyone had broken in.

But I did. Well, not break in, and not that day. I liked reading in the garden, and there was a tree with a nice comfortable low branch for reading, but one day I finished my book and just wandered around the place for a while until a way in kind of appeared.

That sounds nuts, I know. And I suppose what happened was that I hung out long enough to get used to the looks of the place and noticed that the siding in one place was cut into a rectangle, maybe two feet high and one and a half wide. When I looked closer, I saw that it was a small door just set into the side of one wall. It was probably just the pattern of shade from the roofline that had stopped me from seeing it before, but what it felt like at the time, and ever since then, was that the house decided to show me a way in.

Not to get all Stephen King on you, but it should have been crazy creepy, that feeling. I mean, in a novel, a house that invites you in will turn out to be a house with teeth. But again, it just didn't FEEL like that. What it felt like was a big, lonely place that decided I wasn't about to set it on fire, so it tugged back a kind of mental curtain and showed me how to get inside.

Even then, the house seemed to tease me, getting a little loose when I pulled with my fingernails, then sticking. I took out the pocketknife Mom had given me for Christmas—the one I can't take to school but carry all the other times—and put the short blade into the crack. The door hesitated, and I thought there'd be an inside bolt, but then it sighed and gave way.

That first time, I didn't go in very far. The door opened into this strange metal-lined boxy space that took me a while to figure out was a storage place for firewood, next to a fireplace big enough to roast an ox in, or a pig anyway. The room with the fireplace had been the living room, I guess, and wasn't in all that bad of shape. The windows were covered with spiderwebs, of course, and there was so much dust on the floor that my feet left tracks, but the wallpaper was still mostly up, only a few corners peeling away, and the fancy chandelier overhead looked all in one piece. Which, considering it was in earthquake country, was just about amazing.

That first day I walked through the living room and found a sort of library next door, although the shelves only had a few books on them and they were so thick with dust even I didn't want to pick them up. There was another room farther on that had the remnants of curtains on the windows, although you couldn't tell what color they had been, and I thought that if I so much as touched them, they would fall to pieces.

I followed my tracks back and found the kitchen, which looked like something from the museum in town, and was about to go into the next room when I heard something from outside.

I went over to the window, and heard it again: my mother's voice, a long way off, calling my name.

I scrambled back to the living room, and found the wood box, but for some reason when I pushed at the door, it stuck, hard. I guess I was sort of panicky, because I knew Mom would have a cow if she found out I'd been in there, and I hadn't expected her to be home for a couple of hours yet, so that's why my hands were sort of fumbly and I was probably pushing on the frame of the door instead of the door itself. It didn't move a hair, and I had this really awful feeling that the house wasn't going to let me go, but as soon as I thought that, my hands shifted to the middle of the door and it moved, and the door opened.

I tumbled out into the daylight and ran across the wild garden to the place I'd gotten in. When I turned to look back, I saw that I'd remembered to shut the door, which was hidden again, its seams in the shadow of some of the elaborate trim.

Mom was on the road, halfway between our house and the Weirdman place, her back to me. I ran hard, circling around this sort of warehouse that stands near the main road, so when she finally saw me, she'd think I was coming from there and not the house.

She gave me hell for poking around the warehouse, made me promise never to go there again, and took a while to settle down.

Because the really strange thing? She'd been gone for two hours, and she'd been looking for me more than an hour after that, and in that whole time, all I'd done was find a door and walk through four rooms.

The second time I went inside the house was about six months later. The first time it had been summer vacation, when we'd first moved there, then school started, and at first it was awful like usual, and then I made friends with Bee.

Then AJ found us, and the Kim twins, and it was okay. But the house was just sort of . . . there, in the back of my head, and so during the Christmas vacation when AJ was off seeing his family in Mexico and Bee was off someplace in Europe (her father's the manager of a bank, which may explain why he gets away with what he gets away with) and Mom was working all the hours she could at her temp job at the mall, I found myself standing at the gate again, looking for the wood-box door.

No one had been inside since I'd been there in July. My footprints wandered up and down, and no others. But the house was dim, since it was winter, and the sky was cloudy, so I couldn't tell if there were older footprints, just mine.

I stood in the living room, looking at that humongous fireplace and trying to imagine what it would look like with a fire in it. The thing was about six feet across, plenty of room for me to lie down and stretch my arms out without touching the bricks. You could put whole trees in it. And the heat from it—that would make it impossible to sit nearby, wouldn't it?

I tried to picture the family, maybe three ladies with needlework and a bearded man, and oil lamps maybe on the walls. What would you do, without TV or video games? Books, sure, but how many hours a day could you read?

I couldn't picture it, not very well, so I turned to walk out of the room, when out of the corner of my eyes a flame suddenly flashed up in the cold fireplace, and I heard a sort of creaking noise that reminded me of my grandmother's rocking chair.

But when I whipped around to see, there was nothing, and no sound.

The same thing happened in the kitchen, when I had finished looking in the empty cabinets and started to walk out the door: a sudden feeling of warmth at my back, a gust of frying onion and some spice in the air, and the briefest snatch of conversation in the world tickling my ears.

Then it was gone, and the stove was empty and rusting, the air still and stale.

The third time the ghostly voices came, I ran, and I didn't go back.

Until today, three months later, with AJ and Bee, in the sunshine.

Maybe the house wouldn't show us the door, I thought.

But it did. The outline was right there, tucked under the edge of the peeling paint of the trim. You could even see the dent in the ground underneath it, where I'd hit when I came crashing out last December. I could feel my heart beginning to speed up, just remembering.

"This is your door?" Bee asked. I jumped when she spoke, because I'd been so wrapped up in myself.

"Yeah. We don't have to go in."

"I think we do," she said. "I want to see what's in there, and we need it for the project. And besides, if we don't, this is going to bug you forever."

"I think it's going to bug me forever even if we do," I told her, trying to joke, but she just gave me that look and stuck her fingernails under the edge.

I opened my mouth to warn her that she'd need my pocketknife, but for her, the door gave way without a trace of hesitation. She pulled it open, and we looked in: a box, lined with metal, nothing more. She pulled herself up, I boosted AJ, and followed.

We found nothing that day, although we got all the way through the house, a lot more than I'd managed on my own. Most of the rooms were empty, though there were bed frames in a couple of the upstairs rooms and one mattress that was a condo for mice. I began to calm down, and decided that whatever I'd seen that time, it had been my imagination. Nothing else.

I was standing in the middle of the living room again, the empty and silent living room, when AJ said, "It's getting dark, and I'm hungry."

"You're always hungry," I said, but when I looked at the window, it was true, the entire day had gone. It felt like a couple of hours, but when we dropped from the doorway, the sun was low and the air cold.

"You didn't see anything this time, did you?" Bee asked me, as we clawed our way out through the bushes.

"Nope."

"Maybe there was too much activity, with three of us."

"Maybe there was nothing there the first time."

"I don't know," she said. "There's a reason this place is called what it is. And it does feel strange."

This is why I like Bee: she makes me feel like there are two of us in the world. "You felt it, too?"

"Sure. And like you said, time in there seems to move really fast. I'd have sworn it wasn't even lunchtime."

"But that doesn't make sense."

"Expectations don't make sense. And think about it: When people die, where does their energy go? When a house is built to hold a family, and the family lives there for years, then one by one they disappear, what does the house think?"

"There's a video game," AJ piped up. I'd more or less forgotten he was there, which is about usual for AJ. "It's got this device like a projector that sends characters from the game out into the real world."

"That was a movie," Bee said.

"Yeah, but it was a game, too. You could call up people out of history and use them in real time, or anyway the game's real time. Like if you were having a war and you needed Alexander the Great or something, you could troll through history and snag him. Maybe that's what Brad did, snagged the Weirdmans and put them in the house for a second."

"Weildmans," she said.

"Whatever. But I mean, people don't just go away when they die, do they? It doesn't make sense. It's like when you accidentally dump something on your computer, it's there, if you know how to find it. Same with live people, don't you think?"

"Stands to reason," Bee said. We were both looking at AJ—it was funny, but he sometimes came up with the most amazing ideas, out of the blue.

"Man," I said, "it's really late. You guys agree, that we do our group project on the Weirdman House?"

"Weildman," Bee said.

"Sure," said AJ. "It's better than those natural-history choices."

"What insane teacher assigns middle school kids a paper on toxic plants?" Bee muttered.

"I think the idea is so we avoid them, not so we use them," I said.

"Still, this'll be loads better."

So we were agreed: the three of us would do a group project on the history of the Weird—I mean, the Weildman

House, and present it to the class the week before our trip to the historical museum. The next Saturday we found ourselves back in the jungly garden.

That time, we saw the Weird Man.

We met at my house early, at eight. Bee and AJ and me—the Kim twins were supposed to come, but Bonnie called at seven and said their parents had some kind of party they were going to up in San Jose and they had to go, too. Mom had work that day and left even before that, so when the others came, we got together a bunch of food and drink and put it in a backpack. And the big flashlight Mom keeps on top of the fridge for when the lights go out, just in case we wanted to look into a closet or a basement or something.

The sun was out, and the day was going to be warm, for March. The weeds in the garden were shooting up at a tremendous rate and the first blossoms of the enormous climbing rosebush were out, the size of a teacup and pale pink, with a sweet smell that was almost too sweet. Coming through the garden, Bee paused to take a picture of them with her digital camera and pulled off a couple of petals, dropping them carefully into an envelope she took from her pocket. We couldn't use the pictures for our school report, of course, not without admitting that we'd been trespassing, but what Mrs. Dender didn't know wouldn't hurt her.

She'd brought one of those plastic milk crates with her, too, and set it on the ground under the little wood-box door. She stepped up on it and pulled the door open. AJ and I followed her inside.

The dusty footprints went all over, from our number of trips there. Bee took shots of everything: the peeling wallpaper, the dust-choked chandelier, the kitchen, the dusty books on the shelves.

Near the kitchen door we had found a narrow door leading into the basement, where the cool air smelled of mildew, next to an equally narrow door leading upward. "Which way do you want to go first?" I said. My voice echoed against the bare walls.

"Let's go to the top first and—did you see that?" Bee's voice went tight, and AJ and I whirled around to see what she was looking at. But there was nothing there, not even a doorway, just the corner of the dining room: a wall, a length of surviving curtain, and a window too dirty to see out of.

"Something outside?" I asked.

"No, it was like . . . I don't know what it was, just some reflection I guess."

"If you're going to start on the ghost stories," AJ said, "I'm going home." His voice sounded a little tight, too.

"Probably a bird," I said. "Come on, let's see if the stairs hold us."

We took the stairs up, narrow and steep and so thick with dust, you couldn't see the color of the wood. There was a small landing, then a doorway at the next turn: we opened it and looked out, into the second-floor hallway. I commented that the stairs had no carpeting, unlike the wide, dignified staircase near the front door.

"Servants' stairs," Bee said, and took a photograph.

"You'd think they would put carpet on them, so they didn't have to listen to the servants going up and down."

"They probably made them go barefoot," AJ commented. He was standing practically on my heels and kept taking things from some crackly packet in his pocket and putting them in his mouth.

"Do you have to chew right in my ear?" I snapped at him. Bee gave me a look and continued up the stairs.

The rooms at the top of the house—Bee said they were the servants' quarters—were stifling hot, and so dusty they could have been the set of some horror movie. Bee went to the tiny window between a pair of narrow, rusty bedsteads and worked to slide the latch, then pushed at the wooden frame. I didn't think she'd have any better luck than I'd had with the windows I'd tried in the rest of the house, but maybe they hadn't bothered painting the window frames in the little room at the top of the house, because it creaked and went up.

Immediately, the air began to move, rising from the house below to push out of the window. The temperature dropped five degrees in a few seconds.

"Well, if there had to be one window in the place that would open, I'm glad it was that one," I told Bee. She was still at the window, both hands on the window frame, her chin tucked in, looking down, and I realized that she hadn't moved a hair since the window had slid up. "Bee?"

"Who's that?"

"Who's who?" I asked, and moved quickly to join her.

There was a man in the garden some thirty feet below, looking up. He was dressed in a plaid shirt and baggy pants held up by suspenders, with dirty boots and a battered hat. Automatically, Bee raised her camera and took a shot of him.

"Damn!" He had to be one of the people working on the renovation project, sniffing around to make sure the place hadn't fallen down. "Busted."

"I don't think so," Bee said, her voice kind of distracted sounding. "Look at him."

So I looked at him, but I was looking through two layers of dirty glass and he wasn't exactly clear, so I squatted a little to be more on Bee's level, and looked through the open space below.

Somehow, I didn't seem to be seeing him much better. He was still . . . fuzzy, like, around the edges. I rubbed my eyes, wondering if the dust had gotten in them, and when I took my hands away from my face I saw the man taking his hat off, as if he were trying to see us better, too. I stepped back, pulling at Bee's shoulder, but she shook me off and just kept staring down.

There was nothing to do but go back to the window and look. Without his hat, in spite of the problem with my eyes, he was younger than I'd thought, maybe only twenty or so. But his clothes were old, and somehow old-fashioned, as if they'd been made by hand. His hair was blond and touched his shoulders, standing as he was with his head tilted back, and his eyes were a bright blue. He stared up, Bee and I stared down, and we might have stood there frozen until darkness came and obscured everything except that AJ joined us, on Bee's other side. He took one look at the garden, gave a sort of squeak of fright, stumbled backward, and fell straight into the metal bedstead, which shouted out a chorus of metallic groans and squawks under his weight. Bee and I turned to pull him to his feet.

When we looked back in the garden, the young man was gone. And although we tiptoed downstairs with our hearts in our throats, he didn't appear, nor did we see marks of any big boots on the dust of the floors.

Outside, Bee went directly around the house to where we'd seen the man, but there was no sign of him and no sign that either of the house's doors had been opened.

Thoughtfully, Bee retrieved the milk crate and stashed it under a bush, so if anyone came into the garden, they wouldn't see it against the hidden door, and we walked in silence down to my house.

It was, as always on one of those trips, later than we would have expected, and Mom wasn't pleased at the unplanned addition of two mouths for dinner. But they couldn't leave, not without us talking things over, and so they phoned home and Mom put a frozen pizza in the oven, and after we'd made ourselves eat we went into my room and shut the door.

"Okay," I started. "What did we see?"

"A guy in the garden, and we were damned lucky he didn't see us," AJ said.

"He did see us. Bee and me, anyway."

"Then why didn't he come and kick us out?"

"He couldn't," Bee said.

"What, you mean he was trespassing as well? Jeez, that was sure lucky."

I didn't think that was what Bee meant, but she didn't seem willing to go any further, and frankly, I didn't want to talk about it. I didn't want to go there, ever again.

"I hope you got enough for the report," I said, "because I don't want to go back inside. Ever."

"No?" Bee asked, surprised.

"Really no," I said.

"Is Braddy scared?"

"Don't be stupid, Bee. What if that guy'd been a psycho? What if he'd had a gun? Where would we be now, huh?" Jeez, I thought: Girls are supposed to be even more careful than boys, these days. And she was fourteen, a little older than AJ and me—she should know that.

I could see her thinking about what I meant, and to my relief, she sort of deflated a little. "Yeah, I guess you could be right."

"I am right. We've got plenty to do our report on. Let's leave it at that."

"Still, I wish I knew who that man was."

"Why?"

"Didn't you see the way he was dressed? He must have been some kind of reenactor, dressed in period costume."

When she said that, I realized she was right—if the guy had been just checking the pipes or working in the garden, he'd have been wearing normal work clothes like jeans, not baggy cotton pants held up by suspenders.

"He was probably just a hippie," I said, sounding more sure than I felt. "Runs one of those organic farms and plows with horses."

"Even that would be interesting," she said, and I could see that it gave her an idea. Which was good, because she might forget about the house if she was out talking to horse-plowing organic farmers.

AJ's mom came then, to take him and Bee home.

"E-mail me those pictures," I told Bee, as she was leaving.

"Sure. See you Monday."

But she didn't e-mail me the pictures. And she wasn't at school Monday morning.

Before first period, I borrowed AJ's cell phone and texted Bee. When I saw him after second period, he hadn't had an answer. At lunchtime, I used his phone again and called Bee's cell and home phones, but there was only the recording. At the end of lunch, I couldn't stand it, and went to the office.

"Beatrice Cuomo? No, I think she's absent today."

"Did anyone call in for her?"

"I don't think so. Why?"

"It's just, we were supposed to get together and talk about an assignment, an important one, and she's never flaked on me before. It's not like her."

There wasn't much the secretary could do except put Bee's name on the home-call list, which she'd already done. Her father wouldn't get the message until he got home that night.

I nearly took Bee's bus that afternoon, but then I thought about my answering machine at home, and my e-mail, and how stupid I would feel if I got myself stuck clear across town and there was a message from her waiting for me.

But there was no message. And she didn't answer her phone, or her e-mail, or anything.

I must have been nearly in tears when my mother drove up, because she looked shocked at my face. But she didn't argue, just got back in the car, tired as she was, and drove me to Bee's house.

I didn't tell her about the Weirdman House, just that I was worried about Bee.

Bee wasn't home. Her father drove up twenty minutes later, and let us in. We watched as he listened to his phone messages, from the school and from his sister, who was flying in from Miami later in the week, and that was all. There were no messages in Bee's room, no indications of where she'd gone, no nothing.

Nothing, but her digital camera.

When we got home, I told my mother about the Weildman House.

And while she was making phone calls, trying to find the detective in charge of Bee's case, I went to my room and downloaded Bee's camera into my computer.

She'd put in a new memory stick for the trip to the house, so it started with AJ and me in the garden. Photos of the dusty living room, the dusty library, the dusty kitchen—I kicked through them fast, looking for the one she'd taken from the top room.

It was there, the bar of the window cutting at an angle across the top, and the garden was clear, but there was no young blond man looking up.

I went forward, and back, thinking she'd taken some that I hadn't noticed her taking, but that was the only one of the garden from above, and there was no one there.

No one.

And when I called AJ to tell him about it, he started to cry and said he didn't remember, that he'd tripped and fallen and hadn't seen any man in the garden.

Over the next days, a full investigation rose around us. I was questioned, and AJ, and Bee's father. Bee had left her house Sunday morning, telling her father she was working on a school project, and had walked off into the blue. Two people had seen her, on a line drawn between her house and mine— or, between her house and the Weildman House.

A week later, someone at the police department figured out Bee's password and opened her computer. They found the Weildman House photos, which was a relief because I'd begun to feel that I really would have to admit to taking the camera. They also found a diary, where she wrote, among other things, about her father. They picked him up, but didn't arrest him—without evidence, who was to say a young girl's stories about her father taking a belt to her weren't fiction? But people talked, and in the middle of the night a few days later, a brick went through the front window of his house.

But he wasn't arrested. And the police went over every inch of the Weildman House and found no evidence that she had gone back on her own. They found no evidence that a young blond man in old-fashioned clothes had been there. And two weeks later, some kids broke in, on a dare, and started a fire in the big fireplace to keep warm.

The glow of the flames woke me before the first sirens started up.

Bee vanished, as if she had never been. The school talked about holding some kind of memorial, and grief counselors prowled the halls with stuffed bears for a few days, but when no body was found, no one quite knew what to do. Kids did run away, after all, although not usually so spectacularly, involving a rich abusive father and a haunted house.

In the end, the question of Bee Cuomo was more set aside than faced openly. Mrs. Dender decided that the local history project might as well go ahead with the trip to the museum, although she rescheduled it, thinking maybe it wasn't in good taste to go and have a fun outing when this . . . thing was still raw. AJ and I dropped any mention of the Weildman House—he wrote an essay on the technology of the horse-drawn wagon, I did one on poisonous plants of the Central Coast, thinking all the while of how to get one into Mr. Cuomo's dinner.

I nearly didn't go to the museum. I sure didn't want to, because all I could think of was going there with Bee, but by that time, she'd been gone nearly a month, and I had half convinced myself that she'd run away and joined a commune or something. And my grades had slipped and Mom was worried, because it would mean I didn't get into

the advanced classes in high school in September, and Mrs.
Dender said we'd get extra points for doing the trip, so . . .
I went.

And to my relief, it was okay. Bee had taken me there
back in September, when we'd known each other only a few
days, and the building had changed a little since then. The
kitchen had a bunch of new gadgets, another upstairs room
had been opened, and there were more people in the place
than there had been when the fair was going on a quarter
mile away.

It was one of those historical museums made to look like
the people had just stepped out for a minute—pans on the
stove, a half-written letter with an ink pen in its holder, some
pretty lame toys in the kids' room, a bunch of really
lumpy-looking beds. The museum docent was dressed in an
old-time dress and starched white apron, with a bonnet on
her head that looked pretty uncomfortable, and she talked
about life in the early twentieth century and how much work
it was.

I stayed at the back, sick with thinking how Bee would
have eaten all this up. I missed her, all the time, and the hole
in my mind that came with wondering what had happened
to her only seemed to grow bigger as time passed.

Then the docent said something about the Weildman
House, which acted like a slap across my ears.

"This house you're in was once standing across the field
from the Weildman House, and was donated to the historical
society to move here. You can see it in the pictures on the
wall of the study, along with the family members."

To my horror, I felt my eyes prickle and turned my back
on the others to study an arrangement of strange kitchen
tools. When they moved on, I lagged after them and felt

Mrs. Dender's hand brush my shoulder in sympathy. The class went outside to visit the pigs, but I went back into the rooms we'd already come through, to look at the photographs.

Sure enough, this place appeared in the background of a photograph of the Weildman House, taken when the gingerbread was sparkling and all the shingles were straight. The garden looked like the bones of what I had seen, what now lay crisp and blackened by the fire, and a blur of a walking figure could be seen at one side.

I made my way down the line of sharp, black-and-white pictures, of the Weildman House, the town in the distance, the hills rising in the background, just like they still did. Then came a half dozen photos of local landmarks, the old hotel, the train depot that no longer had trains stopping there, a big building I'd never seen before that the description said was the library.

Then came a photograph that kicked me in the gut.

It had been taken inside the Weildman House, in the room with the big fireplace and the chandelier. Only now the chandelier was sparkling, the wallpaper fresh, the furniture crowding the room. And there were people.

Three men and two women, posed to stare at the lens without moving, so the photo wouldn't blur. To the left sat an older woman with a man standing behind her, his hand on her shoulder. To the right was a small sofa, the kind they call a love seat, with two prim women in high-necked dresses. The one on the right had been moving her head when the shutter clicked, and her features were unclear. But behind her, perched on the arm of the love seat, was a face I had seen before.

He could have been the same man I'd seen standing in the

Weildman garden looking up. Only in the picture he was a little older, and he was wearing a suit, a high-collared white shirt, and a necktie. But the same blond hair, the same light eyes, the same intense focus that he'd shown looking up.

The man in the garden must have been a descendant of the Weildmans, returned to the family home.

And then I saw the last picture, and the framed letter beside it.

Mrs. Dender found me. She thought I'd had a fit of some kind, since I was sitting on the floor against the wall, staring at the photographs and unable to speak. She called 911, they called my mother from the hospital, all kinds of questions and tests and poking went on, and I just sat and nodded.

They decided in the end that it was the shock of the terrible coincidence that had made me go gaga for a while, and I never argued with that. It was a shock, all right, although I don't think coincidence had much to do with it.

The last picture on the wall had shown the blond man again, in a different room. He had been sitting on a similar seat, with his hand resting on the shoulder of a young woman, a gesture of great affection. She, too, was looking at the camera, no blur this time, although one foot of the infant in her lap had been kicking, and the white blanket had stuttered onto the film.

The caption below it read:

Marcus Weildman (30), Beatrice Weildman (24), and baby Bradley, taken in the studio of local photographer Ralph Kurzen, May 20, 1909. Marcus Weildman was killed as a soldier in France during World War I. Beatrice (maiden name Collins) arrived in town as an unclaimed orphan in 1899 and married Marcus Weildman in 1905. Their children were Bradley (whose plane went down over the English Channel in 1943), Arthur John (who moved to Spokane in the thirties), and Bonnie. Beatrice Weildman lived in the family home until her disappearance, as mysterious as her arrival, in 1957. She was 72.

The letter beside it, its ink faded but in a writing I knew well, said:

My dear "cousin" Amy,

I send you a studio portrait of your cousin Marcus and his new family, to add to your wall, that you might assure yourself that he is well and happy with his peculiar, rootless wife. I thank you for your friendship, and know that you remain in my affections always.

*   The baby's name, I should add, comes from a young boy who befriended me long ago, whose loss I regret, and whose memory I wished to honor.*

Your cousin by marriage,
Bea

I have to say, in the picture, she looked happier than I'd ever seen her.

Appetite for Murder

by Simon R. Green

I never wanted to be a Detective. But the call went out, and no-one else stood up, so I sold my soul to the company store, for a badge and a gun and a shift that never ends.

The Nightside is London's very own dirty little secret: a hidden realm of gods and monsters, magic and murder, and more sin and temptation than you can shake a wallet at. People come to the Nightside from all over the world, to indulge the pleasures and appetites that might not have a name but certainly have a price. It's always night in the Nightside, always three o'clock on the morning, the hour that tries men's souls and finds them wanting. The sun has never shone here, probably because it knows it isn't welcome. This is a place to do things that can only be done in the shadows, in the dark.

I'm Sam Warren. I was the first, and for a long time the only, Detective in the Nightside. I worked for the Authorities, those grey and faceless figures who run the Nightside, inasmuch as anyone does, or can. Even in a place where there is no crime, because everything is permitted, where sin and suffering, death and damnation are just business as usual . . . there are still those who go too far and have to be taken down hard. And for that, you need a Detective.

We don't get many serial killers in the Nightside. Mostly because amateurs don't tend to last long amongst so much professional competition. But I was made Detective, more years ago than I care to remember, to hunt down the very first of these human monsters. His name was Shock-Headed Peter. He killed 347 men, women, and children before I caught him. Though that's just an official estimate; we never found any of his victims' bodies. Just their clothes. Wouldn't surprise me if the real total was closer to a thousand. I caught him and put him away; but the things I saw, and the things I had to do, changed me forever.

Made me the Nightside's Detective, for all my sins, mea culpa.

I'd just finished eating when the call came in. From the H P Lovecraft Memorial Library, home to more forbidden tomes under one roof than anywhere else. Browse at your own risk. It appeared the Nightside's latest serial killer had struck again. Only this time he'd been interrupted, and the body was still warm, the blood still wet.

I strode through the Library accompanied by a Mr. Pettigrew, a tall, storklike personage with wild eyes and a shock of white hair. He gabbled continuously as we made our way through the tall stacks, wringing his bony hands against his sunken chest. Mr. Pettigrew was Chief Librarian, and almost overcome with shame that such a vulgar thing should have happened in his Library.

"It's all such a mess!" he wailed. "And right in the middle of the Anthropology Section. We've only just finished refurbishing!"

"What can you tell me about the victim?" I said patiently.

"Oh, he's dead. Yes. Very dead, in fact. Horribly mutilated, Detective! I don't know how we're going to get the blood out of the carpets."

"Did you happen to notice if there were any . . . pieces missing, from the body?"

"Pieces? Oh dear," said Mr. Pettigrew. "I can feel one of my heads coming on. I think I'm going to have to go and have a little lie down."

He took me as far as the Anthropology Section, then disappeared at speed. It hadn't been twenty minutes since I got the call, but still someone had beaten me to the body. Crouching beside the bloody mess on the floor was the Nightside's very own superheroine, Ms. Fate. She wore a highly polished black-leather outfit, complete with full face mask and cape; but somehow on her it never looked like a costume or some fetish thing. It looked like a uniform. Like work clothes. She even had a utility belt around her narrow waist, all golden clasps and bulging little pouches. I thought the high heels on the boots were a bit much, though. I came up on her from behind, making no noise at all, but she still knew I was there.

"Hello, Detective Warren," she said, in her low, smoky voice, not even glancing round. "You got here fast."

"Happened to be in the neighbourhood," I said. "What have you found?"

"All kinds of interesting things. Come and have a look."

Anyone else I would have sent packing, but not her. We'd

worked a bunch of cases together, and she knew her stuff. We don't get too many superheroes or vigilantes in the Nightside, mostly because they get killed off so damn quickly. Ms. Fate, that dark avenger of the night, was different. Very focused, very skilled, very professional. Would have made a good Detective. She made room for me to crouch down beside her. My knees made loud cracking noises in the Library hush.

"You're looking good, Detective," Ms. Fate said easily. "Have you started dyeing your hair?"

"Far too much grey," I said. "I was starting to look my age, and I couldn't have that."

"I've questioned the staff," said Ms. Fate. "Knew you wouldn't mind. No-one saw anything, but then no-one ever does, in the Nightside. Only one way into this Section, and only one way out, and he would have had blood all over him, but . . ."

"Any camera surveillance?"

"The kind of people who come here, to read the kind of books they keep here, really don't want to be identified. So, no surveillance of any kind, scientific or mystical. There's major security in place to keep any of the books from going walkabout, but that's it."

"If our killer was interrupted, he may have left some clues behind," I said. "This is his sixth victim. Maybe he got sloppy."

Ms. Fate nodded slowly, her expression unreadable behind her dark mask. Her eyes were very blue, very bright. "This has got to stop, Detective. Five previous victims, all horribly mutilated, all with missing organs. Different organs each time. Interestingly enough, the first victim was killed with a blade, but all the others were torn apart, through brute strength. Why change his MO after the first killing? Most serial killers cling to a pattern, a ritual, that means something significant to them."

"Maybe he decided a blade wasn't personal enough," I said. "Maybe he felt the need to get his hands dirty."

We both looked at the body in silence for a while. This one was different. The victim had been a werewolf and had been caught in midchange as he died. His face had elongated into a muzzle, his hands had claws, and patches of silver-grey fur showed clearly on his exposed skin. His clothes were ripped and torn and soaked with blood. He'd been gutted, torn raggedly open from chin to crotch, leaving a great crimson wound. There was blood all around him, and more spattered across the spines of books on the shelves.

"It's never easy to kill a werewolf," Ms. Fate said finally. "But given the state of the wound's edges, he wasn't cut open. That rules out a silver dagger."

"No sign of a silver bullet either," I observed.

"Then we can probably rule out the Lone Ranger." She rubbed her bare chin thoughtfully. "You know, the extent of these injuries reminds me a lot of cattle mutilations."

I looked at her. "Are we talking little grey aliens?"

She smiled briefly, her scarlet lips standing out against the pale skin under the black mask. "Maybe I should check to see if he's been probed?"

"I think that was the least of his worries," I said. "This must have been a really bad way to die. Our victim had his organs ripped out while he was still alive."

Ms. Fate busied herself taking samples from the body and the crime scene, dropping them into sealable plastic bags and tucking them away in her belt pouches.

"Don't smile," she said, not looking round. "Forensic science catches more killers than deductive thought."

"I never said a word," I said innocently.

"You didn't have to. You only have to look at my utility belt, and your mouth starts twitching. I'll have you know the things I store in my belt have saved my life on more than one occasion. Shuriken, smoke bombs, nausea-gas capsules, stun grenades . . . A girl has to be prepared for everything." She stood up and looked down at the body. "It's such a mess I can't even tell which organs were taken; can you?"

"The heart, certainly," I said, standing up. "Anything else, we'll have to wait for the autopsy."

"I've already been through the clothing," said Ms. Fate. "If there was any ID, the killer took it with him. But I did find a press pass, tucked away in his shoe. Said he worked for the *Night Times*. But no name on the pass, which is odd. Could be an investigative reporter, I suppose, working undercover."

"I'll check with the editor," I said.

"But what was he doing here? Research?"

We both looked around, and Ms. Fate was the first to find a book lying on the floor, just outside the blood pool. She opened the book and flicked through it quickly.

"Anything interesting?" I said.

"Hard to tell. Some doctoral dissertation, on the cannibal practices of certain South American tribes."

I gestured for the book, and she handed it over. I skimmed quickly through the opening chapter. "Seems to be about the old cannibal myth that you are what you eat. You know—eat a brave man's heart to become brave, a runner's leg muscles to become fast . . ."

We both looked at the torn open body on the floor, with its missing organs.

"Could that be our murderer's motivation?" said Ms. Fate. "He's taking the organs so he can eat them later, and maybe . . . what? Gain new abilities? Run me through the details of the five previous victims, Detective."

"First was a minor Greek godling," I said. "Supposedly descended from Hercules, at many removes. Very strong. Died of a single knife wound to the heart. Chest and arm muscles were taken."

"Just the one blow, to the heart," said Ms. Fate. "You'd have to get in close for that. Which suggests the victim either knew his killer or had reason to trust him."

"If the killer has acquired a godling's strength, he wouldn't need a knife any more," I said.

"There's more to it than that." She looked like she might be frowning, behind her mask. "This whole hands-on thing shouts . . . passion. That the killer enjoyed it, or took some satisfaction from it."

"Second victim was a farseer," I said. "What they call a remote viewer these days. Her head was smashed in, and her eyes taken. After that, an immortal who lost his testicles, a teleporter for a messenger service who had his brain ripped right out of his skull, and, finally, a minor radio-chat-show host, who lost his tongue and vocal cords."

"Why that last one?" said Ms. Fate. "What did the killer hope to gain? The gift of the gab?"

"You'll have to ask him," I said. "Presumably the killer believed that eating the werewolf's missing organs would give him shape-changing abilities, or at least regeneration."

"He's trying to eat himself into a more powerful person . . . Hell, just the godling's strength and the werewolf's abilities will make him really hard to take down. Have you come up with any leads yet, from the previous victims?"

"No," I said. "Nothing."

"Then I suppose we'd better run through the usual suspects, if only to cross them off. How about Mr. Stab, the legendary uncaught immortal serial killer of Old London Town?"

"No," I said. "He always uses a knife, or a scalpel. Always has, ever since 1888."

"All right; how about Arnold Drood, the Bloody Man?"

"His own family tracked him down and killed him, just last year."

"Good. Shock-Headed Peter?"

"Still in prison, where I put him," I said. "And there he'll stay, till the day he dies."

Ms. Fate sniffed. "Don't know why they didn't just execute him."

"Oh, they tried," I said. "Several times, in fact. But it didn't take."

"Wait a minute," said Ms. Fate. She knelt again suddenly, and leant right over to study the dead man's elongated muzzle. "Take a look at this, Detective. The nose and mouth tissues are eaten away. Right back to the bone in places. I wonder . . ." She produced a chemical kit from her belt and ran some quick tests. "I thought so. Silver. Definite traces of silver dust, in the nose, mouth, and throat. Now that was clever . . . Throw a handful of silver dust into the werewolf's face, he breathes it in, unsuspecting, and his tissues would immediately react to the silver. It had to have been horribly painful, certainly enough to distract the victim and interrupt his shape change . . . while leaving him vulnerable to the killer's exceptional strength."

"Well spotted," I said. "I must be getting old. Was a time I wouldn't have missed something like that."

"You're not that old," Ms. Fate said lightly.

"Old enough that they want to retire me," I said.

"You? You'll never retire! You live for this job."

"Yes," I said. "I've done it so long it's all I've got now. But I am getting old. Slow. Still better than any of these upstart latecomers, like John Taylor and Tommy Oblivion."

"You look fine to me," Ms. Fate said firmly. "In pretty good shape, too, for a man of your age. How do you manage it?"

I smiled. "We all have our secrets."

"Of course. This is the Nightside, after all."

"I could have worked out your secret identity," I said. "If I'd wanted to."

"Perhaps. Though it might have surprised you. Why didn't you?"

"I don't know. Professional courtesy? Or maybe I just liked the idea of knowing there was someone else around who wanted to catch murderers as much as I did."

"You can depend on me," said Ms. Fate.

Our next port of call was the Nightside's one and only autopsy room. We do have a CSI, but it only has four people in it. And only one Coroner, Dr. West. Short, stocky fellow with a smiling face and flat straw yellow hair. I wouldn't leave him alone with the body of anyone I cared about, but he's good enough at his job.

By the time Ms. Fate and I got there, Dr. West already had the werewolf's body laid out on his slab. He was washing the naked body with great thoroughness and crooning a song to it as we entered. He looked round unhurriedly and waggled the fingers of one podgy hand at us.

"Come in, come in! So nice to have visitors. So nice! Of course, I'm never alone down here, but I do miss good conversation. Take a look at this."

He put down his wet sponge, picked up a long surgical instrument, and started poking around inside the body's massive wound. Ms. Fate and I moved closer, while still maintaining a respectful distance. Dr. West tended to get over-excited with a scalpel in his hand, and we didn't want to get spattered.

Dr. West thrust both his hands into the cavity and started rooting around with quite unnecessary enthusiasm. "The heart is missing," he said cheerfully. "Also, the liver. Yes. Yes . . . Not cut out, torn out . . . Made a real mess of this poor fellow's insides, hard to be sure of anything else . . . Not sure what to put down as actual cause of death: blood loss, trauma, shock . . . Heart attack? Yes. That covers it. So, another victim for our current serial killer. Number six . . . how very industrious. Oh yes. Haven't even got a name for your chart, have we, boy? Just another John Doe . . . But not to worry; I've got a nice little locker waiting for you, nice and cosy, next to your fellow victims."

"You have got to stop talking to the corpses like that," I said sternly. "One of these days someone will catch you at it."

Dr. West stuck out his tongue at me. "Let them. See if I care. See if they can get anyone else to do this job."

"How long have you been Coroner, Dr. West?" said Ms. Fate, tactfully changing the subject.

"Oh, years and years, my dear. I was made Coroner the same year Samuel here was made Detective. Oh yes, we go way back, Samuel and I. All because of that nasty Shock-Headed Peter . . . The Authorities decided that such a successful serial killer was bad for business, and therefore Something Must Be Done. It's all about popular perception, you see . . . There are many things in the Nightside far more dangerous than any human killer could ever hope to be, but the Authorities, bless their grey little hearts, wanted visitors to feel safe, so . . ."

He stopped and looked at me sourly. "You'd never believe he and I were the same age, would you? How do you do it, Samuel?"

"Healthy eating," I said. "And lots of vitamins."

"Why haven't you called in Walker?" Ms. Fate said suddenly. "He speaks for the Authorities, with a Voice everyone has to obey; and I've heard it said he once made a corpse sit up on a slab and answer his questions."

"Oh he did, he did," said Dr. West, pulling his hands out of the body with a nasty sucking sound. "I was there at the time, and very edifying it was, too. But unfortunately, all six of our victims had their tongues torn out. After our killer had taken the bits and pieces he wanted. Which suggests our killer had reason to be afraid of Walker."

"Hell," I said. "Everyone's got good reason to be afraid of Walker."

Dr. West shrugged, threw aside his scalpel and slipped off his latex gloves with a deliberate flourish, as though to make clear he'd done all that could reasonably be expected of him.

Ms. Fate stared into the open wound again. "Our killer really does like his work, doesn't he?"

"He's got an appetite for it," I said solemnly.

"Oh please," said Ms. Fate.

I moved in beside her, staring down into the cavity. "Took the heart out first, then the liver. Our killer must believe they hold the secret of the werewolf's abilities. If he is a shape-changer now, he'd be that much harder to take down."

Ms. Fate looked at me thoughtfully, then turned to Dr. West. "Do you still have all the victims' clothes and belongings?"

"Of course, my dear, of course! Individually bagged and tagged. Help yourself."

She opened every bag, and checked every piece of torn and blood-soaked clothing. It's always good to see a real professional at work. Eventually, she ran out of things to check and test, and turned back to me.

"Six victims. Different ages, sexes, occupations. Nothing at all to connect them. Unless you know something, Detective."

"There's nothing in the files," I said.

"So how were the victims chosen? Why these six people?"

"Maybe the people don't matter," I said. "Just their abilities."

"Run me through them again," she said. "Names and abilities, in order, from the beginning."

"First victim was the godling, Demetrius Heracles," I said patiently. "Then the farseer, Barbara Moore. The teleporter, Cainy du Brec. The immortal, Count Magnus, though I doubt very much that was his real name. The chat show host, Adrian Woss, and finally the werewolf, Christopher Russell."

"This whole business reminds me unpleasantly of Shock-Headed Peter," Ms. Fate said slowly. "Not the MO, but the sheer ruthlessness of the murders. Are you sure he hasn't escaped?"

"Positive," I said. "No-one escapes from Shadow Deep."

She shook her masked head, her heavy cloak rustling loudly. "I'd still feel happier if we checked. Can you get us in?"

"Of course," I said. "I'm the Detective."

So we went down into Shadow Deep, all the way down to the darkest place in the Nightside, sunk far below in the cold bedrock. Constructed . . . no-one knows how long ago, to hold the most vicious, evil, and dangerous criminals ever stupid enough to prey on the Nightside. The ones we can't, for one reason or another, just execute and be done with. The only way down is by the official transport circle, maintained and operated by three witches from a small room over a really rough bar called the Jolly Cripple. If the people who drank in the bar knew what went on in the room above their heads . . . they'd probably drink a hell of a lot more.

"Why here?" said Ms. Fate, as we ascended the gloomy back stairs. "Secrecy?"

"Partly, I suppose," I said. "More likely because it's cheap."

The three witches were the traditional bent-over hags in tattered cloaks, all clawed hands and hooked noses. The great circle on the floor had been marked in chalk mixed with sulphur and semen. You don't want to know how I found out. Ms. Fate glowered at the three witches.

"You can stop that cackling right now. You don't have to put on an act; we're not tourists."

"Well, pardon us for taking pride in our work," said one of the witches, straightening up immediately. "We are professionals, after all. And image is everything, these days. You don't think these warts just happened, do you?"

I gave her my best hard look, and she got the transport

operation under way. The three witches did the business with a minimum of chanting and incense, and down Ms. Fate and I went, to Shadow Deep.

It was dark when we arrived. Completely dark, with not a ghost of a light anywhere. I only knew Ms. Fate was there with me because I could hear her breathing at my side. Footsteps approached, slow and heavy, until finally a pair of night-vision goggles were thrust into my hand. I nearly jumped out of my skin, and from the muffled squeak beside me, so did Ms. Fate. I slipped the goggles on, and Shadow Deep appeared around me, all dull green images and fuzzy shadows.

It's always dark in Shadow Deep.

We were standing in an ancient circular stone chamber, with a low roof, curving walls, and just the one exit, leading on to a stone tunnel. Standing before us was one of the prison staff, a rough clay golem with simple preprogrammed routines. It had no eyes on its smooth face, because it didn't need to see. It turned abruptly and started off down the tunnel, and Ms. Fate and I hurried after it. The tunnel branched almost immediately, and branched again, and as we moved from tunnel to identical tunnel, I soon lost all track of where I was.

We came at last to the Governor's office, and the golem raised an oversized hand and knocked once on the door. A cheery voice called out for us to enter, and the door swung open before us. A blinding light spilled out, and Ms. Fate and I clawed off our goggles as we stumbled into the office. The door shut itself behind us.

I looked around the Governor's office with watering eyes.

It wasn't particularly big, but it had all the comforts. The Governor came out from behind his desk to greet us, a big blocky man with a big friendly smile that didn't touch his eyes at all. He seemed happy to see us, but then, he was probably happy to see anyone. Shadow Deep doesn't get many visitors.

"Welcome, welcome!" he said, taking our goggles and shaking my hand and Ms. Fate's with great gusto. "The great Detective and the famous vigilante; such an honour! Do sit down, make yourselves at home. That's right! Make yourselves comfortable! Can I offer you a drink, cigars . . . ?"

"No," I said.

"Ah, Detective," said the Governor, sitting down again behind his desk. "It's always business with you, isn't it?"

"Ms. Fate is concerned that one of your inmates might have escaped," I said.

"What? Oh no; no, quite impossible!" The Governor turned his full attention and what he likes to think of as his charming smile on Ms. Fate. "No-one ever escapes from here. Never, never. It's always dark in Shadow Deep, you see. Light doesn't work here, outside my office. Not any kind of light, scientific or magical. Not even a match . . . Even if a prisoner could get out of his cell, which he can't, there's no way he could find his way through the maze of tunnels to the transfer site. Even a teleporter can't get out of here because there's no way of knowing how far down we are!"

"Tell her how it works," I said. "Tell her what happens to the scum I bring here."

The Governor blinked rapidly and tried another ingratiating smile. "Yes, well, the prisoner is put into his cell by one of the golems, and the door is then nailed shut. And sealed forever with preprepared, very powerful magics. Once in, a prisoner never leaves his cell. The golems pass food and water through a slot in the door. And that's it."

"What about . . . ?" said Ms. Fate.

"There's a grille in the floor."

"Oh, ick."

"Quite," said the Governor. "You must understand, our prisoners are not here to reform or repent. Only the very worst individuals ever end up here, and they stay here till they die. However long that takes. No reprieves, and no time off for good behaviour."

"How did you get this job?" said Ms. Fate.

"I think I must have done something really bad in a previous existence," the Governor said grandly. "Cosmic payback can be such a bitch."

"You got this job because you got caught," I said.

The Governor scowled. "Yes, well . . . It's not that I did anything really bad . . ."

"Ms. Fate," I said, "allow me to introduce to you Charles Peace, villain from a long line of villains. Burglar, thief, and snapper up of anything valuable not actually nailed down. Safes opened while you wait."

"That was my downfall," the Governor admitted. "I opened Walker's safe, you see; just for the challenge of it. And I saw something I really shouldn't have seen. Something no-one was ever supposed to see. I ran, of course, but the Detective tracked me down and brought me back, and Walker gave me a choice. On-the-spot execution, or serve here as Governor until what I know becomes obsolete and doesn't matter any more. That was seventeen years ago, and there isn't a day goes by where I don't wonder whether I made the right decision."

"Seventeen years?" said Ms. Fate. She always did have a soft spot for a hard-luck story.

"Seventeen years, four months, and three days," said the Governor. "Not that I obsess about it, you understand."

"Is Shock-Headed Peter still here?" I said bluntly. "There's no chance he could have got out?"

"Of course not! I did the rounds only an hour ago, and his cell is still sealed. Come on, Detective; if Shock-Headed Peter was on the loose in the Nightside again, we'd all know about it."

"Who else have you got down here?" said Ms. Fate. "Anyone . . . famous?"

"Oh, quite a few; certainly some names you'd recognise. Let's see; we have the Murder Masques, Sweet Annie Abattoir, Max Maxwell the Voodoo Apostate, Maggie Malign . . . But they're all quite secure, too, I can assure you."

"I just needed to be sure this place is as secure as it's supposed to be," said Ms. Fate. "You'd better prepare a new cell, Governor; because I've brought you a new prisoner."

And she looked at me.

I rose my feet, and so did she. We stood looking at each other for a long moment.

"I'm sorry, Sam," she said. "But it's you. You're the murderer."

"Have you gone mad?" I said.

"You gave yourself away, Sam," she said, meeting my gaze squarely with her own. "That's why I had you bring me here to Shadow Deep, where you belong. Where even you can't get away."

"What makes you think it was me?" I said.

"You knew things you shouldn't have known. Things only the killer could have known. First, at the Library. That anthropology text was a dry, stuffy, and very academic text. Very difficult for a layman to read and understand. But you just skimmed through it, then neatly summed up the whole concept. The only way you could have done that was if you'd known it in advance. That raised my suspicions, but I didn't say anything. I wanted to be wrong about you.

"But you did it again, at the autopsy. First, you knew that the heart had been removed *before* the liver. Dr. West hadn't worked that out yet, because the body's insides were such a mess. Second, when I asked you to name the victims in order, you named them all, including the werewolf. Who hasn't been identified yet. Dr. West still had him down as a John Doe.

"So, it had to be you. Why, Sam? Why?"

"Because they were going to make me retire," I said. It was actually a relief, to be able to tell it to someone. "Take away my job, my reason for living, just because I'm not as young as I used to be. All my experience, all my years of service, all the things I've done for them, and the Authorities were going to give me a gold watch and throw me on the scrap heap. Now, when things are worse than they've ever been. When I'm needed more than ever. It wasn't fair. It wasn't right.

"So I decided I would just take what I needed, to make myself the greatest Detective that ever was. With my new abilities, I would be unstoppable. I would go private, like John Taylor and Larry Oblivion, and show those wet-behind-the-ears newcomers how it's done . . . I would become rich and famous, and if I looked a little younger, well . . . this is the Nightside, after all.

"Shed no tears for my victims. They were all criminals, though I could never prove it. That's why there was no paperwork on them. But I knew. Trust me; they all deserved to die. They were all scum.

"I'd actually finished, you know. The werewolf would have been my last victim. I had all I needed. I teleported in and out of the Library, which is why no-one saw me come and go. But then . . . you had to turn up, the second-best Detective in the Nightside, and spoil everything. I never should have agreed to train you . . . but I saw in you a passion for justice that matched my own. You could have been my partner, my successor. The things we could have done . . . But now I'm going to have to kill you, and the Governor. I can't let you tell. Can't let you stop me, not after everything I've done. The Nightside needs me.

"You'll just be two more victims of the unknown serial killer."

I surged forward with a werewolf's supernatural speed and grabbed the front of Ms. Fate's black-leather costume with a godling's strength. I closed my hand on her chest and ripped her left breast away. And then I stopped, dumbstruck. The breast was in my hand, but under the torn-open leather there was no wound, no spouting blood. Only a very flat, very masculine chest. Ms. Fate smiled coldly.

"And that's why you'd never have guessed my secret identity, Sam. Who would ever have suspected that a man would dress up as a superheroine to fight crime? But then, this is the Nightside, and like you said; we all have our secrets." And while I stood there, listening with an open mouth, she palmed a nausea-gas capsule from her belt and threw it in my face. I hit the stone floor on my hands and knees, vomiting so hard I couldn't concentrate enough to use any of my abilities. The Governor called for two of his golems, and they came and dragged me away. They threw

me into a cell, then nailed the door shut and sealed it forever.

No need for a trial. Ms. Fate would have a word with
Walker, and that would be that. That's how I always did it.

So here I am, in Shadow Deep, in the dark that never
ends. Guess whose cell they put me next to. Just guess.

One of these days they'll open this cell and find nothing
here but my clothes.

A Woman's Work

by Dana Stabenow

As small and mean and dirty as Pylos was, Crowfoot was profoundly glad to see it on the horizon. The voyage from Dorian had been speedy but less than smooth, the Ocean of Aptikos in its usual bad temper. When at last they made fast to the dock, Crowfoot had Blanca and Pedro first up out of the hold and down the gangway to a terra that was blessedly firma beneath her feet. The Sword was strapped to her back and the saddle on Blanca's before Sharryn had finished taking leave of the *Barka*'s captain. Avel was his name, he of the laughing hazel eyes and the tight brown curls and the quick, charming tongue. He had been the only bright spot in Sharryn's voyage from Epaphus. Sailors.

He knew his business, though. The *Barka*'s crew made short work of off-loading what little cargo in its holds was destined for Kalliopean vendors. There was nothing to load, evidently, the primary export of Kalliope being tragic poetry, it was said sold by the yard. It was a joke over the other eight provinces that it was most welcome in the necessary out back.

"Crowfoot?"

A voice made her turn. "Aeron. I wondered if you had waited to greet us."

"Not for long." His grip was firm and quickly released. "We're leaving on the ship you came in on, if the captain will give us passage."

He was a spare man with gray hair and a stern face, as tall as the Staff he held in his left hand. A shorter man stepped out from behind him, and Crow felt her face break into a smile. "Thanos."

That man was younger and built along more generous lines, with the bronze skin and dark hair of the native born Pthalean. His Sword was belted around his waist in such style as the hilt was never very far from his right hand. "Crow!" He gave her a hearty embrace, but his eyes slid past her to the ship. "Is that our outbound transportation?"

"You're in a hurry," she said.

"So will you be, in a year," Aeron said.

"In a week," Thanos said.

She looked from one to the other. "We could probably use a little introduction."

"You'll find out all you need to know between here and Ydra," Aeron said.

"I see." She busied herself with Pedro's saddle to hide her annoyance, and said in a carefully casual tone, "Kalliope not quite the garden spot it's reputed to be?"

Thanos gave Aeros a sidelong glance. "Not quite."

"No," Aeros said, his face grim, "and I don't know why they sent the two of you here. It's going to make the job twice as hard, and the nine gods know it's hard enough already. Especially now."

"Aeron! Thanos!" Sharryn trod down the gangway in a flurry of mulberry skirts and embraced both men with her usual enthusiasm. Even Aeron's stony visage cracked a smile, but further greetings were forestalled by Avel's call. "All aboard!"

"He's calling my name," Thanos said, and kissed first Crow's cheek, then Sharryn's. He shouldered his bag, grasped the hilt of his Sword, and quick-footed it up the gangway. Aeron nodded at both women and followed, the Staff striking the wooden surface every second step like the rhythmic tolling of a death bell.

The *Barka* cast off and stood out in short order. There was a shout from the rail. "There's a good inn about a league out of town! The Soldier's Rest!"

"Thanks, Thanos!" Crow said. "Safe voyage!"

"Good luck!"

"Ominous," Sharryn said. "He sounds like he thinks we might need it." She looked at Crow. "They could have stayed to fill us in a little on what we could expect. We would have."

"Maybe," Crow said, and looked around at the gathering crowd. They were all men, some curious, some lascivious, some distinctly unfriendly.

"Witches," someone said in a voice meant to be heard.

"And maybe not," Crow said. The remark had come from a group of young men better dressed than the rest of the crowd, with gold and gemstones at their wrists and throats. One arrogant dandy with a supercilious arch to his very long nose waited until he caught Crow's eye and spat deliberately before Blanca's hooves.

Sharryn gave a sunny smile. "Ready?"

Without answering, Crowfoot touched a heel to Blanca's

side. The dandy waited to give way until Blanca and Pedro were almost on top of them, his red cloak actually brushing Crow's stirrup. His eyes were dark with contempt and, yes, hatred, Crow thought, but there was something else there as well. The Sword against her back seemed to hum in agreement.

She decided to put him to the test. "Pardon me, good-man," she said mildly, "but Blanca doesn't care much for being crowded." She smiled. "And I would just hate it if she mussed your pretty red cloak."

Next to her she heard Sharryn's startled gasp, quickly repressed. In response to a discreet heel, Pedro turned to face opposite from Blanca and stare down the menacing crowd. Crow's attention remained focused on the dandy. His face had darkened at her words and his hand went to the hilt of his sword. Crow gazed at him steadily, her face expressionless, waiting.

She saw the exact moment when he decided not to push it, anticipated, then saw the scornful shrug. He spat again and said something in an undertone to his friends. They laughed, a jeering, heckling kind of laugh that had nothing of true mirth to it, and fell in behind when he turned with a swish of his pretty red cloak and stalked away.

"Shall we go then?" Crow said, still in that mild tone of voice, and nudged Blanca forward.

"Have you completely lost your mind?" Sharryn said beneath her breath. "He could have brought that whole mob down on us."

Crow thought of the hatred she had seen in the dandy's eyes, so strong it was almost palpable. Hatred that intense, that concentrated, was a force to be reckoned with, something anyone who had been present when Nyssa burned knew first-hand. "And isn't it interesting that he chose not to?"

The Hecates rose behind Pylos on the southern horizon, high, bleak and sharp-toothed. None of the buildings of the town were more than two stories high, most built of wood that had been too long from the tree and fashioned with too little care to begin with. "This place looks like it'd fall over at the first puff of a dragon's breath," Sharryn said, surveying it with disfavor.

The men of Pylos were tall, dark-eyed, dark-haired, and built like whips, all long bone and tensile muscle.

"Spooky," Sharryn said. "They look so much alike."

"Years of inbreeding will do that," Crow said.

In addition, the men of Pylos were dressed alike, in cloaks of dark red, each clasped at the throat with a miniature shield, made of various metals and each stamped with a different design. She saw several designs repeat themselves on different wearers. Separate cohorts, perhaps. The social structure of Kalliope was organized on military lines.

Of women they saw none, all the windows and doors of the houses they passed closed firmly against the road. No female children, either, and very few male children.

On the outskirts of town they found the inn, a long, low building made of solid, well-dressed blocks of stone beneath a sturdy thatched roof. The sign hanging over the door was a wooden man in a red cloak leaning against a spear with his eyes closed.

Their host was a tall, burly individual, polite even as he kept his face averted, refusing to meet either woman's eyes after the one swift glance of recognition at the crests on their shoulders. He was able to offer stalls in a snug stable for Blanca and Pedro, and a small, clean room at the back of the house for them.

Crowfoot dropped her saddlebags on one of the two nar-

row beds and went to unbar the shutters and swing them
wide. "What time is dinner served below, goodman?" Sharryn said behind her. Stars were winking into existence in the
night sky. The cold air had a bite to it, not unpleasant, just
crisp on the inhale, clearing one's lungs and head in equal
measure.

The innkeeper coughed. "In an hour, Seer. But why bother
yourselves with coming downstairs again this evening? I
could serve your meals here, in your room, where you can be
quiet and private."

Crow turned in time to see Sharryn give him her sunny
smile. "I find I have no liking for my own company this evening, goodman. We will take supper in the room below."

He didn't look happy but he didn't argue, and with an
inclination of his head delivered impartially between the two
of them, he was in the hall and the door was closing gently
behind him.

Crow raised an eyebrow at Sharryn. "Perhaps we should
dine armed."

"Certainly not!" Sharryn said bracingly. "We are Seer and
Sword, the King's Justice in Mnemosynea, welcomed in any
of the nine provinces as the personification of the Great
Charter and the Treaty of the Nine. There is no need for
arms."

And so, Crow keeping her inevitable misgivings to herself, Sword and Staff remained behind in their room when
they descended the stairs to the common room at the front of
the house. It was large, with ceilings high enough that it felt
almost airy in spite of the well-aged oak wainscoting and the
stripped and sanded tree trunks holding up the roof. It was
furnished with large round wooden tables sliced from the

trunks of larger trees, attended by low-backed stools, all filling up rapidly.

It wouldn't be fair to say that conversation ceased when
they entered the room, but there was certainly a momentary
pause, followed by a somewhat self-conscious resumption.
Heads turned when they walked by, but away, not toward.

The landlord emerged from a door at the back, through
which Crow caught her very first glimpse of a feminine Kalliopean face. Inquisitive eyes caught hers for a brief moment
before the landlord shut the door firmly and without haste
behind him. "Here is your table, goodwomen," he said, gesturing.

"Thank you, goodman." Sharryn rustled forward, her nose
very much in the air, and accepted the seat offered in the
darkest corner of the room with a regal nod. Crow went
around her to a seat with its back toward the wall, and the
third person at the table coalesced out of the gloom.

"Goodman," the third person said. "A light for the table,
if you please, so I may see my dining companions."

A lamp was brought and set alight with a snap of the
landlord's fingers, and their new companion was revealed to
them. "Seer and Sword," he said, inclining his head.

Crow felt a smile spread across her face. "Bard," she said.

Sharryn noted the wristband with the translucent bone
pick tucked into the back of it. "Bard," she said, a little belatedly.

He was a tall, angular man with weather-beaten skin and
deep-set eyes, and fair enough of hair and skin to be of the
Hesperides. His leathers were neatly made and well kept for
all the leagues on them. His movements were studied and
graceful, his voice deep and resonant. A lutina stood against

the wall behind his chair, its wood polished to a high gloss and its six strings evenly taut from bass to treble.

The landlord brought a pitcher, and the Bard poured. He raised his stein in a toast. "To the King."

"The King," they echoed and drank. The lager tasted of tart apples, and autumn mists, and deep-running mountain streams. As with most innkeepers, the landlord's Talent must be for brewing.

Crow said, "So, Bard, what brings you to Kalliope?"

"Why," he said easily, "like you, I serve at the pleasure of the King."

"Just spreading the news," Sharryn said.

He inclined his head.

"And gathering it," Sharryn said in a lower voice.

He inclined his head again. "As you say, Seer."

Crow watched Sharryn make up her mind. "My name is Sharryn, Bard, and this is Crowfoot."

He inclined his head a third time. "I'm honored."

Sharryn waited. The Bard said nothing more. Crow felt a tickle of laughter begin at the back of her throat, and coughed to cover it. Their host arrived with dinner, and Sharryn maintained a dignified if indignant silence while they worked their way through a selection of hard cheeses, crusty rolls warm from the oven, and a savory venison stew. The pitcher of lager refilled itself, and for a while silence settled in around the table.

When the food was nothing but a memory—the Soldier's Rest had a Talented cook, and Crow wondered if the eyes she'd seen peering through the door belonged to her or if women weren't allowed to have Talent in Kalliope—the three of them settled back around large mugs of tea sweetened with honey. Like everything else they had eaten and drunk, it was excellent, with a smoky aftertaste that lingered pleasantly on the tongue.

"So," the Bard said, sitting back at his ease, "you'd be for the Assizes in Ydra."

"We would," Sharryn said, very much on her dignity.

"Ah." The Bard drank tea.

Goaded, Sharryn said, "And of your goodness, Bard, would there be news as to the cases awaiting the King's Justice there?"

He considered his mug in silence for a moment. "There would," he said, and raised his eyes. His expression and his voice both were grave, and Crow felt her spine straighten. "The son of the heir to the count of Ydra has been murdered."

It seemed to Crow as if the room in back of them had stilled. "I see. And who has been held responsible for this crime?"

The Bard meditated on the contents of his mug for a moment, then raised his eyes again. "His aunt." He drank. "The heir's sister, and daughter to the king by his first wife."

A deferential clearing of throat broke the silence that followed his answer. They looked round and beheld one of the townsmen, his eyes fixed firmly on the Bard's face. "Yes?" the Bard said.

"Of your goodness, Bard, we were wondering if you would be singing for us this evening," the man said.

"Of course, goodman," the Bard said courteously, and reached for his lutina. A place was made for him in the middle of the room, a stool drawn up, an attentive circle assembled.

He knew his audience, but then Bards always did. He

began with a march, a brisk beat that had his listeners stamping their feet and beating their hands together and, after the first repetition, joining in the chorus and erupting into cheers at the coda. The Bard inclined his head gravely and gave them a moment before launching into a ditty about a Yranean farmer's wife and a traveling tinker from Aerato that verged on the pornographic and left everyone winking and nudging one another, because everyone knew about the deplorable moral laxity of Yraneans.

He played for an hour, lullabies, love songs, ballads, more marching songs, then made as if to rise. He was shouted back onto his stool. He raised a hand for quiet. "Very well, goodmen, one more song." He looked around the room, lingering for a moment on Crow's face. His fingers hit the strings in a sudden jangle of notes that had everyone sitting up, alert, uneasy.

And attentive, Crow saw. She smiled to herself.

The encore, the song his listeners had demanded of him, was the history of Mnemosynea, beginning with the Wizard Wars, those eleven hundred interminable years when the country was torn and fractured by the struggle for power between the provincial lords and the mage class. Kings died bloodily on the battlefield or were assassinated in their beds. White wizards held dark wizards at bay until the dark wizards triumphed, then turned on each other, laying waste to everything between them. Dark chords played almost with violence, a dissonant rhythm that was jarring and at times almost shocking, and over it all the Bard's voice harsh, abrasive. Many of the faces watching the Bard were stunned and staring.

At the precise moment when the music became a burden to the audience, a subtle refrain crept in beneath the martial rhythm, a repetitive, almost plaintive minor chord that grew until it took over the melodic line. The Bard's voice blended with it seamlessly, the previous callous disharmony giving way to a more gentle and more easily understood rhythm, and a much more hummable melody.

The Bard sang of a child named Loukas, born of a forced marriage between the heirs of Mnelpomenea and Kalliope— which pleased the audience in the Soldier's Rest, Crow saw—who was spirited out of his cradle by his mother, some said by man but most said by magick. Aegina, after all, had been born in Oetatia of a fey line descending from the white wizard Eneas, who at puberty manifested not just one Talent but all the major Talents combined, the only wizard ever to do so.

Loukas grew to manhood attended by Armonea, the white wizard who was sister to his mother. Some say they lived in the Dryad Forest in Pthalea, some say on one of the unnamed isles of the Hesperides, some say in one of the tiny, anonymous seacoastal villages of Aerato. In the outside world the dark wizards continued their struggle for supremacy, until only three were left, one of them Nyssa, greatest and most terrible wizard of them all.

In that year in the temple at the foot of Mount Oeta, the god of the mountain revealed herself and came forth to raise up one of the pilgrims come to worship at her shrine. This pilgrim she revealed to be Loukas, son of Aegina of Mnelpomenea and Ophean of Kalliope. Armonea stood forth and with her staff rallied to his cause what white wizards were left, joined almost immediately by the lords of the southern provinces, Palihymnea, Yranea, Aerato, and, of course, Mnelpomenea. Kleonea soon followed. The northern provinces came more slowly into the fold, Pthalea first, then Pthersikore, then Euterhepe. Kalliope alone resisted. Two years of pitched battles later, the dark wizard Nyssa lay siege to the very walls of Hestia itself, and was defeated due in great part to the last-minute defection of Kalliopean forces to Loukas.

A solemn, stately procession of chords, as the Bard sang of the writing and the ratification of the Treaty of the Nine, swelling to a grand finale with the election of nine Lords and Ladies Governeur, assembled in a Hestia newly and most resplendently restored, to fix their seals to the Great Charter. The focus had shifted, Crow noticed, from King Loukas to the individual rulers of the provinces. That was well-done, and typical of Loukas's attention to detail. His Talent for governing all and governing well was truly, well, magickal.

There followed a series of mellow, descending minor chords, a complete, harmonious whole with no discordant notes. The last chord died away. There was no applause, only a prolonged, almost reverential silence that lasted some moments. One man rose to his feet and opened his mouth. He closed it again without speaking and slipped away. He was followed in twos and threes, as everyone in the room made their way silently to the door to vanish into the night.

The Bard returned to their table, drank deeply, and smiled at Crow. She smiled back.

Sharryn, who had with difficulty been containing her fury at the Bard's unwelcome news during the concert, said with awful restraint, "A regicide? The murder of a royal?"

"Yes," the Bard said. "And an infanticide." He gave a grim nod at the looks of horror that crossed their faces. "The son of the viscount was a babe in arms."

Their departure the following morning was enlivened by the unlooked-for companionship of the Bard on their journey, who rode knee to knee with Crow on a scarred chestnut stallion with alert eyes and a mouth that almost seemed to smile. For the first league, Sharryn examined the characters of Aeron and Thanos, including the doubtful competence of their tutors at the Magi Guild, their complete lack of either personal or professional honor, and the questionable status of their parents' unions.

For the second league, she broadened her reach to include the Guild of the Magi, the King's counselors, and the bureaucrats in the department of the King's Justice.

As the third league ticked over, the province of Kalliope came under review. "They cull the newborns here, did you know that? They have an actual board of review that inspects the babes, and any they find to be inferior they throw off a cliff into the sea. Many," Sharryn said, giving the word bitter emphasis, "many are girl children, because what's one girl in the Kalliopean scheme of things, after all?"

Crow regarded the road ahead through Blanca's ears and said nothing.

"Kalliopean women are born only to breed, to make more Kalliopeans, preferably male. They are forbidden to have money of their own, to learn to read, to own property of their own, and most especially they are forbidden to study the magicks, to enhance and exploit the Talent given them by the nine gods at the sacred moment of their entry into adulthood."

The Bard's stallion reached over and gave Blanca a playful nip on the neck. Blanca gave a come-hither whicker in reply, sidling so that Crow's leg pressed against the Bard's.

"It's a miracle the count of Ydra's daughter even survived to the age of twenty-five years, and now you are telling me that she somehow mustered up enough magick to produce an effective death spell?"

"There are those with that Talent," the Bard said mildly. "And we all know what happens when such a Talent is repressed, or ignored."

"She did not do it," Sharryn stated.

When neither of her companions said anything, she rounded on them. "Crowfoot! Are you listening to me?"

"For three leagues, Sharryn," Crow said without rancor.

"Have you listened to what I've been saying?"

"Every word."

"Aren't you upset by what you hear!"

Crow sighed. After a moment, she said, "The only way Loukas could get all of the nine provinces to sign the Treaty was to promise that each province would be autonomous within its own borders, retaining to each province its own customs, and to respect the borders of their neighbors."

"But they haven't!" Sharryn said, triumphant. "They have murdered so many babies over the centuries that they have become drastically inbred. One in every two pregnancies ends in miscarriage, and one in every four—one in four!—live births produces a child with deformities or limited intelligence. There are rumors the Kalliopeans are raiding into Pthalea and Euterhepe for girl children, so Kalliopean males will have someone to mate with." She looked across Crow at the Bard. "And you laud them in song for producing Loukas's father, and for defecting from Nyssa's side in the Siege of Hestia. At the last possible moment, I might add."

"So I do," the Bard said amiably.

Crow reined to a halt. Sharryn looked around, her lips parted on a question, when Crow's upraised hand stopped

her. Blanca was very still, Pedro no less so at her side, both
with ears pricked, tense, alert.

The road had narrowed and was overgrown by demon
trees. The road curved both behind them and before so that
they had no direct line of sight in either direction.

The Bard brought his hand down to rest casually on the
hilt of his sword. From the corner of her eye, Sharryn saw
him loosen it in its scabbard. Her face a little paler, she
reached up to tidy an errant curl and slid a hand over the
comforting solidity of the Staff snugged against her back.

Crow, her voice the barest breath of sound, said, "Four
ahead, two behind. They mean to kill us if they can. Now!"

She raised her hand. The Sword leapt into it, and in the
same movement she dug her heels into Blanca's sides. As if
she'd only been waiting for the signal, Blanca jumped from a
standing position to a full gallop. Pedro was a second behind
her, the Bard's rawboned roan at Pedro's heels. Ahead, the
Sword flashed lightning as Crow flourished it, cutting swathes
through the air. "Seer and Sword, to arms, to arms!" Crow
bellowed.

"Seer and Sword, to arms!" Sharryn cried, the Staff freed
of its sheath and held at the ready. Blanca's neigh was like
a rumble of thunder, and Pedro's high bray a promise of
death and destruction. The silver runes inscribed on the
blade of the Sword and around the pole of the Staff glowed
with a white light that seemed almost to smoke with rage.
"Seer and Sword, to arms!" The words seemed to grow in
volume and to repeat themselves so that the very leaves
and thorns on the demon trees were stripped away by their
passage.

They galloped around the bend at full tilt, no check, no

pause. Blanca crashed into the four horsemen waiting there and Crow laid about her, the Sword alive with fury in her hand. There, one man disarmed. There, another screamed when the sword in his hand shattered and the bone in the arm holding it shattered as well.

Behind her Sharryn and the Bard had wheeled to face the two horsemen attacking from the rear. Crow heard the meaty sound of wood on flesh, a shriek of pain, and the thud of a body hitting the ground. A horse whinnied in terror, and there was the clang of metal on metal.

The two attackers in front of her were armed with swords and wielded them well, but not as well as Crow, and their swords were no match for hers. One of them realized that before the other, pulled viciously at the reins of his horse, and yelled, "Away! Away to me!" The disarmed man had already vanished. The third man dropped his guard and paused only to haul the man with the shattered arm up behind him before kicking his horse into a gallop.

A touch of the knee, and Blanca turned a neat half circle on two hooves to face behind them, just in time for Crow to see two horses vanishing around the bend of the road in the opposite direction. "I thought I heard one unhorsed!"

"You did," Sharryn said sourly, inspecting her Staff for nicks. She ran a loving hand down its length and settled it back in its sheath. "He got up again. I must be slipping."

The Bard had his sword already in his scabbard. "Who were they?" he said, a little breathless.

Crow shook her head. "I don't know. It was personal, though. Their hatred was very real and very strong." She started to say something else, then shook her head. "Very strong."

"Handy Talent you've got there," the Bard said.

"Just make sure you pronounce my name correctly when you sing the song," Crow said, and he laughed.

She held the Sword upright before her. Thank you, she thought, and pressed her lips to the cross guard.

They rode through the gates of Ydra Castle just as the sun sank behind the jagged peaks of the Kimaera Mountains. It was a large and forbidding structure, built of black granite flecked with mica, so that light seemed to strike sparks from its surface, like a forge constantly at work on a new weapon. The curtain wall was twenty feet thick, topped with ramparts wide enough for two men to walk abreast and pierced with narrow slits spaced an arm's length apart. Assessing the defenses with a warrior's eye, Crow saw that they were only sparsely manned, bowmen present at only every sixth or seventh station.

The walls ended in the perpendicular face of Mount Daemos on either side of the castle itself, which had been hewn from the side of the mountain. The rooms and passageways were rumored to run for leagues beneath the mountain, each king of Kalliope having made his own additions, some of them in secret. It was said that one of the more merciful punishments meted out by a displeased ruler was to be marooned in a disused corridor, sentenced to wander the halls of Ydra Castle for all time.

There was no king of Kalliope, the direct line having died with Opheon in the Siege of Hestia. The Count of Kalliope received them instead, one Moris Naupactus, who was also the Lord Governeur. In Kalliope, the civil authority and the heredity authority would always be one and the same.

He greeted them civilly enough, actually managing to meet their eyes. "Your journey was uneventful, I trust?"

"I'm afraid not, lord," Crow said. "We were attacked on the road early this afternoon."

He sat forward, his brow furrowed as he listened to their account, and when they were done, he snapped to an aide, "Send a troop out at sunrise to see what you can find." The aide bowed and departed. "I am relieved to see that you suffered no hurt," he said, and almost seemed to mean it. "My most sincere apologies for this outrage. I promise you, every effort will be made to apprehend your attackers. When they are caught, I shall deal with them myself."

Crow bowed again. "We could ask no more."

"The Assizes will be held in the Grand Hall through which you entered," the count said, changing the subject. "We trust that is acceptable. Good. Shall we say Mineus, then, after we break our fast?"

He raised a hand as if to dismiss them. Crow forestalled him. "That is three days hence, Count. It was our understanding that we had a month to review the cases before court went into session. We have discovered through experience that many prospective cases can be resolved by mediation."

His smile was bland. "It is our wish that the Assizes begin on Mineus, Sword. You will dine with me this evening. My servant will fetch you."

He turned toward the Bard. "King's Singer."

"Lord," the Bard said.

"What news do you bring us from abroad?"

This time their dismissal was unmistakable, and they retired to their quarters, a large suite consisting of two bedrooms with a parlor between. Like all the other rooms they had seen in Castle Ydra, they had been hewn from the mountainside. The darkness—there were no windows, of course—was alleviated by a series of tapers burning in wall sconces.

There was about the room, as there was about everything they had seen in Kalliope from the port of Pylos on, an air of deterioration, if not outright decay. The sconces and the candelabra were brass, but tarnished. The tapestries were massive but faded and threadbare. The beds were large and ornate but elderly and creaking in their joints. Putting Sharryn's thoughts into words, Crow said, "With the possible exception of the Soldier's Rest, everything in this province seems like it's on a downhill slide, and rather closer to the bottom than to the top."

A small fire was lit, but the fireplace in the parlor was so massive it swallowed up any heat thrown off. "How I wish we were back at the Soldier's Rest," Sharryn said, shivering. "Speaking of which, where were you this morning?"

"What?"

"I woke up, you were gone. You've never been an early riser." An eyebrow lifted in her direction. "Did the innkeeper prove more charming in private than he was in public?"

Crow was spared further inquisition when there was a knock at the door. A servant in the count's livery, patched at elbows and knees, came in, held the door wide, and announced, "The Viscountess Naiche, daughter of Moris."

The lady was reported to be twenty-five years old, but she looked much younger. Slender to the point of thinness, she had large, dark eyes, a high-bridged nose, a firm-lipped mouth, and a very decided chin carried high and proud. She wore a plain black dress, belted with a narrow girdle with a plain silver buckle. Beneath the hem of her skirt, Crow saw leggings and flat-heeled shoes made of sturdy leather.

Crow exchanged a swift glance with Sharryn. "Lady Naiche. I am Crowfoot the Sword. This is Sharryn the Seer."

The lady inclined her head. "My father the count sends me to see that you are comfortable in your lodgings, and well provided for."

"We are, lady, I thank you," Crow said.

She had entered the room with a long stride, her head high, and she met Crow's eyes with a direct, unflinching gaze. "It is said that you were attacked on the road from Pylos. Our court physician is able, should you have sustained any hurts."

"We did not, lady."

"That is well."

Crow exchanged another look with Sharryn, and said delicately, "Perhaps someone else has reported to the physician for aid."

A wintry smile crossed Naiche's face. "Perhaps."

They waited, but the viscountess said no more. Crow meditated for a moment, and decided on a frontal assault. "Lady, we are told you will stand before us on Mineus."

The viscountess nodded, her expression impassive. "That is correct."

Again they waited. Again, the count's daughter waited with them. Goaded, Sharryn said tartly, "Accused of a most heinous crime."

"Yes," the viscountess said, and no more.

Sharryn, at a loss, looked at Crow. Crow said bluntly, "Lady, we have not long been in your province, but it is plain to see that any woman would have a very poor hearing before any court held in Kalliope."

Naiche, Viscountess of Kalliope, inclined her head. Her hands were clasped before her, and Crow could see her knuckles white with strain. Looking closer, Crow saw the folds of her skirt shaking, as if the young woman's knees were trembling. "Lady," she said, "if you have any evidence to offer in your own defense, and if you have no reasonable expectation of being allowed to lay that evidence in open court, now would be the time to lay it before Seer and Sword."

Naiche's face was white to the lips, and she spoke stiffly. "I thank you for your concern, Crowfoot the Sword, but the customs of Kalliope do not permit it." She turned, and the liveried servant hastened to open the door.

"Then perhaps, lady," Sharryn said to her retreating back, "it is time for the customs of Kalliope to change."

Naiche stopped short of the threshold. Without turning around, she said in a low voice, "Impossible. There is nothing you can do for me." A pause. "Except, I beg you, cause the Sword's judgment to be rendered as swiftly as possible."

The door closed gently behind her, and Sharryn and Crow were left staring at each other.

"Hear ye, hear ye. The Grand Assizes of Mnemosynea, created by Charter and ratified by Treaty, is now in session. All who stand in need of the King's Justice, draw near to be heard. The King's Seer is summoned to hear the truth."

"The King's Seer answers," Sharryn said, striding forward, the Staff in her hand striking the stone floor with a clear ring.

"The King's Sword is summoned to render justice."

"The King's Sword answers," Crow said, and drew the Sword from its sheath on her back and raised it before her in both hands. She took her place at Sharryn's side. Mindful of both their office and of local custom, they had taken care with their attire, clean, neat, badges of office clearly displayed on their shoulders. Above all, Crow thought, no unseemly exposure of bare flesh to offend the Kalliopean gentry who had flooded in from the countryside to view personally this abomination of women in public and to take the tale home again to their shires and villages.

Our bare faces are affront enough to this lot. The link from mind to mind had as usual kicked in at the drawing of the Sword.

Peace, Crow replied. *They have offered us no insult since we have been here.*

Tolerating our presence among them doesn't mean they have any respect for us.

They don't have to respect us. Just the office.

You were gone again this morning.

Crow was spared a reply by the bailiff's summons. "Hear ye, hear ye, draw all ye near to bear witness, hear ye, hear ye."

The words echoed hollowly up into an arched stone ceiling so high there was a perceptible echo. The Great Hall had been cleared of everything except a dais at the far end, upon which were placed two chairs. At a slow, measured pace Sharryn and Crow progressed down the center of the hall, the crowd drawing back to make a path for them, and took their seats on the dais. Crow reversed the Sword and let the tip rest on the dais but kept it upright, a shining blade of tempered steel wrought by the alchemy of the Lycian smiths, the cross-guard silver chased with sapphires, the hilt made to fit Crow's hand, the pommel set with another, much larger sapphire, the length inscribed with silver runes.

Sharryn's Staff was cut from one of the sacred boles of the

Forest of Arthemeus, its length chased in silver runes by the
same Talented artisan and its head set with the twin of the
sapphire in Crow's Sword.

The king's secretary acted as bailiff. He was a thin, nervous man with scant hair and a mouth pursed in perpetual
disapproval as he read out cases from the docket.

The kidnapping came first before them. It wasn't kidnapping the accused was charged with, however. It was
rather the dispossession of a valuable asset—to wit, one
daughter, the loss of whom had deprived her family of, not
her Talent (unspecified), no, no, nothing so inconsequential,
but of her womb, which in Kalliope was the property of her
father and as such to be dispensed with to whom he saw fit.
Her father didn't approve of his daughter's new husband,
and, of course, his daughter wasn't called to bear witness,
but there was enough evidence to bring the charge home.

Simple theft, Sharryn thought.

Proven, Crow thought, and wondered what the Sword
would make of it.

The rape and the subsequent stoning to death of the victim and three revenge murders took up the next three days.
On the fifth day, the Great Hall was crowded with what
seemed to be most of the population of the keep jostling for
space. The count himself was there, standing to one side in
a small circle of deferential space. The Bard was also there,
making polite conversation with the mirror image of the
count, only much younger and considerably better dressed.
The son, Crow thought. *The Viscount Kerel.*

*I see him. But not the daughter, heavens no. You recognize him,
don't you?*

Indeed Crow did. It was the arrogant little nobleman

from Pylos, who had called them witches and spat at Blanca's hooves. Crow had wondered if perhaps he might have had something to do with the attack on the road.

The charge was murder, lodged against the daughter of the Count of Kalliope. Worse, it was infanticide, the murder of a child, a baby not out of its crib. And most horrible of all, a male child, the putative heir to the hereditary ruler of the province of Kalliope.

Why did they send us here for this case? What possible motive could they have for pulling out Aeros and Thanos only halfway through their assigned year? And replacing them with us, of all the Seers and Swords? They must have known that our very presence would alone be an incitement to riot.

Trust in the Sword.

Sharryn's snort was audible and drew glances. She raised her chin and looked around the Great Hall, deliberately catching the eyes of those men not quick enough to look away.

The bailiff stepped forward and called the first witness, the head of the palace guard and the investigating officer, one Captain Sergeus. A burly man in his midfifties, he wore the black livery of Ydra Keep and held his uniform cap beneath one arm as he testified in a steady voice, shoulders squared, eyes straight ahead. His voice was deep and calm, relating the facts of the case in chronological order.

Count Moris Naupactus was that rarity among Kalliopeans, a man with two children. The first was a daughter of twenty-five, Naiche, born to his first wife, unnamed in the record.

Imagine that, Sharryn thought.

The second child was a son of twenty-three, Kerel, born to Moris's second wife, also unnamed.

The brat preens at the mere mention of his name, Sharryn thought.

He did, too, but what interested Crow more was the way his father kept his face turned away from his son. Come to think of it, they were even on opposite sides of the room. She wondered if that was by accident or design.

Last year, in the month of Numina, Kerel had become the proud father of an infant son.

Three months later, on the morning of the third day of the Festival of Freya (*Festival, my eye,* Sharryn thought, *call it an orgy and be done with it*), the baby's crib had been found empty. A hue and cry had followed, Captain Sergeus said, in his dry recounting of the facts. The entire population of Ydra had been turned out, and no corner of the Keep had been left unsearched.

A deep ravine cut between Mount Yrdra and a section of the Keep, with a swift, narrow river below. A postern opened onto a small plateau that overlooked the ravine. One of the searchers had seen something on a ledge halfway down, where the baby's body had been found, broken and cold in death.

Next to the body had been found the personal seal of Na-iche, daughter to Moris, sister to Kerel, and aunt of the deceased.

"The personal seal?" Sharryn said.

"Yes, Seer," Captain Sergeus said, indicating a table set near him.

"Bring it forward, please."

He picked it up and took it to the dais. Sharryn examined it closely and passed it to Crow. The seal was made of some dark, hard stone with a device inset into one side, that of a small hawk, so swift, so fierce it seemed almost in motion, so marvelous was the Kalliopean carver's art.

A curious symbol for a female of this province, Crow thought.

Very, Sharryn thought. Aloud, she said, "And this seal has been recognized as belonging to Naiche, daughter of Moris?"

"It is, Seer. It has been so attested to by the count, the viscount, and the viscountess."

There was a stain on the seal, a thin film dried a rough dark brown. Crow sniffed it. Blood. Her eyes met Sharryn's. "There is blood on the stone, Captain."

"There is, Seer. With your permission, I would call Petros, the court physician, to testify."

"Bring him forward."

The captain raised his voice. "The Count of Kalliope summons Petros, son of Kostas, born of Ydra, physician to the Count of Kalliope, to come forth and give testimony in this matter."

A tall, gaunt man garbed in the gray of the physician came forward with a deliberate pace, halting before the dais. He looked up at Seer and Sword with an unwavering stare. When he spoke, he spoke as an equal, without deference, but also without the general Kalliopean contempt to which they had become accustomed. He spoke directly and to the point. Yes, Sergeus had brought him the seal. Yes, he had identified the blood on it as that of the child's.

"How?" Sharryn said.

"It is the first spell every physician learns after his Talent manifests itself, Seer," Petros said. "Blood is the foundation of life. The health of the blood is the health of its owner. Every diagnosis begins with the blood spell."

"Have you examined the body of the child?" Crow asked.

"Sword, I have."

"And the cause of death?"

"A blow to the head by a small object, struck hard enough to cause a significant impression on the skull." Petros's mouth was a straight line. He took no joy in the tale, and Crow liked him the better for it. "I shaved the skull and found something imprinted in the skin over the broken bone by the force of the bone. I traced it, here." He held up a translucent piece of parchment, and they saw the unmistakable outline of the small, fierce hawk on Naiche's seal.

"Naiche must be allowed to speak to the charges laid against her," Sharryn said.

"It is not our way," the count said.

"A woman to speak in open court," his son said. "Impossible. Father, the people will not stand for it!"

"You mean the men won't," Sharryn said.

An ugly look crossed his face, and he half raised his hand. Crow stepped between them, her back to the Seer. She was a little taller than Kerel. He didn't like it. His sneer deepened, and Crow felt something building in the air around him, pressing against her spirit, something dark and spiteful and menacing. She gave Kerel a thoughtful look. It was something very like what she had sensed during the attack on the road to Ydra.

"If you must speak with Naiche, you must," the count said in a mild voice, and the feeling vanished as Kerel gaped at his father. "Kalliope is a full signatory to the Great Charter and the Treaty of the Nine. We are bound by those accords."

"Father!"

Moris continued as if his son had not spoken. "I will have

the court cleared, however. Whatever she has done, my daughter shall not be so shamed in public."

You mean you won't, Sharryn said, but only so Crow could hear her.

The hall was cleared but for Sword, Seer, Count Moris, Viscount Kerel, Sergeus, Petros, and the bailiff, and somehow the Bard had managed to remain behind as well.

Sharryn was incredulous. *He wants to sing about this?*

It's what he does, Crow said. *He bears witness to the tale, then he tells the tale everywhere he travels, so that all of Mnemosynea may bear witness through his songs. Loukas knew what he was about when he created the King's Singers.*

Sharryn sighed. *I suppose an eyewitness account is better than a wild rumor.*

Naiche appeared promptly, attired in the same simple black dress. On the surface she was very calm, too much so for one on trial for her very life.

Crow came directly to the point. "Naiche, daughter of Moris, Viscountess of Kalliope, you are called to answer for the murder of the infant, your brother's son, your own nephew. How do you plead?"

Naiche looked at Count Moris. "Father?" she said. He would not meet her eyes. "Father, please?"

There was no response. Sharryn shifted in her chair.

Naiche turned to face them, her face flooded with color. She started to speak, failed, tried again. At last she gathered what appeared to be every scrap of courage she had, and said in a voice that started small, "I am innocent of this crime. I did not kill the babe! I am innocent!" The last sentence came out with a force and passion that startled everyone, even the speaker. "I am innocent of this most foul crime," Naiche said more calmly. "Aside from every other consideration, I am Kalliopean. I could not raise my hand in anger to a babe, but most especially I could not raise my hand in anger to the heir to the stewardship of Kalliope."

"Step forward," Sharryn said crisply.

Numbly, Naiche did so.

"Place your hand upon the staff."

Naiche's eyes widened, but she did as she was told, one shrinking hand laid against the silver-chased Staff.

"Again, Naiche, daughter of Moris, lady of Kalliope. Did you kill your brother's son?"

Naiche closed her eyes tightly and took a deep breath. "May Freya attest to my honor! I did not kill the babe!"

There was a charged silence. Nothing happened. The Staff did not wax wroth at a lie spoken in its presence.

She's telling the truth.

Don't sound so surprised.

There is something, though, Sharryn said, *something she's more afraid of than being found guilty of murder.* Aloud, Sharryn said, "Where were you the night of the Festival of Freya?"

Naiche started, flushing crimson, but Sharryn was inexorable. "Where were you on the night of the Festival of Freya?"

"I—I—"

"Come, come," Sharryn said impatiently, "you were with someone, the rituals of the Festival of Freya are well-known across Mnemosynea. Do you not understand yet, daughter of Moris, that whoever you were with, provided you were with him long enough, he is the one man who can corroborate your testimony and clear your name?"

Naiche shook her head. "I cannot, Seer. I must not!"

Sharryn leaned forward, and said fiercely, "And I say you must!" The Staff gave off a faint glow. "Speak!"

Naiche tugged frantically at her hand, but the Staff had caught it fast. The sweat beaded her brow and the pain drove her to her knees but she did not cry out, and still she would not speak.

The count looked on, impassive. Kerel looked on, gleeful. He was enjoying this, and again Crow felt that stirring of some unnamed force, growing ever stronger, as if magick invoked in its presence fed on it.

"Stop!" Sergeus said. "Stop this now!"

Surprised, everyone looked at him, with the exception of Crow, who happened to be looking at the count. The count was regarding his shoes with an impenetrable expression. Her gaze traveled to the count's son and heir, who, as Sergeus spoke, looked in turn astonished, revolted and, finally, enraged.

Uncaring of anything his betters might or might not be feeling, Sergeus strode forward and raised Naiche to her feet. He glared at Sharryn.

Well?

Let's see where this goes, Crow said.

Sharryn shook Naiche's hand free of the Staff and bent a stern look on Sergeus. "You have something to add to your testimony?"

"The lady was with me that night," Sergeus said flatly.

The viscountess stood erect next to him, head high, not looking at her father or her brother.

"For how long?" Sharryn said.

"The whole night," Sergeus said. "I went to her chambers after the feast, just as the bell sounded the first exchange of favors. She met me there within five minutes. I didn't leave her until dawn."

"Is this true?" Sharryn said to Naiche.

The viscountess, still with her head carefully turned away from her father and brother, said, "Seer, it is."

What's all the fuss about? Sharryn said. *The Festival of Freya was specifically engineered by Ophean to mix up the Kalliopean gene pool, to try to up the birth rate and increase the viable births.*

I get the feeling the plan wasn't meant to include royalty mixing in with the common clay. Kerel is very unhappy about it. Moris is either better at hiding his outrage, or he doesn't feel any. Sharryn, we haven't asked the question. Who benefits from the murder of the child?

Sharryn cast Crow a quick, startled glance. *No one that I can see.*

Nor I, and that's the problem. What would Naiche gain? It's not as if she would become heir after Kerel, not in Kalliope. She had no reason to kill the babe.

Then who did?

Out loud, Crow said, "The Sword summons Moris Naupactus, Count of Kalliope, to testify in this matter."

What! Crow, what in the name of the nine gods do you think are you doing?

"Lord," Crow said into the shocked silence that had fallen over the room, "come forward and place your hand upon the Staff."

"What do you mean by this!" Naiche said. "Surely you do not suspect my father!"

Kerel said hotly, "Father, do not! This is some witch's trick!"

Crow met the count's eyes. She and Sharryn between them could compel Moris to testify, and he knew it.

"Lord," Sergeus said, and was stopped by one raised hand. The count stepped forward to stand before the dais and without hesitation placed his hand upon the Staff. He met Crow's eyes without fear. "Ask your questions."

But it was Sharryn who spoke first. "Was the babe healthy?"

The count looked at first startled at the question, then reddened with understanding. "Seer, he was," he said curtly.

"No physical imperfections?"

"None."

He's lying, Sharryn said.

I don't think so. "Did you murder your grandson?" Crow said baldly.

There was a collective intake of breath around the room, not excluding Sharryn. "No, Sword, I did not," the count said.

The Staff remained quiescent. *Truth,* Sharryn said, sounding relieved. Finding the hereditary ruler of one of the nine provinces guilty of infanticide might be a little more justice than even King Loukas the Just had bargained for.

The count looked only at Crow, however, and in his eyes she fancied she saw a plea. "Tell me about your grandson, lord," she said softly.

There was a brief, charged silence. "He was a babe," the count said at last, heavily. "Handsome, healthy, cheerful. Innocent, as yet unformed as to character."

Crow said, "Whereas your son, his father, was not?"

What? Sharryn said.

Kerel hissed. "Insolent bitch! Who are you mongrel Hestians to call the rulers of Kalliope to account for any action!"

"What has your son done to displease you, lord?" Crow said without looking at Kerel, though she could feel the Summoning, and when Sharryn tensed next to her, knew she had felt it, too. Once felt, two years before, at the burning of Nyssa, the last, most powerful, and most vengeful of the Dark Wizards, it could not be mistaken for anything else. Sword and Staff responded as if to a call to arms, and Crow took a firmer grasp on the hilt, which had begun to vibrate within her grasp.

For the first time, Moris looked Kerel full in the face. "Sword. Kerel, son of Moris, Viscount of Kalliope, has been practicing the dark magicks."

Crow looked at Naiche, who looked agonized but unsurprised.

She knew, Sharryn said.

They all knew, Crow said, looking from Naiche to Moris to Sergeus, the court physician, the bailiff. The Bard was the only one who appeared surprised. Aloud she said, "The study of dark magicks has been outlawed since the signing of the Great Charter by the Nine."

"Sword, it has," Moris said.

The Summoning gathered in strength, amassing like an invisible black cloud around the count's son and heir.

"When did you discover your son was practicing the dark arts?"

"Sword, I—had suspected for some years. Things happened around him. Accidents at first, small injuries to people who challenged him or disagreed with him. His nurse fell ill. One of his tutors suddenly lost his Talent and was dismissed. Then a boy who defeated him at sword practice died. A rival suitor was maimed horribly in a fire. And there were other incidents. Just before the babe was born, I confronted him with the knowledge. He didn't deny it." The count looked again at Kerel then, and away again, as if he couldn't bear the sight of his own son. "He didn't deny it."

Oh, Sharryn said. *I had thought the child was deformed, and had thus been destroyed according to Kalliopean custom. But that wasn't it at all, was it?* "You decided to disinherit him," she said out loud. "When your grandson was born, you had an alternate heir, and you were going to disinherit Kerel in favor of the child."

The count's chin lifted. "I had no choice," he said bleakly. "I knew that Kerel's taste for black magicks would be found out sooner or later and that Kalliope would suffer as a result. Loukas has been very clear on that. I had to act for the good of the province."

"But you made the mistake of telling Kerel what you were going to do," Sharryn said.

Crow looked at Kerel. "And Kerel killed his own child."

In one swift smooth movement that Crow recognized from the encounter on the road to Ydra, Kerel pulled his sword, its length lit with a red glow. "Yes!" he cried, "I killed him! I threw him from the edge of the cliff with mine own hands! And with that death my Summoning of the dark power was complete! No one can defeat me now!"

"You are wrong," Crow said, and she leapt from the dais to confront him, Sword raised. The two blades crashed together with a crackle of power that rang off the stone walls.

They fought the length of the Grand Hall, Kerel at first very much on the attack. Crow let him beat her back, watching for an opening. He didn't offer many. She dropped her guard once and received a cut on her sword arm to remind her to be more careful, and after that she was.

They both had the Talent for making war. He had more muscle and a longer reach, but she had far more experience, and she fought a delaying action, exerting every skill she had

with wit and guile, making him work for every lunge and
thrust.

After what seemed like hours but what Sharryn told her
later was less than fifteen minutes, Kerel was sweating and
exhausted. He stumbled, tripping over his own feet to drop
to one knee and left himself wide open. Crow gripped the
Sword in both hands, turned on a graceful half step, and
swung the blade in an arc to deliver the coup de grâce.

Kerel, enervated, defenseless, screamed. "Father! Father,
help me!"

Moris did not move.

Crowfoot was the Sword, and the Sword was Crowfoot,
and with one will they came around in a sweeping arc. But as
the edge touched the skin on Kerel's neck, it froze in place,
reverberating all the way up Crow's body.

She felt the words bubble up into her throat and opened
her mouth to let them out before they choked her. "Let the
Sword sing!"

The silver runes on the blade of the Sword glowed with a
piercing light. "Lord," Crow said, "call your court back!"

The blade of the Sword made a tiny cut in Kerel's skin,
and blood trickled into his collar as the room filled again
with an awe-struck crowd, silenced by the display of the
magick that bound the provinces together, wielded by the
instrument of king and mage.

Sharryn, her voice cold, clear, and commanding, spoke.
"In the matter before the sitting of this Assideres—"

The Sword's hum became audible to all.

"—in the city of Ydra this third New Year in the reign of
King Loukas the Just, I, Sharryn the Seer, find Kerel, Viscount of Kalliope, guilty of the wanton murder of his own
son, by words out of his own mouth, and in trial by battle."

She paused, waiting for the cries of astonishment and fear to die down. "Let the Sword of Justice render judgment!"

The Sword raised its voice, a clear, cold call that could not be denied.

Kerel tried to jerk back from its edge, only widening the cut on his throat. "No! Keep it away from me! Father, Naiche, help me!"

The Sword rose in Crow's hands, held before her as an ensign of her command, as an emblem of the King's Justice newly wrought upon a war-torn, weary land. The blade brightened to a silver that seemed almost transparent, the blue sapphire on the hilt as bright with right and rage. The court of Kalliope cried out and cowered before its might.

When Crowfoot spoke, her voice was as cold as Sharryn's and as clear as the song of the sword. "In the name of the Great Charter of Mnemosynea and the Treaty of the Nine, by the power vested in me by king and mage, let justice be done!"

And then something odd happened, something Crowfoot the Sword did not know could happen, a power manifesting itself in her and through the Sword that until that moment she had not known existed. "The Sword speaks," she said, her voice a deep, resonant roll of sound clearly audible to everyone in Ydra Keep whether they were in the room or not. "Draw near and heed the word of the Sword of Justice."

She felt rather than saw Sharryn come to stand beside her, the Staff brought to stand next to the Sword.

"Let it be known that the Sword names Naiche, Viscountess of Kalliope, as the true heir of Kalliope. Kerel, son of Moris, is heir no more. He is stripped of Talent and wears the brand of the Sword, so that all who look upon him for the rest of his life shall know him for the murderer that he is."

Kerel screamed again, the miniature brand of the Sword etching itself upon on his forehead as Crow spoke the words. The Sword released him, and he fell back to the floor, sobbing. He clawed at his forehead, tearing at the skin, but the sign of the Sword shone clear and merciless through the blood.

"Further," Crow said, "it is the Sword's judgment that from henceforward, all men of the province of Kalliope shall wear upon their foreheads the brand of the Staff of Truth."

There were screams and a frantic scrambling among the men present, but there was no escaping the unbending justice of the Sword. "By this brand shall the men of Kalliope be known among all other men of the nine provinces, for a generation to come."

The men of Kalliope looked at one another, incredulous, each raising his hand to touch the miniature Staff as it was carved into his forehead.

"If, at the end of that generation, all men of Kalliope have served the heir to Kalliope wholeheartedly and well, the mark of the Staff will disappear."

Crow's voice deepened. "If the Lady Naiche, viscountess and heir to the throne of Kalliope, is for any reason unable to fill out her allotted span, no Kalliopean man will ever father another child on a Kalliopean woman.

"And the mark of the Staff will be worn by every generation of Kalliopean men, down through the history of recorded time.

"The Sword has spoken."

The Bard cleared a way through the riot that was the Kalliopean Assizes and hustled them to their room, shutting the door securely behind them and setting his back to it.

Sharryn looked at Crow. "I didn't know we could do that. Did you know we could do that?"

"Sit in judgment on an entire province?" Crow said. She worked her shoulders, which were beginning to stiffen from the fight. "No. We're going to have a few words with Loukas, not to mention the Magi Guild, when we get back to Hestia. If we live long enough to get back to Hestia, that is." She looked at Sharryn. "I understand it, though. Don't you see? All the cases that came before us in this Assizes, they were all in some way connected to the trouble at the root of the society itself. For centuries Kalliope has ignored, sequestered, subjugated fully half of its population, and as a result it is dying."

"And you think forcing its first woman ruler upon it will make it live?"

"It doesn't matter what I think," Crow said. "The Sword has rendered judgment. The rest is up to the Kalliopeans."

Unbelievably, the Bard laughed. "What a song this Assizes will make," he said. He reached for Crow's hand and brought it to his lips. "Truly, King Loukas chose well when he chose you to bear his Sword."

"So that's where you've been every night," Sharryn said to Crow accusingly.

Crow sighed. "Sharryn, meet Basil the Bard, son of Baruch, of the Isle of Lateum in the Hesperides, King's Singer." She met Basil's eyes with a rueful smile, and added, "And my husband."

Sharryn's jaw dropped. "Husband! Husband? Since when?"

Crow's answer was forestalled by a knock at the door. The Bard opened it a crack, then far enough to admit Naiche.

"Do you realize what you have done?" she said without preamble, strung as taut as one of the Bard's lutina strings.

"Have you any idea? Kalliope has never been ruled by a woman, never in its history."

"Then it's time it was," Sharryn said.

"It is the Sword's judgment, which may not be gainsaid," Crow said more gently. "And the men of Kalliope have only to look in a mirror to remind them of what will happen if they fail to obey."

Naiche paced, her prowling stride long enough to test the width of her skirts. "Can you possibly imagine the task you have set before me? Naming me heir offends every Kalliopean custom and tradition going back a thousand years. It calls our very society into question. Every man's hand will be against me. I will be all alone. I will have no help—"

"You will have Sergeus," Sharryn said.

Naiche paused, arrested. "But he is not of royal blood."

"Then I rather think your first order of business will be to coax a title for Sergeus out of the King," Sharryn said.

"And you will have your father," Crow said. "No, think. He did not protest the judgment of the Sword. And," she added, "you will have us, at least for the first year. King's Seer and King's Sword and King's Singer at your shoulder, should Kalliope's memories of this day fail too soon."

Naiche turned and spread beseeching hands. "How do I begin? Where?"

Crow looked at Sharryn and smiled. "Do you have any women friends?"

ABOUT THE AUTHORS

Like Meg Langslow, the ornamental-blacksmith heroine of her series from St. Martin's Press, **Donna Andrews** was born and raised in Yorktown, Virginia. These days she spends almost as much time in cyberspace as Turing Hopper, the Artificial Intelligence Personality who appears in her technocozy series from Berkley Prime Crime. Although she has loved fantasy and science fiction since childhood, Andrews developed a taste for murder in college (particularly at exam time). After graduation, she moved to the Washington, D.C., area and joined the communications staff of a large financial organization where she developed a profound understanding of the criminal mind through her observation of interdepartmental politics. Her first mystery, *Murder with Peacocks*, won the Agatha, Anthony, Barry, and Romantic Times awards for best first novel and the Lefty Award for funniest mystery of 1999. *The Penguin Who Knew Too Much* (St. Martin's) was #1 on the Independent Mystery Booksellers Association bestseller list for August 2007.

Michael Armstrong was born in Virginia, raised in Florida, and moved to Alaska half a lifetime ago. He now lives in Homer, Alaska, a town the *New York Times* describes as "too rough and too weird to be a tourist trap." His fiction has appeared in *Asimov's Science Fiction, Fantasy & Science Fiction, Powers of Detection, The Mysterious North*, and other anthologies. His latest novel is *Truck Stop Earth*, now in search of a publisher that can decide if it's truth or just science fiction. He covers cops, courts, science, arts, and wayward marine mammals at the *Homer News*.

Mike Doogan is a retired journalist who writes mystery novels and serves in the Alaska State legislature. He and his wife of thirty-seven years, Kathy, live in Anchorage.

Carole Nelson Douglas's *Good Night, Mr. Holmes* was a *New York Times* Notable Book of the Year and "ushered in a 1990s explosion of women-centered history-mystery reschooling us about the ornery presence of women in both social and literary history," said *The Drood Review of Mystery*. Douglas's Irene Adler Sherlockian suspense novels and her Midnight Louie feline PI contemporary mystery series comprise half of her fifty novels, but she's also written high fantasy and science fiction. Her short fiction has been reprinted in seven Year's Best collections, and her work has been short-listed for or won more than fifty awards. Her latest novels are Delilah Street's *Dancing with Werewolves* and *Brimstone Kiss*, and Midnight Louie's *Cat in a Sapphire Slipper*. A former daily newspaper reporter covering women's and social issues, Douglas has written fiction full-time since 1984 and lives in Texas.

Laura Anne Gilman is the author of the popular Retrievers series from Luna Books, which includes *Staying Dead*, *Curse the Dark*, *Bring It On*, *Burning Bridges*, and *Free Fall*. She is also the author of the Grail Quest trilogy and more than thirty short stories published in a variety of magazines and anthologies, including the magazines *Realms of Fantasy*, *ChiZine*, and *Flesh & Blood*, and the anthologies *ReVisions*, *Murder by Magic*, and *Polyphony 6*, among many others. Readers who like Bonnie in this story will be able to follow her adventures in novel form, coming soon from Luna Books.

Simon R. Green was born in 1955 in Bradford-on-Avon, Wiltshire, England. He has an MA in modern English and American literature from Leicester University and has also studied history and has a combined humanities degree. After several years of publishers' rejection letters, he sold seven novels in 1988, just two days after he started working at Bilbo's bookshop in Bath. This was followed by a commission to write the novelization of the Kevin Costner film *Robin Hood: Prince of Thieves*. He is a British Fantasy Society (BFS) member and still finds time to do some Shakespearean acting.

Charlaine Harris is the Anthony Award–winning author of several series, both mystery and paranormal. Her books are published in twenty countries. Charlaine lives in southern Arkansas, on six acres out in the country, with two other humans and three dogs. She loves to read.

Laurie R. King is the *New York Times* bestselling author of eighteen novels and a number of short stories, from the Edgar® and Creasey award–winning *A Grave Talent* to the ninth Mary Russell story, *The Language of Bees* (2009). Her work has also won the Nero (*A Monstrous Regiment of Women*) and the Macavity (*Folly*), and been nominated for the Agatha, the Orange, the Barry, and two more Edgar® awards. "The House" began as a writer's improv project in 2006 to celebrate Santa Cruz County naming Laurie its artist of the year. In what was billed as "Performance Art with a (Plot) Twist," she was handed a set of prompts—from Aileen Vance, Cassie Shea, Katie Fox, and Kerry Kilburn—and built her story around them in a public event that was also streamed online. The writing process is described at www.LaurieRKing.com.

Sharon Shinn is the author of *Archangel* and five other books in the Samaria world, as well as thirteen other adult and YA science fiction/fantasy novels. She won the William L. Crawford Award for outstanding new fantasy writer for her first book. A graduate of Northwestern University, she has lived in the Midwest most of her life.

Dana Stabenow was born in Anchorage and raised on a seventy-five-foot fish tender in the Gulf of Alaska. She knew there was a warmer, drier job out there somewhere and found it in writing. Her first science fiction novel, *Second Star*, sank without a trace; her first crime fiction novel, *A Cold Day for Murder*, won an Edgar® Award; her first thriller, *Blindfold Game*, hit the *New York Times* bestseller list; and her twenty-fifth novel and sixteenth Kate Shugak novel, *Whisper to the Blood*, comes out in February 2009.

Michael A. Stackpole is an award-winning author, game and computer-game designer, and poet whose first novel, *Warrior: En Garde*, was published in 1988. Since then, he has written forty other novels, including eight *New York Times* bestselling novels in the Star Wars® line, of which *X-wing: Rogue Squadron* and *I, Jedi* are the best known. Mike lives in Arizona and in his spare time spends early mornings at Starbucks, collects toy soldiers and old radio shows, plays indoor soccer, rides his bike, and listens to Irish music in the finer pubs in the Phoenix area. His website is www.stormwolf.com.

John Straley is a novelist and private investigator from Sitka, Alaska. He is the author of the Cecil Younger mysteries, as well as his newest historical novel, *The Big Both Ways*. His first book of poetry, *The Rising and the Rain*, was published in October of 2008. Straley is the twelfth Alaskan writer laureate.

COPYRIGHTS